Saving
Sara

Saving Sara

NICOLA MARSH

Published by Lake Union Publishing, Seattle
www.apub.com

Amazon, the Amazon logo, and Lake Union Publishing are trademarks of Amazon.com, Inc., or its affiliates.

ISBN-13: 9781503935792
ISBN-10: 1503935795

Cover design by Lisa Horton

Printed in the United States of America

For Soraya.
Thanks for believing in me and in this book.
Your friendship means so much.

PROLOGUE

The size of the coffin struck Sara Hardy most, the day of Lucy's funeral.

Small. Incongruously small under the pretentious flowers.

Lilies. Sara hated lilies. Their cloying, overpowering stench pervaded the air, clung to her clothes, her hair.

They draped the coffin in an obscene, cascading wave, obliterating the polished wood, a wood she should know from her past but couldn't remember. Not that it mattered.

None of it mattered. Not anymore.

"Sara? Sure you want to do this?"

She wrenched her gaze from the coffin and focused on Greg, her blinding grief mirrored in her husband's bloodshot eyes.

"People will understand if you can't." He gently squeezed her hand and she flinched, hating the contact, hating the wounded expression crinkling his face more.

He cleared his throat. "Maybe I should—"

"I'll do it."

She was my child, my baby, Sara wanted to scream, as isolated in her grief as she'd been in her marriage even when Lucy was alive.

Greg had cared more about billable hours at the firm than quality hours at home with their child. But he wasn't the only one guilty of putting work before Lucy, and that knowledge tore a gaping hole in her grief anew.

"She's with us, you know." His tremulous smile grated. "Always."

He tapped her lightly on the shoulder this time, not keen to repeat his mistake of hand contact, and she shrugged him off, compressing her lips to stop the angry, bitter words from spilling out in a blistering torrent.

Greg was full of crap, couldn't stop it from flowing even at their daughter's funeral.

Lucy wouldn't be with them always.

She was in that repulsively small coffin with the hideous flowers and that's where she'd remain until they buried her. Then she'd be in the cold, hard ground, subject to New York snow and Atlantic winds and the odd heatwave.

The seasons would change, every mourner in this church would grow older, but her precious Lucy would remain three forever.

Three, dammit. Three freaking years old. Where was the justice in that?

An eerie silence fell over the crowd as Sara stepped up to the podium, taking care not to lean too close to the microphone as she'd been taught early in her career.

Though what did it matter if feedback screeched through the silence? It wasn't as if Lucy would cover her ears and yell "Mommy!" like she always did when a stray fork scraped a plate during the washing up.

She swallowed, twice, desperate to clear the lump in her throat.

She had to do this.

For Lucy.

Placing her hands flat on the podium, Sara studied her chewed nails, the ripped cuticles, and the faint tan line where her wedding ring had resided, testament to more guilt. More pain. More regrets.

The priest cleared his throat from the pulpit, a pointed prod for her to hurry along, and she dragged in a breath, several, before finally raising her head.

Oblivious to the crowd she stared at the coffin, her belly churning with a sickening mix of sorrow and revulsion, hollow yet twisted, her heart gripped in an icy fist that squeezed with relentless persistence.

Her baby was in that coffin.

Her gorgeous, cheeky, blonde-curled little girl who lisped, who laughed at anything on Nick Junior, who preferred Thomas the Tank Engine over Dora the Explorer. Who adored purple and despised pink. Who ate green vegetables over orange.

The lump in her throat expanded, slid down, wedging in her chest like a Sumo wrestler pinning her to a mat and sitting on top of her. She could barely drag in a breath but the longer she focused on the coffin the harder she fought.

Sara had to breathe, had to breathe for both of them, and just like that the air forced itself past the tightness in her windpipe and the words followed, tumbling from her icy lips.

"Lucy-Lou, we used to wish upon the stars every night. You wished for so many things. A pony, a trip to Disneyland, a Barbie fun house. I didn't make any wishes because, cuddling you in my arms as we stared up at the sky, I already had my wish. I had you."

Sniffles, a sob, punctuated her pause but she didn't stop. She couldn't. The tidal wave of agony was growing, bigger, faster, threatening to swamp her, to sweep her away from her baby, to whom she had so much more to say.

"But now it's my turn, Lucy-Lou. Now's my turn to wish. I wish I'd bought you those extra Happy Meals. I wish I hadn't told you off for splashing in the bath all those nights. I wish I'd taken you to the park those sunny days rather than placing you in front of the TV so I could squeeze in extra work."

The sobs grew louder but she was on a roll, the words spilling as swiftly as her tears.

"I wish I'd let you wear those awful, patched purple overalls you loved so much every day, rather than forcing you to wear sensible clothes to preschool. I wish I hadn't yelled at you every time you wanted ice cream before dinner. I wish I hadn't worried so much about what you were going to be when you grew up and concentrated more on making the most of every minute we had together."

Greg half stood, took a step toward her, and she realized the loud, heart-rending sobs weren't coming from the congregation: they were bubbling up from deep within her.

Her fierce glare succeeded in placing his butt back on the pew, so she refocused on that obscenely inanimate box of wood, and pictured her daughter smiling and holding out her arms for the last cuddle of the night.

"But most of all, Lucy-Lou, I wish you were here with me now. That I could hold you, squeeze you and tell you how much I love you. You're my world. I'll watch for your star. Always."

Sara collapsed against the podium, her legs boneless, her head smacking the microphone with a thud. The crowd's audible gasp receded as Greg leaped to the rescue, supporting her weary body as he led her back to her seat.

Too little, too late. Where was he when their daughter needed rescuing, needed saving, needed a father?

"Sara, that was—"

"Save it," she hissed through gritted teeth, shrugging off his comforting arm, dashing away the tears streaming from her stinging eyes.

He'd push for a reconciliation—she knew him—but hopefully somewhere during their seven-year marriage he'd learned a thing or two.

Like the fact that Sara valued actions more than words. That all the slick charm and polished promises meant little if he didn't follow through. That love involved more than expensive floral bouquets and chocolates. That seeing him spend quality time with their daughter would've melted her hardened heart more than the obligatory goodnight kiss he'd plant on Lucy's forehead when he eventually got home every evening.

Sure, he'd been supportive after Lucy died, solicitous to the point of overbearing. She'd appreciated his presence, their blinding grief the only thing to unite them. To his credit, he'd stood up in the crisis, organizing the funeral and the wake. Taking care of everything when it took all her energy to lift her head off the pillow in the morning and drag on some clothes.

But it wasn't enough. Not when their marriage had been struggling before Lucy's death.

The mantra echoed again through her aching head: *Too little, too late . . .*

The rest of the service passed in a blur. She didn't hear a thing apart from her silent, fervent wishes, wishes no one could hear, least of all her child lying lifeless in that damn box.

The achingly poignant rendition of Ave Maria, sung by one of Greg's dorky colleagues, pierced her sorrow for a few moments, serving only to make her cry harder, her heart fragment further.

Then it was over.

The drive to the cemetery, the frigid wind whipping the leaves against her legs, the droning of more meaningless words by a robed priest who hadn't known her little girl at all, the wake back at their apartment where well-wishers patted her back and kissed her cheeks and couldn't quite look her in the eye, sapped what little energy she had until she made a run for it, slamming the bedroom door shut before collapsing on the bed.

It took her a full two seconds to realize it wasn't her room.

5

She'd stumbled into Lucy's messy, lived-in, preschooler's room. Stricken, she grabbed Snuffly, Lucy's squishy, one-eared dog, and hugged him to her chest, tight. Rocking back and forth, tears spurting, sobs ripped from so far down in her soul she wondered how she'd ever continue living.

Greg slipped into the room and rested his back against the door, the distance between them indicative of the last few months—the last few years, if she was completely honest.

He held out a hand to her. "I know you're hurting, Sara, we all are, but you—"

"Don't you dare say I need to pull myself together."

She jabbed a finger in his direction, clutching Snuffly with the other hand, drawing strength from the tenuous link to Lucy. Crazy, using a stuffed toy animal to face up to her husband. Giving her courage to say what should've been said a long time ago.

His pained expression irritated her and fed the well of resentment that bubbled from a long-festering source.

"And stop damn well looking at me like that."

"I'm doing the best I can." He dragged a hand through his hair, the messy blond spikes annoying when they'd once been endearing. "What do you want from me?"

"Nothing." Even now, he didn't have a clue. "Absolutely nothing."

The burning anger gnawed at her, urging her to berate him, to castigate him, to hurt him as much as he'd hurt her over the years.

Then she made the mistake of glancing down at the dog, with its skewed, sewn-on red cotton eyes and button nose and lolling felt tongue. An ugly, pilled, fluffy toy with the life squeezed out of it. The memory of placing Snuffly in Lucy's welcoming arms every night slammed into her, eradicating her fury toward her husband.

Their marriage was over. Had been over for years. With Lucy around, they had been able to pretend that they were a family. Hanging their hopes on the occasional outing together on a Sunday. The rare dinner when they all sat down at the dining table and made small talk. The fleeting moments where they made eye contact and smiled in unison over something funny Lucy had done or said.

But with Lucy gone, Sara couldn't pretend anymore. Her love for Greg had dwindled to affection, the kind she might have for a best friend. Without Lucy, they were housemates, nothing more, and she couldn't tolerate it any longer.

She could have said so much to him in that moment but why rehash the pain? There was enough of that going around today for everybody.

He must've seen something in her face, a clue to her ambivalent feelings, because he blanched.

"Sara, we can work this out—"

"Stop."

He took a step toward her and she held up her hand to ward him off.

"Dammit, I can't read your mind," he said, sounding tortured, confusion crinkling his brow.

She flinched at his harsh tone and hugged Snuffly tighter, caught his muttered curse as he jammed his hands into his pockets, shoulders drooping.

He looked as weary, as battered, as resigned as she felt, and the faintest flicker of empathy blossomed as he pinned her with his custom-made, specially-for-her, accusatory glare.

"I can't do this anymore," he said. "Tell me what you want."

She wanted the one thing she'd craved since that devastating phone call had been relayed to her and ripped an irreversible, irreparable hole in her heart.

Meeting his hard, unflinching gaze, she whispered, "Redemption."

1.

REDEMPTION, CONNECTICUT
12 MONTHS LATER

Sara woke to the sun's rays warming her face and a bird rapping at the window.

Confused, she rubbed her eyes and scooted into a semi-sitting position.

Her studio apartment in New York City didn't have a large enough window for sun to stream in and birds sure as hell didn't tap on her window thirty stories up.

She glanced around and reality crashed over her. This wasn't New York City. It was her first morning in her grandma's cottage in Redemption.

Twelve months ago, if anyone had suggested she'd be living in Connecticut after quitting her financial analyst position at a high-flying company, she would've laughed in their face.

But that was before Lucy's death and more recently, Gran's. She could've added the death of her marriage to Greg into the mix but she hadn't grieved for that as much as the other two.

She'd moved out of their apartment after Lucy's death and had thrown herself into work to quell the pain. It hadn't worked.

Nothing had. But she'd discovered that operating on autopilot was better than being surrounded by memories of Lucy in their home and Greg's constant tiptoeing around her.

The isolation—from her husband, her colleagues, her friends—had been cathartic. She'd needed to be left alone to heal and they'd let her.

When Gran had died four weeks ago, she'd seen it as a sign. It seemed almost trite that she now resided in Redemption when it was what she'd craved most. Some kind of absolution from the ever-present guilt that constantly plagued her. The move wasn't quite what she'd anticipated but it was a start. A new beginning, in a new town, in a house she'd always loved. The only place she'd ever called home. Gran had been supportive in a way her mother never had and the fact that Sara's pyrography pieces adorned the walls in the hallway, kitchen, den and sunroom was testament to that.

It had been years since she'd picked up a heated wire tip to scorch designs into wood. Too many years. She'd buried her artistic talent when she'd met Greg. Corporate law and pictures of fairies and gnomes burned into bark didn't mesh in his professional world.

He'd never been to this house, had never visited Gran. Sadly, Sara's visits had tapered off once she'd had Lucy and begun the frantic act of juggling work and motherhood.

Gran hadn't come to Lucy's funeral. She'd been sick—an angina episode. Sara understood. What she didn't understand, and couldn't forgive, was her own mother not being there.

Vera could've come. She should've come. Then again, Sara's childhood had consisted of being dragged from town to city across the States, wherever her mother's whim took her.

When Lucy died, Vera had been in Atlantic City, her latest fad. Distance wasn't the problem with her getting to New York City for the funeral. Selfishness was.

Sure, Vera had made all the appropriate platitudes when Sara had called to tell her the devastating news, and she'd sent a condolence card, but that was it. Then again, what had she expected, from a woman who'd met Lucy, her own granddaughter, a grand total of twice?

Sara had learned to harden her heart toward Vera a long time ago. Had accepted she'd never have a real relationship with her mom. But the fact Vera hadn't shown up for Lucy's funeral guaranteed she never wanted to speak to her mother again.

Her gaze landed on one of her creations, a strap of leather about four feet long, hanging on the wall opposite the bed.

It had been her last piece, a series of scenes burned into the leather from her time spent at Gran's. Tending the garden. Picking herbs. Making bread. Pickling fruits.

Gran must've loved it, as she'd hung it in a place where she'd see it every day when she opened her eyes.

Tears clogged Sara's throat and she swallowed.

No way would she cry the first morning of her new life.

She shrugged the covers off and padded to the window. The view made her chest ache. Countless rows of grapevines in the distance, as far as the eye could see. A small dam bordering Gran's property with her closest neighbors. An apple orchard, a veggie patch and an herb garden that spread a good forty feet from the back door.

Sara loved this place. And it was all hers.

She'd make a new start here. It had taken her a long twelve months to realize she owed it to Lucy to start living her life rather than existing.

Increasingly maudlin at the thought of Lucy and how much she would've loved it here, Sara headed to the kitchen. She'd stocked up on groceries in town yesterday on her way here, knowing she'd be exhausted from the drive and the overwhelming emotion, a sense of coming home.

That's exactly what had happened. She'd managed to unpack the car, put away the perishables and dump her suitcases inside the front door, before bone-deep fatigue had set in and she'd fallen into bed, half-clothed.

As she walked the long hallway, more of her pyrography caught her eye. A bunch of plump grapes embossed into birch wood. An intricate sprig of rosemary. A fruit bowl. A towering oak. She'd been going through a nature fad and Gran had adored everything she'd made.

She reached out and touched the first piece, traced the outline of a grape, her fingertip tingling with the urge to *feel* wood again.

As she stood in the hallway, surrounded by evidence of her past, she wondered if she could still do it.

If she found the perfect piece of wood and picked up her tools, could she create again?

Only one way to find out.

2.

Cilla Prescott felt more alive at dawn than any other time of the day. When the first streaks of mauve, marigold and sienna streaked the sky, she was already up, dressed and tending to the plants that were the basis of her naturopathy business.

Not that she could call it a business per se, considering she didn't advertise or sell online. But she'd been helping the folk of Redemption cure their ailments for nineteen years and it made her feel worthy in a way that marriage or motherhood never had.

As she puttered among the sage, lemon verbena and tarragon, she spied movement next door. A good half acre separated her house from Issy's, who'd passed away a month ago, and Cilla had been looking out for a glimpse of her new neighbor ever since.

There wasn't much that happened in Redemption that Cilla didn't know about, and Bud the lawyer had informed her that Issy's granddaughter Sara would be moving in.

A sad business, Sara losing her young daughter a year ago. Issy had adored Sara and the old lady had been heartsore. On her philosophical days, Cilla liked to think Issy was playing ring-around-the-rosie with her great-granddaughter in heaven.

Cilla slipped off her gardening gloves and hung them on a hook by the back door. As she did, she caught a glimpse of herself in the window and chuckled. What right did she have to think of Issy as old when she wasn't far behind? She'd turned sixty the week before and looked it. Short grey hair cropped into a spiky style, too many laugh lines to count and a chin that was fast defying gravity.

She'd never bothered about her looks, not since Vernon had died twenty years ago. She'd never forget that day when the local sergeant knocked on her door, telling her he suspected Vernon had deliberately driven his car into a tree at high speed.

No one was told the truth but her and Tam. No one needed to know. So Cilla had moved on. Completed the naturopathy course Vernon had deemed a waste of time. Started dispensing natural remedies to the community. Embraced her new lifestyle.

Every day when she looked in the mirror and saw her paisley kaftan tops and her striped leggings and her beaded sandals, it proved how far she'd come.

A car pulled up in her drive and she walked the length of the house, curious to see who'd be visiting her at eight a.m. As she rounded the corner, she caught sight of an attractive man. Tall. Broad-shouldered. Chiseled jaw. Expensive charcoal suit. Not the kind of visitor she was used to, and her hand unconsciously fluttered to her hair.

The closer she got, the more familiar he looked. When he flashed a welcoming movie-star smile, she recognized him.

Bryce Madden. A much older Bryce Madden since the last time she'd seen him, when he'd finished his medical degree and made a brief visit home to see his parents and friends before moving on to a job in LA.

He'd dropped by to see Tamsin, unaware that Tam hadn't been home since she left for college. They'd been good friends once, Tam and Bryce. Tam had had the biggest crush on him and Cilla had seen the attraction.

Six-three, muscular, with wavy dark hair and piercing ebony eyes, Bryce had been memorable. Now, with the man in question smiling at her like she'd bestowed a gift basket of her best remedies on him, she could see that not much had changed. Sure, grey streaked his hair to make it almost match her color, and grooves bracketed his mouth, but he was just as handsome in an obvious kind of way.

"Bryce, this is a surprise. How are you?" She held out her hand, feeling foolish when he ignored it to step closer and kiss her cheek.

That foolish feeling was quickly replaced by another feeling altogether: shock. Since when did her daughter's friend greet her with a kiss?

"It's good to see you, Cilla," he said, his deep voice triggering a memory of him strumming a guitar in her backyard, singing some soulful song that had Tam almost swooning. Her too, if she'd been completely honest.

Having Tam at eighteen meant she'd openly shared her daughter's crushes on actors and rock-stars. She'd liked it. It had bonded them in a way she'd never envisaged, having a child so young. But she'd never had a crush on Bryce. It would've been too weird, secretly lusting over her daughter's crush.

It should still be weird, despite the fact the eighteen years between them now didn't seem as great as it had back then.

Increasingly uncomfortable under his scrutiny, she glanced past him to see an expensive black convertible parked in her driveway. "If you're looking for Tamsin, she's not here."

"I didn't come to see her."

"Oh?" It came out an odd squeak and Cilla cleared her throat, wondering what it was about Bryce that had her so off-kilter.

He took a step closer. "I came here to see you."

Cilla wondered if it was his proximity and the intoxicating smell of his crisp, citrus aftershave or the fact she hadn't been this close to a man in twenty years that overpowered her sensibilities, but she found herself actually grinning at his bizarre proclamation.

"Why on earth would you want to see me?"

He touched her arm, a glancing brush that made her skin tingle. "Because I'm the new locum in town and I want to hear more about the amazing natural remedies my patients raved about yesterday."

Cilla didn't know which snippet of information to process first. The fact Bryce had moved back to town. The fact he'd be here for the foreseeable future. Or the fact he'd come to see her on his second day here. Albeit professionally, and for an insane moment she was almost disappointed.

Heck, what had she expected—that he'd actually come all this way out of town to see her?

She really was turning into a silly old woman.

"Sure, come on in. I'll make coffee and we can talk."

He glanced at his watch. "Actually, I've got a home visit to make shortly, so I was hoping you'd agree to have dinner with me."

"Dinner?" Cilla mimicked, making it sound like he'd asked her to run through her herb garden naked.

The smile that curved his lips transformed him from handsome to devastating, and damned if her heart—and other body parts long neglected—didn't twang. "Yeah, dinner. You do take time out from curing the town to eat?"

"I don't cure the town," she snapped like a schoolmarm, sounding every one of her sixty years and way too defensive. "That's your job, isn't it?"

"It will be for the next three months." His smile broadened. "I've got loads of catching up to do with patient files, trying to familiarize myself with everything, so I'm busy the next few nights. But how about Friday? Dinner at seven?"

For an insane second, Cilla found herself contemplating his invitation. How long since she'd been out to dinner, to any kind of meal that didn't involve sitting in front of the TV? Vernon had been stingy as well as mean and since he'd died, she'd preferred her own company for meals than to have people pity her at a restaurant's table for one.

"It doesn't have to be in Redemption," he said. "We could drive to Fairfield or Bridgeport."

"But locals eat there too and might see us," she blurted, then wished she hadn't said anything when he laughed. A rich, genuine laugh that tugged on something deep inside, demanding a response.

"It's only dinner. It's not like I'm asking for anything else." He ducked his head to murmur near her ear. "Yet."

Cilla had to say no. Bryce was flirting with her, for goodness' sake, and he was young enough to be her son.

But as he stepped back and stared at her with nothing but kindness, the sort of kindness she'd never had from a man, ever, she found herself wishing she could say yes.

"I'm sorry, I can't," she said, adding a frown along with a glower for good measure.

He nodded. "Fair enough, but I'm not giving up," he said, with a brisk salute before strolling away, whistling under his breath.

"Don't waste your time," she yelled at his retreating back.

He whistled louder, as if trying to drown her out.

As her wistful gaze focused on his butt for a moment, and registered how taut it was, she knew she'd done the right thing in refusing him.

Hadn't she?

3.

The moment Jake Mathieson heard his sister murmur, "I need your help, I'm desperate," over the phone, he'd broken the land speed record to get to her crummy studio apartment in Manhattan.

As his nephew, Olly, opened the door to him, wearing torn shorts and a grubby T-shirt streaked with ketchup down the front, Jake sent up a silent prayer of gratitude.

Rose had problems, always had, yet she'd never approached him for help despite his many overtures. So the moment he'd heard her heartfelt plea, he'd known things had to be bad and his first thought was for this innocent six-year-old who didn't deserve to suffer because of a troubled parent.

If anyone knew what that was like, he did. He'd borne the brunt of his father's abuse, trying to deflect attention off Rose and protect her. He wanted to be Olly's protector too but he couldn't be there for the kid twenty-four-seven because Rose wouldn't let him. It broke his heart, looking into Olly's big brown eyes. Eyes that seemed to bore right down to his soul and find him lacking.

"Hey Ol, where's your mom?" He ruffled Olly's curls, glad when the kid didn't shrug away like he did sometimes.

"She's lying down." Olly's somber tone made the dread in Jake's gut solidify. "In there."

Increasingly worried, Jake pulled a chocolate bar from his pocket and presented it to Olly. "I'd love one of your great shark pictures, so why don't you go draw me one and eat this while I chat to your mom?"

"Okay." Olly grabbed the bar with eager hands and proceeded to tear the wrapping.

"Manners?" The gentle admonition slipped out but Jake wasn't sorry. He tried his best to instill values into the boy whenever he was around.

"Thanks, Uncle Jake," Olly said, cramming half the bar into his mouth in one go before bounding toward the kitchen.

Olly was a good kid but he didn't have a lot of friends and was behind in class. Rose didn't seem to think this was a problem. Then again, his sister was becoming increasingly self-absorbed and he knew why.

He'd seen what too much alcohol had done to their father and he could see the signs in Rose. Not good.

Jake dragged in a deep breath and blew it out. He'd always been gentle with Rose. Supportive. Because of what they'd been through growing up. He'd backed her when she'd left home at sixteen and worked in a local diner. He'd financed her cooking course at night school. He'd been there for her during her accidental pregnancy by a celebrity chef who'd died of a drug overdose at a fancy party in the Hamptons before Olly was born.

And he'd been around ever since.

A sliver of guilt wormed its way into his conscience. He hadn't always been there for Rose and Olly. He'd been AWOL the last six months, too caught up in his own misery to give a crap about anyone else.

He'd been selfish and he hoped Olly hadn't paid the price.

Rolling his shoulders to release some of the tension, he took a few steps into the living room. When he saw Rose lying on the sofa, pale and lifeless, his chest squeezed.

"Rose?" He ran to her, unable to breathe until her eyelids fluttered open. "You scared the crap out of me."

"Sorry." She winced and struggled into a sitting position. "So tired. Can't keep my eyes open."

Then stay off the booze, he wanted to say, but considering she looked as disheveled as Olly, it wasn't the time.

For Olly's sake, Rose kept it together. She worked long hours at an all-night cafe, she provided good meals for Olly and she always dressed them well on a budget.

Today, she wore a faded grey T-shirt and sweatpants, and her hair hung in lank strands around her heart-shaped face, devoid of makeup. She looked . . . ill.

"What's going on, Sis?" He reached for her hand and she let him hold it for a few seconds before yanking away.

She glanced over her shoulder toward the kitchen, half-fearful. "I want you to take Olly."

"Sure, I'm happy to give you a break." He'd offered many times before but Rose had always refused. "Do you want him back today or can he stay overnight—"

"You need to take him for a month or two," she murmured, her hands unconsciously wringing the end of her top. "While I'm in rehab."

Jake heard Rose's heartfelt plea but it took a few seconds for the enormity of what she'd asked to compute.

"Rehab?"

Were things that bad? Hell, he knew Rose drank but she'd been able to control it. He'd suspected she might have a problem from a few of their late-night conversations but he'd put it down to her using alcohol as a way to wind down after work.

She functioned well regardless, taking Olly to school and holding down a job. Alcoholics couldn't do that. Their father sure as hell hadn't been able to and it had made him all the meaner, taking out his frustrations on them.

"Something happened today . . ." Rose covered her face with her hands and Jake's heart twisted.

She looked so small, so sad, so bereft, curled up on the sofa, and he knew he'd do whatever it took to help her.

"What happened?"

She lowered her hands and this time, when he took hold of one, she let him. "I forgot to pick Olly up from school."

Jake let out a relieved breath he'd been unaware he was holding. "That's not so bad. I'm sure plenty of parents have done that—"

"I was passed out after going on a bender," she said, self-loathing lacing every word. "I got fired last night and I drowned my sorrows."

Jake knew if Rose had got to the stage of benders, she needed help. There had to be more she wasn't telling him but he needed to broach the subject carefully.

"Passed out?"

"Not literally. Just so tired from drinking too much last night that I needed an afternoon nap and ended up sleeping for hours." Tears filled her eyes and spilled onto her cheeks as she gripped onto his hand for dear life. "The last few months have been tough. Olly's a handful and the new boss at work was constantly on my case no matter how many extra shifts I did, so I drank to make myself feel better."

Sorrow lodged in Jake's throat and he swallowed. "You know that's not the answer—"

"Of course I bloody know." She scowled and tried to remove her hand from his. He didn't let her. "I hate myself every freaking day when I look in the mirror, see the bloodshot eyes, my sallow skin, and know I look like *him*."

Jake squeezed her hand, encouraging her to continue. The more she talked, the more time he had to formulate a response that wouldn't have her pulling back when she'd finally reached out.

"I thought I could control it." She swiped at her tears with her free hand. "Because of Olly. I'd never do anything to put him in jeopardy. But today . . ." Self-disgust twisted her mouth. "The thought of that poor kid waiting for me to turn up . . . alone . . ."

Her solemn stare fixed on him and he read her silent plea. "I need help, because I'll be damned if I end up like our old man. Olly deserves better than that."

"He does." Jake nodded slowly, the enormity of what his sister had been going through making his bones ache. Or maybe that was the guilt, because he hadn't been around when she'd needed him the most. "You've found a place?"

"Yeah, a recovery center, one of those holistic places that focuses on general wellbeing rather than addictions only, and I can check in as soon as you take Olly—" Her voice broke and her eyes grew glassy again. "I can't imagine life without him, even for a day, but I have to do this, for both of us."

"Have you told him?"

She shook her head. "I wanted to make sure it was okay with you first."

"Of course it's okay." He ducked down to kiss her cheek. "I'm always here for you, Sis. Whatever you need. Any time."

"Thanks." She hugged him, a rare show of affection that made him wish he could fix everything with a simple embrace.

When she eased away, her relief was palpable. "I know you've got your own stuff to deal with at the moment, so are you sure this is okay?"

"Absolutely," he said, knowing that looking after a kid was probably the last thing he needed right now but unable to say no to Rose.

He'd been through hell the last six months, wallowing in guilt on a daily basis, but no way would he let Rose know that. She needed him. He'd be there to help. It was the way it had always been from the time they were kids and living in a nightmare after their mom died.

"I'm fine," he said, so brusquely that Rose startled. "Let's tell Olly he's going on a little holiday with Uncle Jake."

Thankfully, Rose allowed the abrupt change of subject. "I hate lying to him, so let's tell him the partial truth, that I haven't been well and need some medical help."

Jake frowned. "Won't that scare him?"

"He's a smart kid," she said. "He's seen the bottles. He's seen me blurry-eyed sometimes." She hesitated, before continuing. "I knew about Dad's drinking when I was Olly's age."

"That's because he was a nasty bastard, but you're nothing like him," Jake spat out, his fingers curling into fists as he wished for the umpteenth time that he'd retaliated earlier when his father came at him rather than waiting until his teens to stand up to him physically.

"I'd never hurt Olly physically, but what do you think seeing me like this all the time is doing to him?" Rose's eyes teared up again and she blinked rapidly. "I'm telling him the truth."

Jake knew nothing about raising kids so he had to give his sister the benefit of the doubt. Because despite her drinking, she had done a good job raising Olly.

"Okay." Jake stood and stretched out the kinks in his back. "I'll go get him."

"Jake, wait." Rose snagged his hand. "Do me a favor?"

"Bigger than the one I already am?" He'd aimed for levity but it fell flat when the corners of Rose's mouth turned downward.

"Don't let the guilt eat away at you." She released his hand to pat her chest. "All I've done for the last few months is feel guilty. Over doing a lousy job as a mother, over not providing enough for Olly, over not being here for him every night because I have to work." She shook her head. "That guilt has got me to this point and I don't want you to suffer the same fate."

"But I don't drink," he said, almost defiantly, wearing his teetotaler status like a badge of honor.

He'd never touched the stuff after he'd seen what it did to their father. Mainly out of fear he might not be able to control himself and stop at one, like dear old Dad.

"I've hit rock-bottom, Jakey, and it's not just because of the alcohol." She struggled into a standing position, her legs wobbly, and he helped her. "You're a good guy. You don't deserve to feel like this."

"I'm fine," he said, for the second time in as many minutes. It was the same trite response he'd trotted out to concerned colleagues for a month after the accident until he couldn't take it anymore and had finally quit. "Now let's go tell that son of yours he's in for a world of fun with Uncle Jake."

Rose's lips compressed into a thin line, as if biting back whatever she wanted to say.

Good. Because Jake didn't want to rehash what he'd gone through the last six months. The vivid nightmares. The avoidance of friends. The struggle to get out of bed most mornings.

As Olly strolled into the room, chocolate stains around his mouth, Jake knew he'd have to get his act together now.

He had a kid to care for and he was determined to do a damn sight better job than his father ever had.

4.

Sara spent the day wandering through the house, exploring every nook and cranny. She'd need to eventually clean out some of Gran's junk but not today. Today was for remembering.

She found a box filled with dog-eared Mills and Boon books in a closet and remembered Gran scolding her for reading them when Sara had been thirteen.

She found a stack of old CDs and remembered dancing around the living room to Hootie and the Blowfish and The Smashing Pumpkins, Gran breathless from laughter as she tried to keep up.

She found a garbage bag filled with old toys: puzzles and skipping ropes and balls, stuff she'd played with as a kid but Gran had never thrown away. Surprising, as the house was reasonably tidy and Gran hadn't been a hoarder.

But she'd kept the things that had meant the most to Sara and that made her want to hug Gran all the more.

Blinking back tears, Sara searched the final cupboard for her greatest treasure, knowing if Gran had kept all that other stuff she wouldn't have got rid of her pyrography tools. But there was nothing but a pile of old photo albums in the cupboard.

Damn.

If the tools weren't in the house, Sara knew where they would be. In the shed down by the dam.

She'd had no intention of heading down there. She couldn't. Not when the shed bordered the back of the property . . . and a camp. For kids.

She couldn't face it. Couldn't face seeing the excitement on their faces or hearing the children's chatter and laughter. It would be a stark reminder of all she'd lost and she couldn't do it. She wasn't strong enough. Not yet. Maybe not ever.

Rubbing her chest where the residual pain flared whenever she thought of Lucy, she flipped open her laptop. If she couldn't face the work shed to get her tools, she'd have to order a new set.

Throughout the day, the urge to resume pyrography had grown until it was all consuming. She had to try again, had to see if she could still create.

New life. New beginning. New creations.

It was somehow all tied together in her mind and she wanted to make a start ASAP.

It didn't take long to buy what she needed. She even threw in a few sample pieces of leather, to get her hand back in the game. Alongside new tools, she'd ordered her favored woods but would source more later with a stroll past her favorite trees, where she'd touch the bark and feel something for a piece she wanted to create.

Gran had never laughed at her when Sara had talked about knowing what to draw on which piece of wood simply by touch. Gran had always supported and praised her, and while Sara didn't believe in ghosts—she couldn't, because if she started talking to Lucy's spirit she'd never stop—coming back to this house, being surrounded by her grandmother's things, she could almost imagine Gran still being here for her.

Intolerant of the nebulous direction her thoughts had taken, Sara dusted herself off and closed the cupboard door. She'd ordered the tools to be delivered express and they should arrive in the morning.

In the meantime, she'd finish her walk down memory lane for the day with her favorite meal that Gran used to make: grilled cheese on toast, potato salad and apple crumble for dessert.

It would be fitting and as she bustled about the kitchen, trying not to think of how she'd rarely made dessert for Lucy, she knew she'd done the right thing coming back here.

When she sat down to eat her comfort food, she idly flicked through an old photo album she'd found tucked away behind the box of novels earlier.

It made her smile to think of Gran painstakingly arranging the photos in an album when these days most people swiped their phone or tapped at their keyboard to bring up photos.

Sara preferred the old-fashioned way, liked the feel of flipping cardboard pages to see the past come alive. The first few pages held pictures of Sara's youth, captured during each visit to the cottage. Making mud-pies in the back garden. Picking bunches of flowers. Riding a tricycle.

One photo stood out and made her peer closer. Sara running around the garden wearing a pale pink tutu and fairy wings, glancing over her shoulder with a cheeky grin for the camera.

She looked so much like Lucy it made her chest ache.

Most people had said Lucy looked like Greg but this photo proved them wrong. It somehow made Sara feel closer to Lucy and she reached out a finger to trace the photo, wishing Lucy could've been here to see it.

With her appetite gone, she pushed away the food and continued flicking through the album. Gran had documented every stage of Sara's life, eight pictures per double page for each age, culminating in her wedding photos.

Sara remembered sending these to Gran, a few professional shots as a keepsake of her love for the man of her dreams.

What a crock.

Had she ever been that naïve? A resounding yes if the pictures were anything to go by. Photos of her hand in hand with Greg. Gazing up at Greg. Kissing Greg. Waltzing with Greg. She looked carefree and ecstatic in them all, the epitome of a blushing bride.

Too bad the blush had worn off in the first six months of marriage when Greg's hours at the firm meant he missed more dinners than she could count, stood her up for her work functions, and consistently crept into the apartment around midnight, too exhausted to do anything but sleep.

Not that she'd been a sex maniac, but Sara had expectations of her husband that had petered out pretty damn fast in the first few months of marriage because of his precious job.

Conceiving Lucy had been a miracle of good timing and luck, on one of the rare times Greg had been home early, on Christmas Eve.

She'd roasted a chicken, steamed vegetables and made a pineapple upside-down cake from scratch. They'd eaten, exchanged gifts and made love on the sofa. A perfect evening. With a perfect result nine months later.

They hadn't been trying to have a child. Sara had already been too disillusioned in her marriage. But she'd had a bout of food poisoning a few days earlier, so her contraceptive pill hadn't worked.

Later, she'd thought it was a godsend, having a gorgeous daughter like Lucy to bestow all her love on. Love Greg didn't seem interested in anymore.

Losing Lucy had gutted her and while she didn't love Greg any longer, staring at their wedding photos, tangible proof that they had once loved each other, made her wonder how he was doing.

He'd tried to stay in touch after she moved out but she'd wanted a clean break. In some warped way, Greg reminded her of Lucy and all that she'd lost. She blamed him, just as much as she blamed herself for Lucy's death.

Tears burned her eyes and she snapped the album shut.
No point lamenting all that she'd lost in the past.
Time to focus on the future.
She owed her daughter that much.

5.

"Hey Olly, time to brush your teeth," Jake called out, running a hand across the back of his neck to ease a kink. It didn't help. The tension still knotted his muscles, giving him a headache.

Or maybe the most stubborn, recalcitrant six-year-old he'd ever met had caused that. Not that he'd had much to do with kids, but Rose coped admirably with her son despite her shortcomings so how hard could it be?

After a day and night caring for Olly, he had a newfound respect for Rose. All parents, for that matter. Kids were tough. Damn tough. Or was it because he was lousy at it? He refused to consider it, as that meant he was as useless as his father in the parenting stakes and no way would he accept that.

He had to try harder. Read some books. Brush up online. And breathe.

"Don't wanna." Olly leaned against the bathroom doorway and scowled. "You get up too early. And you don't have Pop-Tarts. And you're grumpy."

Couldn't fault the kid there. But not wanting another battle like the one they'd had over dinner last night—who knew kids didn't like store-bought sushi?—Jake forced a smile. "If you brush your teeth real fast, we'll have extra time at the park."

A spark lit Olly's steady gaze. "That's bribery."

How old was this kid—six going on sixty?

"Is it working?"

Olly tilted his head to one side, studying him, before nodding. "Sure. I like the park. Better than here."

Jake's heart dropped. He was doing the best he could but if Olly hated it here after only a day, how the hell would they cope for the next few months? The entire summer vacation stretched before him, a minefield filled with dinners Olly wouldn't eat, toys he wouldn't like and activities he'd despise.

Jake was in way over his head.

As Olly pushed past him to get to the sink, a vivid memory flashed across Jake's mind of him doing the same thing to his Aunt Cilla. She'd been filling the tub with water and adding bubble bath when he'd barreled into the bathroom and accidentally bumped her elbow, resulting in her tipping way too much liquid into the bath. The resultant bubbles had ensured he and Rose had the best fun ever.

His aunt had laughed at their antics. His uncle, not so much. Vernon had been the spitting image of his brother, Jake's dad. Like two mean, nasty peas in a pod. The only reason their father had ever taken them out to Connecticut to visit his brother was because he knew Cilla would care for the kids while he sat around on his ass drinking beer.

Jake had enjoyed those rare visits because Cilla would act as a buffer, so no matter how much his dad drank or how mean he got, he couldn't lay a finger on Jake. Cilla wouldn't stand for that.

Not that she'd ever said anything, of course, but Jake knew his aunt understood. It was like an untold secret, something they both knew but never spoke of. Besides, Jake often wondered if his Uncle Vernon took his frustrations out on Cilla, or even Tamsin, their daughter. He'd rarely seen his cousin; she'd been a decade older than him and never home once she'd left for college. Considering how grouchy Uncle Vernon was all the time, he didn't blame her. He empathized. Boy, did he empathize.

As Jake gazed at Olly, who was concentrating fiercely on squeezing the right amount of toothpaste onto his toothbrush, he had an idea.

Olly was used to having only Rose around. He related better to a female. And while Jake believed Olly needed a male role model in his life, he wasn't delusional enough to think that he could be a good parent for Olly over the next few months when he had no clue how.

Cilla would know, though. Cilla had been excellent with him and Rose. She'd been funny and thoughtful and caring, yet strong on discipline too. She'd be perfect to help out with Olly.

Only one problem. Jake hadn't been in touch in years. In fact, since his uncle Vernon had committed suicide by driving into a tree, he'd seen her a grand total of three times.

He'd been twelve at the funeral. Thirteen when she'd dropped in on an impromptu visit but been driven away by his dad. She'd tried again a year later, bringing a basket of lavender cookies and banana muffins. His father had thrown the lot in the trash and told her to go to hell, that they didn't want her guilt gifts, seeing as she had driven Vernon to his death.

That was the last Jake had seen of his aunt and it irked him that he hadn't contacted her in eighteen years. He'd always viewed family as meaning him and Rose against the world.

Maybe it was time to change all that.

"You finish up here, get your shoes on and I'll meet you out front," Jake said, placing a hand on Olly's shoulder. Considering the awkward, tension-filled evening they'd had yesterday, he wasn't surprised when Olly shrugged it off. Disappointed, but not surprised.

The faster he engaged his aunt's help, the better.

Leaving Olly to finish up, he strode to the front door and grabbed his cell out of his pocket. Once the door was closed and Olly safely out of earshot, Jake scrolled through the contacts he'd transferred from cell to cell ever since he'd had his first at the age of twelve.

Hoping Cilla hadn't moved—and that she wouldn't verbally flay him for ignoring her all these years—he found her name, hit the call button and waited.

The phone rang once, twice. A total of eight times. About to give up, Jake glanced over his shoulder to see Olly through the front window, trying to tie his shoelaces, his tongue poking out in concentration.

Jake didn't have long. On the ninth ring, someone picked up.

"Hello, Priscilla Prescott speaking."

So she'd ditched the Mathieson name and taken back her maiden name. Good for her.

"Hi Aunt Cilla, it's Jake."

Silence. A long, taut silence filled with awkwardness and sadness and regret. On his part, anyway.

"I know this is crazy, me ringing you out of the blue like this, but I was hoping I could come visit today."

Damn, did he sound as desperate as he felt?

After what seemed like an eternity, she finally spoke. "It's been a long time, Jake. Is everything all right?"

"Yeah. Just thought it would be good to catch up."

"After eighteen years, that's a lot to catch up on." Typical Cilla, a gentle rebuke without much rancor.

"I know, and I feel terrible for losing contact with you, but after Dad died I had my hands full with work and looking after Rose . . ." Could he sound any weaker?

He should 'fess up and say he was a selfish prick who'd become used to looking out for himself and Rose only, and there wasn't much room in his life for anything else.

34

"I guess your father got his wish, keeping me away from you kids after Vernon died."

He found himself nodding. "I'd like to change that, starting today."

Cilla's pause lasted several seconds and he'd almost given up hope when she said, "Sure, come by today. I'll make some of those oatmeal cookies you used to love."

Relief made him sag against the wall. "That'd be great. See you in a few hours."

"I'll look forward to it."

Cilla hung up quickly, but not before Jake heard a quiver in her voice.

He should've told her about Olly. If his phone call had surprised her, he had a feeling she'd be shell-shocked when she discovered that Jake planned on staying awhile in Redemption so Olly could get the attention and care he needed from his great-aunt.

6.

Cilla had hung up the phone and was trying to absorb the shock of Jake calling after all these years when she heard a knock at the front door.

No one used her front door. Townsfolk knew she stored and dispensed her remedies from a small room branching off her sunroom at the back, so that's where they came.

Heck. Was it Bryce again?

She didn't want to think about his dinner invitation. Didn't want to dwell on how put out she felt after he'd left yesterday because she hadn't accepted. Didn't want to rehash all the names she'd called herself, ranging from cougar to stupid old biddy.

If this was Bryce she'd send him away again, with a sterner warning this time to leave her alone. Yes, she'd definitely do it. But she opened the door to a tall, thin blonde woman dressed in city clothes. A leisure suit, but citified nonetheless. She was beautiful in that elegant, timeless way that only some women could pull off. With her big blue eyes and elfin features, she had the kind of face that turned men's heads.

There was something familiar about her. Something about her tentative smile . . .

"Can I help you?"

"I hope so." The woman held out her hand. "I'm Sara Hardy and I've moved in next door."

"Oh my word." Cilla's hands flew to her cheeks. "I should've known. You're the spitting image of Issy." Cilla waved her in. "Please come in and I'll put the kettle on."

"Actually, I can't stay. There are some important documents I need to post in town and I was hoping you could do me a favor." Sara spoke quickly, like she was used to doing everything in a hurry. City folk were like that.

"Sure. What is it?"

"I'm expecting a delivery that needs to be signed for. I've left a note on my door asking if they could deliver it here if I'm out . . ." Sara sounded almost desperate and Cilla quelled the urge to bundle her into her arms for a hug.

"Not a problem; I'll take care of it for you," Cilla said, saddened by the shadows in Sara's eyes.

She knew what it felt like to be haunted by memories.

"Thanks. I appreciate it." Sara turned to go, then paused on the top step and glanced over her shoulder. "Did you know my grandmother?"

Cilla nodded. "We were friends. She was a lovely lady."

Sara smiled and it transformed her face from pretty to beautiful. "I'd love to hear your stories about her one day, if you've got the time?"

"I've got all the time in the world to talk about Issy," Cilla said. "And get to know you."

An unexpected joy lit Sara's cautious gaze and it struck Cilla anew how fragile the girl appeared.

"I'd like that," Sara said, before turning away and continuing toward her car, a small red hatchback.

"See you soon," Cilla called out, and Sara responded with a wave.

Cilla watched Sara drive away, pondering the strangeness of her week. She didn't get many visitors, bar the townsfolk wanting remedies. Yet so far, she'd had Bryce and Sara drop by, and soon Jake would arrive.

For a woman who valued her peace and quiet, it had been an eventful few days. As she glanced at her watch and realized she had to make those oatmeal cookies she'd promised Jake, plus her signature brownies as a treat, she thought it was nice to have her staid life shaken up every now and then.

7.

Are we there yet?" Olly whined for the umpteenth time and kicked the back of Jake's seat.

Like every other time he'd been asked on this interminably long trip, Jake forced his jaw to relax so he wouldn't grind his teeth to dust, and remembered that Rose needed his help.

"Almost, buddy. Another five minutes or so."

"That's what you said last time." Olly blew him a raspberry. "I hate you."

Jake had put up with worse insults from his father but the hint of vulnerability in Olly's voice slayed him. He'd seen the distrust in Olly's eyes when Rose had explained she had to go away for a while to get better and that Uncle Jake would be taking care of him.

Olly had fixed those big, brown eyes on him in accusation, as if to say, "What the hell would *you* know about taking care of a kid?"

Unfortunately, for both their sakes, Jake knew jack about children, a fact that had been consistently rammed down his throat over the past twenty-four hours by Olly.

"Hate's a strong word, pal. And it's not very nice to use it." He glanced in the rearview mirror in time to catch another scowl.

"Mom uses it," Olly said, his defiance admirable and so reminiscent of himself as a kid that Jake had to stifle a smile. "She hates her job. She hates our small apartment. She hates not being rich." He spoke so solemnly it broke Jake's heart. "She thinks I don't hear her when she says it softly but I do." Olly's bottom lip wobbled a little. "So if Mom says *hate*, I can too."

Hell, the last thing Jake needed was a tear-fest, but he understood where Olly's attitude was coming from. The kid must be petrified, being dumped on an uncle he'd rarely seen over the last six months. Olly needed reassurance, something Jake was ill-qualified to give considering the mess he'd made of his own life lately, but he'd give it a damn good shot.

"Your mom's great, isn't she?"

"She's the best." Olly nodded, so solemn Jake's chest ached. "I wish she didn't have to go away."

Olly's slight hiccup and muffled sob almost undid Jake's intentions to reassure his nephew by talking about Rose, but he persisted. "Sometimes when grownups don't feel well, they need to spend time in a place away from home to get better."

Olly perked up. "Like a hospital, you mean?"

"Yeah, though the place your mom's in is more like a hotel than a hospital."

Jake had done a thorough search on the rehab facility Rose had chosen and had been suitably impressed. It made him feel better, knowing his sis was in reputable hands.

"Mom told me she's been getting headaches . . ." Olly frowned. "And she's been really sleepy lately. Sad, too. And forgetful. I notice stuff like that." He brightened. "So maybe it's a good thing she's going away to this hotel hospital for a while."

"Sure is, buddy," Jake said, relieved they'd had this conversation and that Olly seemed okay with opening up to him a little. Progress at last. "And guess what? You can tell your mom all about this trip to the country."

"Will there be cows and horses and stuff?"

Annoyed with himself that he'd have to disappoint his nephew again, Jake shook his head. "Not at Aunt Cilla's, but I'm sure some of her neighbors have animals, so we can go exploring."

Olly's momentary enthusiasm faded. "Don't go making promises you can't keep. That's another thing Mom says, because apparently people keep disappointing her."

Wow, this kid was observant. He'd have to let Rose know that Olly's perception exceeded his years.

"We'll ask Aunt Cilla about it." It was the best he could come up with, and it sounded lame, even to Jake's ears.

Thankfully, Olly shrugged and remained silent as Jake followed the winding road, slumping in relief when Cilla's cottage came into sight.

It had been a long time since he'd been back here but Jake could've sworn an invisible weight lifted off his shoulders now and floated away.

Cilla would welcome them, like she'd done for him and Rose all those years ago. She'd envelop Olly in her warmth and care for him like he deserved, doing a damn sight better job than Jake ever could.

Yeah, everything would be okay once they reached his aunt's.

It had to be.

8.

Cilla glanced around the kitchen, hoping it looked welcoming.
She'd laid out plates piled high with oatmeal cookies, banana
cake and brownies. All Jake's favorites.

A vase of roses clipped from her garden took pride of place
on the table, their velvety soft crimson petals catching the rays of
sun spilling in from the windows, their fragrance battling with the
freshly baked cookies, lacing the air with homeliness.

Jake had been a good kid and he'd once told her this place was
better than his home. Considering Ray had been the spitting image
of Vernon in every way, including his fondness for the bottle, she
could only imagine.

She'd spent many a sleepless night wondering what Jake and
Rose had endured at home, away from prying eyes. Any time they'd
visited here, she'd watched for signs of abuse. But Rose had seemed a
happy child, if a little shy. It had been Jake who'd borne the brunt of
Ray's alcohol-fueled temper; she'd bet her life on it.

Even as a child, he'd had that wary glint in his eyes, like he'd
seen too much. She'd tried to mother the kids as best she could,
spoiling them with home-cooked meals and long walks in the fresh
air, but there hadn't been much she could do when they went home.

She'd grieved more for the loss of her relationship with Jake and
Rose than she had for Vernon. After her husband's death, she hadn't

been surprised when Ray cut off contact between her and his kids. She'd expected it but, regardless, she had kept hoping he'd allow her visits for the sake of Jake and Rose.

But Ray had been as downright cussed as Vernon and she'd given up. As the kids grew older, she'd hoped they'd contact her. But they hadn't, and she hadn't pushed the issue out of respect. She'd left her past behind when Vernon died and she imagined Jake and Rose had done the same. Maybe they didn't need an aunt who reminded them of times they'd rather forget.

So the fact Jake had contacted her again after eighteen years meant one of two things: he'd grown a conscience or he was in trouble. She hoped it wasn't the latter.

A car pulled up in the drive and the engine was shut off. Curiosity drove her to the front door and she had it open before Jake had made it halfway up the garden path.

His size struck her immediately. Jake had grown into a strapping young man, too handsome for his own good. Though a vague resemblance, something around the mouth, or the cheek-bones, reminded her of Vernon. Or maybe it was the way he carried himself, with a slight swagger that oozed confidence. Yeah, Jake was a Mathieson through and through.

Even more startling than his resemblance to her husband—he wasn't alone.

A young boy slouched beside him, scuffing his shoes deliber-ately with every step, shooting the occasional scowl Jake's way while trying not to appear too excited as he glanced around. He had curly brown hair in need of a trim, was a tad too skinny and wore a faded blue T-shirt and shorts.

The boy didn't look like Jake but why else would Jake have a child with him unless it was his son?

Fixing a welcoming smile, she stepped out onto the front porch.

"Good to see you, Aunt Cilla." Jake took the steps two at a time, like he'd always done, and the memory brought a lump to her throat. "You look amazing."

"I look old," she said, surprised to feel her cheeks heating with a blush. "And you're all grown up."

He enveloped her in a bear hug. A good, strong hug that alleviated some of her fears that their first meeting would be awkward after all this time.

When they eased apart, Jake laid a hand on the boy's shoulder, urging him forward. "And this is Olly, my nephew. Rose's son."

Olly shrugged off Jake's hand as if he abhorred the contact so Cilla quelled her first instinct to hug the boy too.

So Rose had a son. She must've had him young, judging by the boy's age, around six or seven. The question was, why was Jake bringing him for a visit after all this time, without Rose?

"Nice to meet you, Olly." She held up her hand for a high-five. She spent a fair bit of time with the youth group in town and if there was one thing she'd learned, it was that they favored this weird ritual over a handshake any day.

Olly stared at her hand in surprise before slapping his palm against hers. "Hey."

He hadn't ignored her so that was a start. She noted the relief on Jake's face, the way his concerned gaze darted between her and Olly, and she wondered what the real reason was for this visit.

"Come on in." She climbed the steps and beckoned them to follow. "Hope you like cookies and cake and brownies, Olly."

"Wow." Olly stared at her like she'd promised him a trip to Disneyland. "I don't get treats very often."

Cilla didn't know what to say to that so she settled for a smile.

"Thanks." Jake looked like he didn't know whether to hug her again or make a run for his car, leaving the boy behind. "I remember your baking."

As Olly bounded into the house ahead of them, she lowered her voice. "Pity you didn't keep in touch after your dad died."

Guilt twisted his mouth. "That's another thing I remember. Your bluntness."

Cilla shrugged. "Why waste time not saying what you mean? Life's too short."

"True." Jake held up his hands, palm up, like he had nothing to hide. "Sorry. I've got no excuse other than after Dad died I moved on. Concentrated on aircraft mechanics. Supported Rose as best I could." He blew out a breath. "Left my past behind."

"Don't blame you for that." She laid a hand on his shoulder, patted it. "Did the same myself."

"I bet you did."

They exchanged a long, loaded glance filled with understanding and empathy.

"Anyway, that part of our lives is over," she said, bustling him into the house. "You can tell me about Rose and Olly later."

"There's a lot to tell," he muttered, his expression pained as they entered the kitchen, where Olly hovered near the laden table, his eyes wide as saucers.

Jake lowered his voice. "If it's not too much of an imposition, can we stay the night?"

"Absolutely," she said, secretly pleased she'd have more time with Jake. "We'll have a good natter when Olly's in bed."

He nodded, suddenly grave. "Thanks, Aunt Cilla. You owe me nothing, after the way I've ignored you all these years, yet you're as welcoming as ever—"

"Stop. You're family." She slipped an arm around his waist and hugged. "And family sticks together. Always."

He slung an arm across her shoulders and hugged her back. "That's what I'm hoping to instill in Olly."

Who lost patience with them at that moment and started shifting his weight from foot to foot. "I'm starving," he declared, crossing his arms and glaring at Jake with intense dislike. "Really starving."

"Have you washed up?" Cilla said, ushering Jake toward the table and heading for the fridge.

Olly frowned. "I don't usually wash my hands before eating at home."

"Well, it's a good habit," Cilla said. "You don't want the yumminess of those cookies spoiled by yucky germs, do you?"

Olly pondered for a moment, before nodding. "Where's the bathroom?"

"Please," Jake added. "We make manners a habit here too."

Olly's gaze swung between them, ascertaining how hard he could push, before shrugging. "Okay."

"You can wash up through there." Cilla pointed to the mudroom. "Would you like some lemonade? It's homemade."

"Yes," Olly said. "Please," he added, after a pointed glare from Jake.

"Seems like a nice kid," Cilla said, as she took the jug from the fridge and poured lemonade into three glasses.

"Rose does her best." Jake took the glasses and placed them on the table. "It's been hard for her."

"She's a single mother?"

Jake nodded. "Olly's father died before he was born."

"Poor girl." She sat at the table. "She must've had it tough."

"You don't know the half of it," Jake said under his breath, as Olly ran back into the kitchen and waved his hands in the air.

"All clean, so can we eat now?" Olly sat in the chair next to Cilla and scooted closer to the table.

"You bet." Cilla nudged his glass closer. "And here's your lemonade."

"Thanks," Olly said, as he piled two brownies, three cookies and a slice of cake on his plate, garnering a raised eyebrow from Jake.

"You're welcome," Cilla said. "Your uncle Jake used to eat that much, you know."

"Not anymore." Olly crammed a cookie into his mouth and demolished it in a few chews. "Now he only eats yucky black stuff wrapped around rice."

Jake laughed. "We had sushi last night for dinner."

"It's horrible," Olly said, a second before he took a giant bite of brownie.

"I agree," Cilla said, stifling a laugh at the solemnity of Olly's expression as he chewed like a maniac. "I'm not a fan of Japanese food either."

When his mouth was empty, Olly took a sip of lemonade and wiped his mouth on his sleeve. "What's your favorite food?"

"Steak and barbecued corn, followed by apple pie and ice cream," Cilla said, increasingly charmed by the little boy.

It had been so long since she'd had anything to do with kids beyond the youth group in town that she'd forgotten their innocence and copious questions.

"That sounds amazing," Olly said, reaching for another cookie.

"It is," Jake added, relaxing for the first time since he'd arrived as Cilla watched him settle into the chair and nibble at a cookie. "I remember Aunt Cilla used to make the best apple pie ever."

"Can you make it for me tonight?" Olly pressed his hands together in prayer pose. "Pleeeeease."

Jake stiffened. "Olly, your aunt has made all these yummy treats for us. She's probably tired."

Cilla hadn't made an apple pie in years but she found herself softening, responding to the plea in Olly's eyes and the concerned look in Jake's.

There was a lot of tension between Jake and Olly, and she wondered about the cause. Jake seemed uncomfortable with Olly, out of his depth, like he didn't know what to do or say. She hoped she could help with whatever had brought him all the way out here when they talked later tonight.

"I'll make you a deal. If you eat all your veggies with dinner tonight, I'll whip up an apple crumble, which is like a pie but without all the pastry." Also took half the work, something Cilla remembered from the pies she had toiled over, not that Vernon had ever appreciated it. "How does that sound?"

"Awesome," Olly said, before his face crumpled a little. "But what kind of veggies? Mom knows I like orange ones more than green."

Cilla's heart broke a little at the audible quiver in Olly's voice. He must miss Rose. For his sake, she hoped Jake looking after him was only temporary and he'd be back with Rose ASAP. If anyone knew a child needed its mother, she did. Pity Tam didn't share the same philosophy.

Cilla missed Tam something fierce.

"In that case, how does carrot and pumpkin sound and we give broccoli a miss?"

Olly's smile radiated pure joy. "You're nice."

"She sure is," Jake said, looking at her like she'd handed him the keys to a new Mustang. "Aunt Cilla is the best."

She felt another blush flush her cheeks. "If you're trying to butter me up for something, Jake, stop right there. I'm not as gullible as I used to be."

"You were never gullible," he said, patting her hand. "Kind and generous, definitely. And you still are."

Oddly flustered by his praise, she pushed back from the table and stood. "I better go pick some carrots and a pumpkin from the garden."

Olly's forehead crinkled in consternation. "But you get carrots and pumpkin from the grocer's?"

"They originally come from a garden," she said. "Would you like to help?"

"Yeah." Olly stood so fast his chair toppled and she grabbed it before it hit the floor. "Let's go."

Olly didn't look at Jake once, and it saddened her to see their fractured relationship.

"Jake, you up for a bout of vegetable gathering?" Only when Cilla mentioned his name did Olly glance his way, and even then only for a second.

Jake shook his head. "Thanks, but I've got a few phone calls to make."

Olly perked up. "Are you calling Mom? Can I talk to her?"

"Not today, champ, but we'll call her in a few days."

Jake's gaze met hers, beseeching her not to ask any questions in front of Olly. As if she would. She'd been the epitome of discretion her whole life. She'd had to be, being married to Vernon and putting up with his crap.

Interesting, though, that this wasn't an overnighter for Olly and Jake. A few days, Jake had said. The fact they couldn't call Rose tonight, or tomorrow, meant there was definitely something going on.

"Okay," Olly said, not sounding okay at all, as his bottom lip wobbled.

"Ready to get those hands dirty in the garden?" Cilla pointed at the back door. "My gardening tools are outside."

"But you just told me to clean them." Olly inspected his hands. "You're funny with hands."

Cilla chuckled, and thankfully, Olly joined in.

As Cilla guided Olly out the back door, she glanced over her shoulder to see Jake staring into space, a frown creasing his brow.

He looked tired, like he had the weight of the world on his shoulders. Whatever problems Jake and Rose were having, she hoped she could help.

It was nice to be needed again.

9.

ara knew she should never have dawdled over those wedding photos in the album yesterday. Shouldn't have reminisced. Because as the incoming videoconference button flashed on her computer and she noticed who it was, she knew she'd tempted fate.

She could've ignored Greg. But he'd been her husband for seven years and despite the way their marriage had fizzled out, she didn't want to have bad blood between them. Not when the divorce was one step away from being finalized.

Jabbing at the answer button on her computer, she exhaled the breath she'd been unaware she was holding. When his face popped up on the screen, her heart thudded in remembrance.

He'd made her breathless the first time they'd met, at a coffee shop near her work on Wall Street. With hair the color of ripening wheat, clear blue eyes and a smile that dazzled, she'd been smitten. Then he'd opened his mouth and charmed her further with sincere compliments and genuine interest.

She'd dated sporadically in college but had never experienced the overwhelming urge to spend every spare second with a guy. Greg had done that and she'd allowed herself to fall for him.

Too fast, as it turned out, because if she'd taken the time to get to know him better, to live with him, she would've seen the flaws earlier. His propensity for boasting, for immersing himself in his work at the expense of everything and everyone, for shutting off emotionally and justifying the withdrawal by citing his prowess as a provider.

Those faults had emerged over time, solidifying when they had Lucy. By then, Sara had fallen out of love with Greg and in love with her beautiful baby daughter. It had been enough to sustain their marriage. So it was no great surprise that losing Lucy had meant the death of their marriage too.

"Hey Sara, how are you?" He smiled, the way his eyes crinkled in the corners as endearing as always. "Thought I'd see how you're getting on in your new home."

"I'm fine. Busy getting Gran's house livable again. How are you?"

"Manic at the firm." He shrugged. "You know how it is."

Sadly, she did.

As if realizing his gaffe, his gaze dipped, before he cleared his throat and refocused. "Are you seeing anyone?"

Alarmed by the swift change in topic, she shook her head. "Not that it's any of your business, but no."

She wanted to know why he'd asked but, becoming increasingly uneasy at this impromptu call, she clamped her lips shut.

"It's been a long time, Sara. I thought . . ." His brows knitted in a frown. "It's just that our divorce is almost final and if there's any chance for us—"

"There isn't." She cut him off, her tone clipped, while she ignored the traitorous flare of hope deep inside.

She didn't want a second chance with Greg. They'd had a second, third and fourth chance while they were married, as far as she was concerned.

No good could come of rehashing the past or trying to resurrect something that had died a slow, painful death over the years.

She'd come to terms with their marriage imploding a long time ago. Time for Greg to do the same.

"Would you like some time to think about that?" His forehead puckered in irritation before he swiped a hand over his face, eradicating the tension. "Look, I know this comes out of left field, but we were good together, Sara. We fit. And before Lucy died—"

"Stop." She held up her hand, the inevitable stab of powerlessness and remorse whenever Lucy's death was mentioned making her want to disconnect instantly. "We're over, Greg. We'd been over for years before Lucy, so don't try and fix something that broke a long time ago."

Stubbornness flashed in his eyes. "I know we can make this work. You just have to give me a chance—"

"A chance to do what, Greg? Try to make me fall in love with you again? Try to make up for the past?" She dashed her hand across her eyes, swiping away tears of frustration, infuriated that he'd put her in this position. "Don't you get it? I fell out of love with you a long time ago. Way before Lucy was born."

She jabbed a finger at the screen, resentment tightening her throat. "Losing her the way we did . . ." She trailed off, biting back the ultimate insult.

But he knew. He knew what she'd been about to say. Resignation darkened his eyes to indigo as his shoulders slumped.

"You blame me and you can't get past it," he said, despair lacing every word.

After what seemed like an eternity, she nodded. "She was sick but you called me a helicopter mom, made me feel like an overprotective parent. So I listened to you—" She broke off on a sob, but had to get the rest out. Had to purge the resentment that she'd bottled up for too long. "—and she died. So yeah, I blame you as much as I blame myself."

Greg stared at her, remorse waging a battle with devastation in the depths of his eyes.

In that moment, she felt sorry for him and some of her bitterness faded.

This wasn't doing either of them any good. Attributing all the blame in the world wouldn't bring Lucy back. Time to end this, once and for all.

"So that's it?" He reached for the screen, as if to press his palm against it, before letting his hand fall.

Greg was a smart guy. He knew when to call it quits.

"When the divorce goes through, I'd prefer it if you didn't contact me again." Her voice quivered but her resolve stood firm.

She needed a clean break.

He stared at the keyboard for an eternity before eventually raising his head, the sheen in his desolate eyes slugging her to the gut. "If that's what you want."

"It is."

Not wanting to shed any more tears, she raised a hand in farewell. "Take care." Before he could respond, she hit the disconnect button and Greg's face faded to black.

Sara didn't move for a long time, tears she'd been unable to stop trickling down her cheeks.

She mourned her marriage. She mourned her daughter. She mourned the life she'd once had.

When the tears dried she stood and squared her shoulders.

When those divorce papers went through, she'd finally be free to face her future.

10.

Jake nursed the whiskey Cilla had poured him, staring into the amber depths without drinking a drop.

Though he never touched the stuff, he thought a sip might give him courage to ask for the monumental favor. But the stench made him want to fling it down the drain instead. While his father had been a beer man, any alcohol would do and at times, when Ray drank spirits, he'd turn particularly nasty.

"You going to drink that or meditate with it?" Cilla sat on the sofa opposite and tucked her legs beneath her, looking comfortable in this house in a way he'd never known.

When his Uncle Vernon had been alive, she'd been a bundle of energy, never sitting still. She'd buzzed around, feeding them and cleaning up after them and doing endless chores. Back then, Jake had wondered if keeping busy was her coping mechanism; that if she moved around enough she wouldn't have to spend much one-on-one time with Vernon.

"I don't drink," he said, placing the glass on a coaster on the coffee table between them.

Her eyebrows rose and he felt compelled to explain why he'd let her pour it in the first place. "Thought it would help give me some Dutch courage."

"Why?"

"I need a favor," he said, pinching the bridge of his nose.

Yeah, like that would stave off the blinder of a headache that was building. Tension did that to him. Usually work stress, but he hadn't had that for six months, not since he'd turned his back on the only career he'd ever known.

"I don't bite, Jake," she said, snuggling into the cushions. "It's been a while but you can still tell me anything."

Astounded by her generosity, he shook his head. "You're amazing. You welcome me back into your life like the last eighteen years never happened. You take Olly under your wing to the point he helped you cook dinner, ate every scrap, then went to sleep in a strange bed without a protest. Now you're sitting there, making me feel like I did when I was a boy around you, comfortable enough to really talk to you."

She shrugged, as if his praise meant little, but he saw a glimmer of pride in her eyes. "I've always liked you, Jake, and I miss having young people in the house."

"Tamsin doesn't get home too often?"

"Try never." Sadness downturned her mouth and he cursed inwardly.

"Sorry."

"Don't be." She waved away his apology. "Tam left home for college and didn't come back, and I don't blame her."

Hoping he wasn't prodding old wounds, he said, "Uncle Vernon?"

Cilla nodded. "Tam couldn't wait to escape the tension in this house. She came back for the funeral. That was it."

Jake struggled to hide his surprise. "So you haven't seen her in . . ." He tried to do the math but had forgotten when Vernon had died.

"Twenty years," Cilla said, sorrow deepening her voice. "We talk on the phone occasionally. The obligatory calls at birthdays,

Thanksgiving and Christmas along with posted cards and gifts. That's about it."

"I had no idea," Jake said, feeling like an idiot for dredging up an obviously painful subject.

He wanted to ask where his cousin was and what she was doing, but that wasn't conducive to bringing up the favor he needed.

"I think Tam blames me for tolerating Vernon's abuse all those years." She fiddled with the tassel on a cushion, absentmindedly twisting it around and around. "I'm guessing she lost respect for me . . ." She trailed off, sounding so forlorn Jake wanted to go to her and hug her tight. "I've never told anyone but it was a relief when he drove into that tree. Nothing I did was good enough. I wore the latest fashions, hairstyle, makeup. Cooked gourmet meals. Provided a welcoming home. Raised Tam. He'd still find fault, not holding back on the vitriol 'til he had me in tears, cowering or both."

She took a deep breath and Jake let her speak. He had a feeling she needed to offload, to expunge the past.

"The day he died, I'd snapped. I'd usually placate him when he was in a mood, try to soothe him with soft words by pandering to his ego. But that day I yelled back . . ."

She blinked rapidly. "When I heard the news, I didn't shed a tear. I think some of the townsfolk initially judged me for my lack of grief. But most of them knew Vernon was a mean bastard and they eventually rallied around and became my clients once I opened my naturopathy business."

She looked at him like she expected him to judge her. "Do you think I'm a bad person?"

"We do what we have to do at the time to cope," he said. "Whatever it takes."

She nodded. "Vernon's abuse never turned physical; I wouldn't have put up with that. But the verbal stuff was bad enough. And while I tried to shield Tam from most of it, it must've had an impact."

"Dad was the same, though he took his fists to me a couple of times." Jake had blocked those memories but there was something about being in Cilla's living room, with the lights muted and soft rainforest music playing in the background, that tore a hole in the barriers he'd erected a long time ago. "Until I was fifteen, put on more muscle than him, and hit back."

"Good for you," Cilla said, snapping him out of his reverie with her firm tone. "Now, let's forget our maudlin pasts and focus on the present. What's this favor?"

Jake dragged in a breath and blew it out in a long huff. "Rose is in trouble. She checked into one of those fancy wellness recovery centers to deal with her alcohol issues. Called me yesterday, desperate, asking me to look after Olly for a few months."

Cilla's eyes widened. "That long?"

"Yeah, and I'm floundering after day one." He leaned forward and rested his elbows on his knees. "I don't know a thing about kids, let alone a six-year-old who'd rather be with his mom than his uncle who's going through some heavy crap of his own."

Cilla opened her mouth to ask him about it but he stalled her. "I'll tell you about that later, but for now, Olly is my number one priority, and that's where you come in. I hope."

He waited, could almost see Cilla mentally joining the dots as her eyes widened.

"You want *me* to look after him?"

Sheepish, Jake shook his head. "No. I was hoping you'd let us stay here for a while. The kid's used to having a female role model in his life and I can see how quickly he bonded with you, when he barely looks at me. I thought staying here would be good for him."

Good for Jake too, if he were completely honest. He'd felt more relaxed here than he had in months. He didn't know if it was the fresh air, the familiarity of Cilla's home—the only place he'd felt safe as a kid—or Cilla's calming presence, but whatever it was, he wanted more of it. Looked like Olly wasn't the only one who needed a little of Cilla's special TLC.

When Cilla continued to stare at him like he'd gone crazy, he continued. "I know it's a huge imposition and a lot to ask after ignoring you all these years. But I always felt safe here as a kid and I think it'll be good for Olly too."

"You can stop laying it on so thick," she said, her expression softening. "You can stay."

"Thanks." Jake leaped from his chair and leaned down to hug her. "You're just as amazing as I remembered."

She batted him away but looked suitably pleased. "On one condition."

"What is it?"

"That you spend some quality time with that boy and really get to know him." She jabbed a finger at him. "Olly needs his uncle. He needs to trust you."

She hesitated before continuing. "Because Rose may have relapses, so this may not be the first and last time you're the boy's caregiver."

Damn, Jake hadn't thought of that. He'd been so busy trying to get Olly to like him that he hadn't contemplated beyond the next six weeks or so.

What if this wasn't a one-off? Cilla was right. He needed to bond with his nephew, needed to be the one guy Olly could trust in this world. Jake would've given anything to have that growing up, because his rotten father sure as hell couldn't be trusted.

"You're right." He nodded and sat again. "And while we're here, if there's any jobs you need doing, please put me to work."

An odd expression flickered across her face. "You mentioned being an aircraft mechanic before. Have you taken time off work to care for Olly?"

Jake's heart sank. He didn't want to talk about this, not when he was still digesting the thought of being Olly's caregiver now and possibly sometime in the future. But he owed Cilla an explanation and it would be easier to get it out in the open now.

"I resigned from my job six months ago." He eyed the whiskey and wished he did drink. "There was an accident. One of the planes I serviced crashed soon after takeoff, killing all eighty-nine on board."

"I'm so sorry, Jake. That must've been tough." Her audible pity didn't help. He didn't need to be pitied. He needed to be made accountable. Maybe that's why he'd taken on Olly. It was a way to redeem himself, if only in his own eyes.

"I was cleared of any wrongdoing," he said.

"But you still feel guilty anyway." It was a statement, not a question, and he marveled at how the aunt he hadn't seen in eighteen years understood him better than anyone else had after the accident.

He nodded. "I was tired on the job that day. Had been on the phone to Rose late the night before, after she finished her shift at the restaurant where she works. We had a huge argument. About Dad, ironically."

He swallowed the bile that rose whenever he thought of his father's demise. "Ironic, because after the massive argument I had with Dad, he drank himself into a stupor and fell down the stairs. Though he only killed himself by accident. I killed eighty-nine."

Cilla puffed up like an outraged bullfrog. "Now you listen to me, young man. You did not kill anyone. Accidents happen. You're not to blame. You hear me?"

He appreciated his aunt's protectiveness but he *was* to blame. He'd bowed to pressure from his superior, who demanded they get all flights that day out on time. So he'd ignored a niggle in his gut that one of the routine checks, one he'd done a thousand times as an aircraft mechanic, wasn't quite right, despite being unable to pinpoint where that niggle came from.

He'd cleared the plane for takeoff and it had crashed.

That faulty plane hadn't taken eighty-nine innocent lives.

He had.

He'd killed those people. A horrific nightmare he confronted every single day.

Being cleared of wrongdoing by the aviation authority hadn't helped. For Jake knew the truth. His actions—or inaction—that day had impacted the lives of countless people and he'd never forgive himself for it.

Cilla stood, towering over him, hands on hips. "You think I don't know what guilt is? I live with the thought I drove Vernon to his death every single day. I'd had it with his perpetual moaning about how he was going to kill himself, so I plucked up the courage to finally answer back."

Her chest heaved with the breaths she dragged in. "I told him to go ahead and do it. To stop whining and do us all a favor and follow through on his hollow threats. I taunted him . . ." She pressed the pads of her fingers to her eyes. "When I learned he'd driven his car into that tree deliberately, I beat myself up over it."

Blown away by her confession, Jake stood and enveloped her into his arms. Cilla let him comfort her for a moment before pushing away.

"But you know something? Guilt can eat away at you. It can stifle your future." She patted her chest. "After all I'd been through because of that man, I decided I wanted to embrace a new future. He owed me that much."

Jake could see the point she was trying to make but Cilla's actions, or words, more precisely, had inadvertently resulted in the death of one man. Jake's recklessness had killed way too many.

"Promise me you'll use your time here to put the past to rest and let go of your guilt." She cupped his face in her hands, forcing him to eyeball her. "Promise me."

Jake gritted his teeth. "I won't make promises I can't keep, but I'll try to work through my stuff."

She frowned but released him. "As for your father, your argument didn't drive him to drink. He did a fine job of that on his own most days."

"Yeah," he said. "When Mom died, he hit the bottle pretty hard. Do you remember that time?"

Cilla scrunched up her eyes, thinking. "You were eight and Rose was four?"

"Yeah. Mom had always been a buffer between us and Dad when he drank, but with her gone . . ." Jake had taken on that role. He'd turned into a rebel on purpose, to take his father's attention off Rose. He had happily borne the brunt of his dad's nasty streak if it meant Rose was safe.

"You did what you had to do to protect Rose," she said, staring at him with an admiration he didn't deserve.

He nodded and she continued. "I did the same with Tam." Sadness twisted her mouth. "I did anything I could to take Vernon's focus off her."

"We did what we had to do to survive," Jake said, wishing for the umpteenth time since he'd arrived earlier today that he hadn't lost touch with his aunt. A strong, resilient woman who'd had it as tough as he had, probably tougher, with the Mathieson men.

"Gardening was my savior," she said, glancing out the window into the inky darkness of a country sky. "Kept me sane."

"Tinkering with engines was mine." He had no idea why he was telling her about his past, but in a strange way, it felt cathartic. "Our neighbor was a mechanic and he took pity on me. Probably heard our arguments but never mentioned it. Instead, he taught me everything he knew. Used a contact at the airport to get me into aircraft mechanics because he knew I loved planes. He's a good guy."

"I'm glad we had our special go-to places to escape," she said. "We've come a long way, you and I." She blinked several times and Jake hoped to God she wouldn't cry. He hated tears. Didn't have a clue how to handle a woman when she cried.

"Right, I think it's time for bed," she said, suddenly brusque. "If Olly's like other kids, he'll be up at the crack of dawn, starving and eager to explore."

Which was testament to how lousy he was as an uncle, considering Olly had had to be all but dragged out of bed this morning and hadn't even wanted to walk down to the bakery for fresh bagels.

"Okay." Jake hugged his aunt again. "I can't thank you enough for letting us stay with you."

She squeezed him tight before releasing him. "I get it. You both need some time to heal." She glanced around the room fondly. "This place is perfect for that."

He hoped she was right.

11.

For the next two days, Sara fell into a routine. She woke early, ate a bowl of porridge drizzled with maple syrup, strolled through the herb garden, and spent countless hours cleaning out Gran's things, before having a light dinner of toasted cheese sandwiches, taking a shower and falling into bed, too aware of every single muscle in her body.

Cleaners had been through Gran's place when she died, but Gran's personal things had needed to be boxed, a job Sara needed to tackle and complete before she could feel like the house truly belonged to her.

Thankfully, Gran hadn't been much of a hoarder. Sara had all the books, knick-knacks and clothes boxed for charity on the first day. She'd dithered on the second day because she'd spent hours sorting through Gran's filing cabinet filled with paperwork and mementos, caught up in memories of times spent here.

She'd always wanted to live here, not be a gypsy like her mother, and thanks to Gran's generosity, now she could.

But on the third day, when she sat at the dining table contemplating her empty porridge bowl, she knew she couldn't avoid the inevitable.

She had to open the parcel.

It had arrived after she'd got home the other day and the largish brown box had taken pride of place on a sideboard ever since.

Sara had cited the clean-out as her excuse not to open the box but now that she had time, she still couldn't do it. Crazy, considering she'd ordered new tools and materials online because she wanted to try pyrography again. So what was holding her back?

She knew. Fear. The same fear that haunted her every waking moment: that nothing she did would ever make her feel good again. It was like Lucy's death had sucked all the hope out of her. That nothing was important anymore.

If pyrography, the art that had once been her world, failed to provide a spark, Sara would have to admit she'd hit rock bottom and nothing could save her.

She glared at the box and stood. She *would* open it today. She'd force herself to. After she took her morning walk.

A stroll through the herb garden couldn't be classed as a walk so she ventured farther today, striding out toward the small dam. Sure, it was an avoidance technique but hopefully the clear air would help her headspace and make her face that box on her return.

She followed the path along the hedge that bordered her property and Cilla's. She liked having no fences, liked the feeling of freedom that came with having trees and shrubs rather than wooden palings.

Sunlight dappled the ground and she was so busy studying the patterns it made she didn't see the child until it was too late. Too late to pretend she hadn't seen him and avoid any contact, which is what she would've done if she'd been more aware.

She couldn't face kids. Not yet. The pain was too raw, the gaping wound in her chest from losing Lucy unfixable.

"Hey," he said, his big, brown eyes fixed on her. "Whatcha doing?"

Sara swallowed, trying to ease the tightness in her throat. She couldn't speak.

65

The child didn't seem fazed by her lack of response. "I'm Olly. I live over there." He jerked his thumb toward Cilla's. "My mom's sick and my uncle Jake isn't very good at taking care of me, so he brought me here to stay with Cilla." He stopped, and clapped his hand over his mouth. "I mean, Aunt Cilla. Uncle Jake said I have to call her that, even though she's not my real aunt. She's too old. She's Jake's aunt." He rolled his eyes. "Uncle Jake, I mean."

The kid talked. A lot. Listening to him should've been painful, but as he rambled, the tightness in Sara's throat eased. She remembered Lucy talking like that, like she couldn't get the words out fast enough, tumbling over one another in a rush to be heard.

"You're quiet." Olly tilted his head, studying her. "What's your name?"

Sara cleared her throat. "Sara." It came out a squeak but it was a start.

Olly giggled at her high-pitched voice. "Do you have any kids I can play with?"

Sara felt her face crumple at Olly's innocuous question and tears filled her eyes as a man appeared through the hole in the hedge where Olly had wriggled through.

"Olly, why don't you head back? Aunt Cilla has a snack waiting for you." The man stood and dusted off his jeans, staring at the kid like he was as terrified of him as she was.

"Okay," Olly said, his gaze solemn as he looked up at the man. "Don't be mad, but I made Sara cry."

The man turned his attention to her and damned if she didn't want to cry harder.

He reminded her of Greg.

Something in his clear blue eyes . . . an inner confidence, a knowing, like he could take on the world and still come out on top.

It made her bristle and she clamped down on the urge to yell at him to follow the kid and to not come back.

"Run along, Olly, it'll be okay." The man gave Olly a gentle nudge toward the hole in the hedge. "See you soon."

"Sorry, Sara," Olly said, before scrambling through the hedge and disappearing from view.

For someone who hadn't wanted to converse with the child, Sara suddenly wished he'd hung around. For now she had time to study the man who, in turn, was staring at her with a little curiosity and a lot of caution.

On closer inspection, he was nothing like Greg beyond the same self-assured gaze. He was tall, a good five inches taller than her, with wavy light brown hair the same shade as her favorite caramel. He had incredible eyes, the kind of blue that was digitally altered for advertisements of the Caribbean. Tanned, with light stubble covering his jaw, he exuded the rugged handsomeness associated with sports stars. With the body to match, if her quick glance at his chest and the way the navy cotton molded to it was any indication.

The fact she noticed how damn *physical* he was annoyed her anew.

"I'm Jake Mathieson." He held out his hand. "I'm staying next door with my aunt for a few months. Olly's my nephew."

"I know. He told me," she said, managing a brief shake before releasing his hand, disconcerted by how warm it felt. "I'm Sara Hardy. This was my gran's house and I moved in a few days ago."

If he noticed the past tense, he didn't say so and she was glad. Last thing she needed on the heels of Olly's devastating question was to discuss how she'd inherited the house after Gran's death.

"I'm sorry if Olly upset you," he said, eyeing her the same way he would a jittery filly, like he expected her to kick him before bolting. "He's a good kid but going through some tough stuff at the moment."

"Aren't we all?" she said, the response slipping out before she could censor it.

"Yeah, you got that right." As he continued to eyeball her with that same hopeful yet wary expression, she wondered what had made him so sad.

Because he was. Sad. He wore it like an invisible cloak, draped around his shoulders, too heavy to bear. She recognized it because she felt the same way.

Disgruntled, not wanting to empathize or have anything else in common with him, she crossed her arms and glowered, hoping he'd get the message to leave her the hell alone.

"Anyway, sorry to intrude." He backed away, almost having to bend double to squeeze through the hole. "Maybe I'll see you around."

"Maybe." *Like never.*

Sara had no intention of following through and didn't know why she said it, but when Jake smiled, a tentative smile that lit his face and transformed him from handsome to gorgeous, she couldn't help but think *maybe* wasn't so bad after all.

As she headed back to the house, she pondered her reaction to him. That jolt she'd felt when he smiled had been sexual. The flush of warmth. The odd tingle. Reactions she hadn't felt in a long time.

When was the last time she'd had sex? She'd been separated for twelve months—and was officially divorced as of yesterday. Before that, Greg had been too busy chasing partnership in his firm and she'd been too tired at the end of each long workday followed by caring for Lucy to even think about it. Eighteen months, maybe? Longer?

If she couldn't remember, it had clearly been too long. And while she had no intention of doing anything about the lack of intimacy in her life, she couldn't help but appreciate a fine male when he looked like Jake Mathieson did.

For a split second, when he'd stared at her and smiled, she wondered what it would be like to *be* with a man again.

She clomped indoors, kicked off her boots at the back door and spied the box. It still taunted her, beckoning with its crisp brown paper wrapping and shiny label featuring a pyrographed feather and inkpot. She liked the analogy, associating etching and burning into wood with old-fashioned writing. What she didn't like were the nerves making her stomach churn with dread.

"This is crazy," she muttered under her breath, stomping across the kitchen to lift the box off the sideboard and place it on the table.

She rummaged in the junk drawer, found scissors, and carefully slit into the paper and tape. Opened the box flaps. Inhaled.

She'd always loved the smell of wood. Birch. Maple. Cherry. Each unique in its own way. It had been so long since she'd touched a piece of specially prepared wood that her hands shook as she lifted several pieces out of the box and laid them carefully on the table.

When her fingers wrapped around the solid-point tool, some of the tension in her stomach dissolved. She pulled it out of the box, staring at the state-of-the-art, electrically heated implement, whose temperature could be adjusted to produce a greater range of shades. Subtle. Bold. Various tones achieved by changing the temperature, pressure, type of wood and tool point.

After her earlier reticence, she couldn't wait to get started.

Her hands drifted over the wood until she settled on a piece. Birch. And as she waited for the tool to heat, she flipped open her wallet and extracted the picture she would attempt to burn into the wood.

Lucy, with her chin resting on her hands, smiling at the camera, fairy wings protruding over each shoulder in the background. It was Sara's favorite picture. Whimsical and cheeky and happy. Lucy all over.

Tears slid down her cheeks as she picked up the tool and swept it across the wood. Again and again and again. She didn't stop. She couldn't. All her pent-up helplessness and frustration and sorrow flowing through the soldering iron onto the wood until she sat back, exhausted.

She stared at the piece of birch, stunned. She'd captured Lucy's likeness in a way she'd never thought possible after being away from her craft so long.

The quirk of her lips. The tilt of her head. The glint in her eye.

Lucy.

Drained yet exalted, she rested her forearms on the table, laid her head on top, and bawled.

12.

I met Sara," Jake said, helping Cilla hoist two baskets brimming with herbs onto the bench in her work shed. "What's her story?"

Cilla cast him a funny sideways glance as she slipped off her gardening gloves. "If she has a story, it's hers to tell."

She turned her back on him, busying herself with firing up the burners to simmer or boil or do whatever she did to the herbs to make her concoctions.

Her evasiveness piqued his curiosity. "She definitely has a story, then?"

"Don't we all?"

Eager to learn more, he propped himself against the workbench so he could see his aunt's face. "She got pretty upset when Olly asked if she had any kids he could play with."

Cilla dropped the pipette in her hands and it hit the bench with a clatter. "Olly was with you?"

Jake nodded. "We were exploring the garden. He found a hole in the hedge and climbed through. I was content to let him go 'til I heard him talking to someone. When I followed, that's the question I heard him ask and she looked like she was about to burst into tears."

Cilla sighed, rested her hands on the bench top and hung her head. "Sara had a daughter, Lucy, who died about a year ago.

Sara's grandmother Issy owned the place. Then Issy died last month and left the house to Sara, and she moved in earlier this week."

When Cilla raised her head to look at him, her sharp gaze skewered him. "That girl needs time to heal. Seeing Olly probably isn't the best thing for her, so keep your distance."

Jake gaped at his aunt. Was she warning him off Sara because she sensed his hidden motives for asking questions?

If so, then damn, she was good. Because Jake did have other reasons for asking about the ethereal blonde who had captured his attention from the moment he'd poked his head through that hedge and caught sight of her staring at Olly like she'd seen a ghost.

Losing her daughter must've been tough. But the stark fear he'd glimpsed in her eyes spoke to other demons and he'd felt a connection. Tenuous at best, but still there, linking them in their . . . sadness?

Because that's what he felt every day when he opened his eyes, an all-pervading sadness that tainted everything he did. Food didn't taste the same anymore. Jogging had lost its appeal. Reading or movie marathons did little to distract. But he did them all anyway, moved through his life by rote, unable to dodge the constant guilt that gnawed away at any potential he had for happiness.

As for women, his deliberate dating drought suited him fine. If he couldn't muster enthusiasm for much in his life, he'd be useless with a woman. Until he dealt with his guilt, he couldn't move on.

When Sara had looked at him with that mix of fear and sorrow, a certainty in his gut told him she knew the feeling.

"Is there a husband in the picture?"

"No." Cilla's eyes narrowed, fixing him with a disapproving glare. "Issy didn't think much of him. Said she'd only seen him once, at the wedding, that he never came to visit. An uptight city type, according to Issy. More in love with his cell than with anyone else, apparently. Didn't have much time for Sara or their daughter."

Jake couldn't fathom the relief at Cilla's pronouncement. He had no intention of starting anything while he was in town, least of all with a grieving mother. "Then she's better off without him."

"Issy agreed." Cilla picked up a bunch of thyme and tied it with a string. "What about you? Anyone special in your life?"

Jake shook his head. "Relationships aren't my thing."

Cilla frowned. "Never been close to marriage?"

"I'd need to be in a long-term relationship for that to happen, so no." Increasingly uncomfortable with discussing his lack of interest in forming a lasting bond with a woman, he pushed off the bench. "Give me a holler if you need help in here."

Thankfully, she accepted his abrupt change of topic.

"I've been doing this on my own for a while, but thanks." She turned back to her mint and basil and rosemary, effectively dismissing him. "But remember what I said: Sara needs time to heal."

According to the shrink he'd seen at work to debrief, the day of the crash, he did too.

No one understood the darkness he struggled with on a daily basis.

Who knew—maybe he and Sara could heal together.

Mentally chastising himself for being foolish, he bounded up the back steps and into the kitchen, to find Olly hunched over the dining table, crayons scattered across it.

For the first time since he'd taken custody of Olly, his nephew's face lit up at the sight of him.

"Uncle Jake, check this out." Olly bounced up and down in his chair, brandishing a folded piece of paper with a giant red balloon on the front. "I've made a card for Sara to cheer her up."

Jake's chest ached for this incredibly intuitive boy who wanted to make someone else happy, when he still must be feeling disoriented himself.

He crossed the kitchen to crouch next to Olly. "That's great, buddy."

Olly grinned. "Want to see the inside?"

"You bet."

Olly opened the card with a flourish. "I hope Sara likes sharks. Because that's what I drew. And seaweed. And some fish. See?"

Jake looked at the colorful drawings and his chest constricted further. "It's brilliant, Olly. Really great."

"Thanks." Olly shrugged like Jake's praise meant little. "But I think you should give it to her. I might make her cry again." Olly's smile waned. "Mom cries sometimes too. At night, when she thinks I can't hear her, but I do. It makes me sad."

Jake wanted to bundle Olly into his arms and squeeze him tight. But Olly rarely tolerated more than a hair ruffle the last few days and he didn't want to push the tentative bond they'd formed.

He straightened and slid onto the chair next to Olly. "You know, buddy, we all get sad sometimes. And crying is a way to express that sadness. It's normal."

Olly studied him with solemnity. "Do you cry?"

Jake nodded, remembering the night of the plane crash, when he'd barely made it through his front door before breaking down and sobbing like a baby. Compared to the tears he'd shed in private as a kid, after another of his dad's brutal putdowns, it had been a doozy of a crying jag.

"Yeah, when I'm really sad."

"Me too," Olly whispered, glancing over his shoulder like he didn't want anyone else hearing. "When Mom's sad, I get sad, and sometimes I cry." He scrunched up his eyes. "And that time I fell off the swing and hurt my leg. And when the class guinea pig died when it was my turn to take it home. And that other time . . ."

Olly glanced away, furtive, and Jake didn't know whether to encourage him or leave well enough alone.

When Olly started pushing the crayons around roughly, Jake felt compelled to ask. "What other time?"

Olly pushed the crayons harder until one tumbled off the table onto the floor and he glanced up, fearful. "That first night at your house. Because I missed Mom and didn't like that seaweed stuff for dinner and I was scared."

"It'll be okay." This time Jake didn't hesitate in wrapping his arms around Olly and hugging hard. "I know being in a new place is scary but you can always count on me." He rubbed his cheek against Olly's curls and battled the burning rising in his chest. "Always."

"Thanks, Uncle Jake." Olly slid his arms around him, tentative, but when he squeezed back Jake knew they'd made serious progress.

When Olly wriggled free, he grabbed the card and thrust it at him. "Can you give Sara my card now please? Because if she has no kids to give her a hug, she won't have anyone to make her feel better like we just did."

The kid was a genius. "Okay, I'll deliver it to her now."

"And tell her I said hi." Olly scooped crayons into a pencil case. "Is it okay if I watch TV 'til you get back?"

"Sure. I'll be back soon." This time, when Jake ruffled Olly's hair, the kid beamed.

A hug might not be much in the grand scheme of things but it was progress in their relationship. And Jake knew he had Cilla to thank for it. She'd been a gentle buffer between them the last few days, getting them to help her with simple things, from weeding one of her many herb gardens to cleaning windows.

Olly had been hesitant at first—city kids didn't get to do stuff like that—but Cilla had been patient and encouraging, and soon Olly had been splashing soap suds and hoeing like a kid enjoying himself.

He'd been wary around Jake, as if he blamed his uncle for taking him away from his mom. But Cilla had advised to give it time, not to rush the boy, and Jake valued her opinion.

So that hug had been huge. A monumental step forward. Jake hoped the peace would continue. But he wasn't a fool. While Cilla had agreed to letting them stay, what happened if she grew tired of having them around? What if Jake had to head back to New York City and care for Olly alone in his sparse apartment? There were no gardens to explore or hedges to crawl through or vegetables to pick there. He had a feeling Olly would revert to being sullen and scared.

Cilla's kindness knew no bounds but the key to staying around was to make himself useful. He was good with his hands. Whatever she needed doing, he'd do it. Maybe see if he could help out in town too.

Satisfied with his plan, he slipped out the front door, wanting to bypass Cilla and a potential lecture if she knew where he was heading. It took a brisk two-minute walk to reach Sara's front door. Her house wasn't as large as Cilla's but appeared upkept, with the shutters painted a pristine white, stark against the red bricks. The garden looked tended too, a riot of color with flowers of different shades. The place looked cozy. Like a home. Something he'd never really had and had always coveted.

For him, home conjured up visions of roaring fires in winter, a hammock on a sundeck in summer and a kitchen filled with food and laughter. Happy people to love and support and nurture.

The closest he'd ever had to it growing up was when he visited next door and Cilla served up her baked goodies. Laughter had been at a premium. The rest had been a pipe dream.

Shaking off his maudlin memories, he knocked at the door. He didn't want to intrude, not after Sara had been upset earlier, but Olly had asked him to do this and at the moment, with their tentative bond slowly solidifying, he'd do anything for his nephew.

The door swung open and Sara stared at him like he'd delivered a pile of horse manure on her front step.

"What are you doing here?" A tiny frown line appeared between her brows as she half hid behind the door.

"Olly was concerned that he upset you earlier so he made you this." Knowing this could be a bad idea he thrust the card at her. "It's his way of saying sorry."

When she stared at the card in growing horror, he said, "He also asked me to say hi."

Almost as an afterthought, he added, "He's a good kid."

Sara didn't speak, her eyes downcast and expression dismayed, but she finally reached for the card. She opened it as if in slow motion and when she glanced at the drawings, a lone tear squeezed out of the corner of her eye and slid down her cheek.

Hell.

"Anyway, I just wanted to drop it off . . ." He trailed off as more tears followed the first, and Sara stumbled back with an anguished cry, before pressing her fist to her mouth.

Jake's gut went into free-fall. This was bad. Really bad. He'd stirred up a hornet's nest of emotions when he should've left well enough alone.

She didn't slam the door and he felt awful leaving her in this state, so he followed her into the house, concern and discomfort making him feel gauche. What did he do in a situation like this? He barely knew the woman so he had no right comforting her, but as the card slid from her hands and she cried harder, he instinctively reached for her.

Surprisingly, she let him hold her. Let him smooth her hair, stroke her back, and whisper trite things like "It's okay."

But it wasn't okay. At least, not for him. Because as he held her, he started to notice things. The way she fit perfectly against him. The way her hair smelled: like vanilla and coconut. The way she snuggled into him and clutched at his shirt, like she never wanted to let go.

At that moment, the hug morphed from comforting to something else for him and he slowly disengaged, not wanting to scare her off completely if she felt exactly how much he liked holding her.

"I'm sorry," she said, swiping at her eyes with her fingertips. "You must think I'm an idiot for blubbering all over you like that."

"I don't think you're an idiot." He glanced at the card on the floor, unsure whether to pick it up or not.

She followed his gaze and her lips compressed, as if she struggled to fight back tears again. "My daughter Lucy died a year ago. I'm coping okay but there are days . . ." She squatted, picked up the card, and straightened. "It's rough."

"I'm so sorry about Lucy." He shook his head, powerless to do anything but offer trite condolences. "I can't imagine what you've gone through."

"Not many can," she said, staring at the card with a glimmer of interest. "Olly seems like a sweet kid. Especially to do this for me when he thought he upset me."

"He is," Jake said. "If seeing him makes things worse for you, I'll make sure he stays out of your way."

To her credit, she didn't offer false protest. Instead, she headed down the hallway and beckoned for him to follow. "Let's see how it goes."

As he followed her, the walls caught his eye. Or more precisely, what covered them. Beautiful pictures burned into pieces of wood and leather. Exquisite drawings made by a very talented artist.

"These are amazing," he said, gently tracing the outline of a rose etched into a pale wood. "Was your grandma an artist?"

Sara paused in the kitchen doorway, shuffling her weight from side to side, uncomfortable. "Actually, I did those."

"Wow, you're good." He stepped closer to another piece of wood, depicting the house. "Exceptionally good."

"Thanks. I haven't done pyrography for years, but I've just ordered some new materials and was planning to tinker."

"You should." He met her gaze, felt that jolt again, the same one he'd experienced in the garden. "Have you ever shown your work professionally?"

Her eyes widened. "Like an exhibition, you mean?"

"Yeah. I've been to a fair share of gallery openings in New York and your stuff is much better than anything I've seen there."

A tentative smile played about her lips and it made something twang in his chest. He'd hazard a guess she didn't smile often these days—he knew the feeling—and it transformed her from pretty to stunning.

"After a compliment like that, I should either offer you a coffee in gratitude or pour you a whiskey in the hope I'll hear more lies like that."

He found himself smiling back at her, the muscles in his face almost creaking at the foreign movement. "A coffee would be great."

He followed her into the kitchen, a huge room that also housed a dining table, a sideboard and giant chest of drawers. Various pieces of wood and a tool that looked like a soldering iron covered the table.

"This your stuff?"

At the sink filling a kettle with water, she glanced over her shoulder and nodded. "Yeah."

"You did all those pieces in here?" It didn't look like much of a workspace.

The light from her earlier smile faded. "No. There's a shed at the back of the property. I loved working down there."

"And now?"

"I prefer to work here." Her tone curt, she busied herself with spooning coffee into cups and he knew there was more to the story.

But he had no right to delve, not when it might precipitate another crying bout.

He picked up the soldering iron and turned it over. Tools fascinated him, always had, hence his interest in mechanics. "So you burn pictures into the wood using this?"

She nodded, the tension of a moment ago fading. "Traditionally defined, pyrography is the art of writing with fire."

She crossed the kitchen and plucked the tool out of his hands. "See this tip? It's electrically heated to scorch designs into the wood or leather, the mediums I work with."

Intrigued by how animated her expression was when discussing her art, he wanted to keep her talking.

"How did you get started?"

"I loved art at school." She wrinkled her nose and gave an unladylike snort that he found cute. "Had a huge crush on my teacher, so it was the only class I paid any attention in." She flipped the tool over, weighing it in her palm. "One day he started talking about some cultures, like the Egyptians and a few African tribes, and how they practiced pyrography. I've been fascinated by it ever since."

She laid down the tool and blinked, as if reawakening from a memory. "But like anyone who led a nomadic life and got dragged around the country and brought up without much money, I ignored my artistic side, did a finance degree at college and became a financial analyst."

She didn't sound bitter but he saw the way she glanced at the paraphernalia on the table. Wistful, with a hint of hope.

Anything that could make her hopeful after what she'd been through, he was all for.

"You're taking a sabbatical?"

She shook her head. "I quit. Gran left me this place and I've got enough saved to have a year off work. After that . . ." She shrugged. "Who knows? I'll find a job around here."

"Or you could concentrate on your art."

She stared at him like he'd suggested she pose naked for art rather than do it. "I couldn't make a living out of that."

"Why not? Other artists do."

She pulled a face. "But they're good—"

"So are you, sweetheart, trust me."

The endearment slipped out and he held his breath, expecting her to renege on her offer of coffee pronto. Instead, she chose to ignore it, and finished making the coffee.

"Cream and sugar?"

"Neither," he said, content to watch her move about the kitchen. There was nothing overtly sexy about her outfit: fitted red tank top, knee-length navy shorts, and beaded flip-flops. But the way the clothes clung to her body, highlighting her trim waist yet curvy hips and breasts, made him wonder why he'd sworn off women until he got his head together.

"Let's take these outside," she said, glancing over her shoulder in time to see him staring at her legs.

Great.

He hoped his rueful grin conveyed he wasn't a perv as much as a red-blooded male appreciating a pretty woman.

Her brows knitted together, as if she were perplexed that he'd find her attractive, and she waited until he opened the back door before stepping through.

Cilla might have warned him off Sara, and he might not want to date while he was still screwed up over the crash, but for a brief moment, when she'd noticed his appreciation of her assets and acknowledged it with confusion rather than a backhander, he wondered if getting to know Sara better could be an option after all.

13.

After living with Jake and Olly for five days, Cilla needed a break. Not that she didn't love the company, but after living on her own for so long, it was tough having her personal space invaded.

She was used to early nights, waking at dawn, then puttering at her own pace. She liked the solitude, having her house sorted and everything in its place. She'd forgotten how kids made a mess and didn't always follow the same routine she did.

As a child, Tam had, because Cilla made her. She hadn't wanted Tam getting underfoot with Vernon and potentially drawing his wrath, so she'd made her follow a strict routine. Tam had rebelled initially, like any sane kid would, but after a vicious tongue-lashing from her father when she'd accidentally knocked over one of his beer bottles, Tam had fallen into line.

She'd been five at the time, only a year younger than Olly, and the thought of what her child had grown up with—the regimented routines, the forced quiet, all because she hadn't wanted to annoy Vernon . . . damn, was it any wonder Tam didn't want to have much to do with her these days?

No child should be made to feel like they're an intrusion in their own home. But fear had been a powerful motivator for Cilla back then and she would've done anything—and had—to protect Tam from Vernon.

She knew that's why she'd allowed Jake and Olly to stay. Saw it as a second chance. For both of them. From what she'd seen, Jake was right; Olly needed a female figure in his life and the way she'd bonded with the child so quickly made her feel useful in a way she hadn't in a long time.

As for Jake, she liked having him around. Liked his dry sense of humor, his ability to detect moods, his valuing quiet in the evenings when she wanted nothing more than to curl up with a good romance novel.

But after almost a week of living under each other's noses, it was time for a break and Cilla headed to her other favorite place in Redemption besides home: the hospital.

Some people hated hospitals; feared them with a passion that bordered on phobia. She liked the antiseptic smell, the orderliness, the notion that people were being healed and helped. For her, death was an inescapable fact of life, sickness something she hoped to avoid but wouldn't fear. She'd already spent half her life living in fear and she was done with that the moment she received news of Vernon's suicide.

She visited the hospital on a weekly basis. Read to the old people. Played games with the kids. Organized fundraisers for new equipment. It made her feel valued in a way she never had before. Today, she'd promised to play rummy with Sergio, an adorable eight-year-old battling leukemia. His parents were struggling, raising four kids eight and under, and the medical bills were adding to their stress.

She'd already mentioned organizing a mini-fair to raise funds to help with Sergio's bills and they'd been ecstatic. In the meantime, she had a date with one cute kid.

Waving at the nurses as she headed for Sergio's room, she didn't notice Bryce until she almost trod on his toes as he rounded a corner.

"You're in a hurry," he said, his hands shooting out to grab her upper arms, his deep voice sending a ripple of awareness through her.

Damn the man and his too-good looks, his too-husky voice and his too-sexy bedroom eyes.

"I'm visiting someone," she said, stepping out of his grasp.

"If it's a patient, you can slow down. Odds are they'll be in their bed waiting for you." His eyes twinkled with mischief and she had no idea if there was an innuendo behind his comment or not.

He took a step closer and leaned down to murmur in her ear. "Ready to have dinner with me yet?"

"No," she blurted, resisting the urge to shove him away. This close, she could see the laugh lines radiating from the corners of his eyes, the faint stubble covering his jaw, and could smell that fresh aftershave that gave the impression he'd just stepped out of the shower.

"You'll have to give in sometime, you know." He straightened and Cilla inwardly cursed the unexpected craving to have him close again. "It's inevitable."

She rolled her eyes, unwilling to admit she was enjoying their banter as much as he was, if his bemused smile was any indication.

"Why don't you go flirt with someone your own age?"

"Is that what you think we're doing? *Flirting?*" His smile broadened. The way he said *flirting*, he made it sound like they were doing something far naughtier.

The thought alone had heat surging to her cheeks.

"And here I was, thinking we're just old friends getting reacquainted." He lowered his voice. "By the way, you're gorgeous when you blush."

Which of course, only served to make Cilla blush harder.

The man was incorrigible and she needed to put him in his place before this went any further.

"We were never friends. You were my daughter's friend." She scowled, hands on hips. "As for getting reacquainted, we weren't acquainted in the first place. And the only old thing in this equation is *me*."

She finished on an outraged huff that made him laugh.

"Are you done?"

She compressed her lips into a mutinous line in response.

"Did it ever occur to you that the only reason I hung out at your house with Tam was to see you?"

Her jaw dropped, shock rendering her speechless when she wanted to give him a tongue-lashing for being so ridiculous.

"I'm not ashamed to admit now that I was a horny seventeen-year-old who had a crush on his friend's very hot mom," he said, eyeballing her with frank admiration while she struggled to absorb the astounding news. "And now, twenty-five years later, I discover you're just as beautiful. And single. So what's a guy to do?"

"Do?" It came out a screech and she lowered her voice when a passing nurse tittered. "I'll tell you what you can do."

She jabbed a finger at his chest, not surprised it felt as hard as it looked. "You can quit badgering me and go find some nice *young* girl to take to dinner."

"Age is irrelevant to me," he said, with a shrug.

"It's not to me, considering I'm sixty." She jabbed him again for good measure. "And sexagenarians don't date guys in their forties, no matter how handsome they are."

"You think I'm handsome?" That infuriating grin was back, devastatingly charming. "And you're mentioning sex before we've even had dinner."

"God, you're annoying," she said, pushing past him and diving into Sergio's room, trying to ignore Bryce's taunting chuckles behind her.

The curtain was drawn around Sergio's bed and she was glad for the reprieve, so she could press her cool palms against her hot cheeks.

She couldn't remember the last time she'd flirted, let alone enjoyed it so much. As for Bryce's declaration, she couldn't fathom it. Back then, she'd been a frazzled thirty-five-year-old, dealing with a hormonal teenager who had never made a secret of the fact she was counting down the months until she left for college. Vernon's moroseness had continued to spiral out of control as he alternated between verbally abusing her and dosing up on pills to anaesthetize his demons. And Cilla had been working as a paralegal secretary, trying to make ends meet and pretend like she had the best life in the world, when in fact her home life was in tatters.

She remembered Bryce trying to talk to her back then, the usual polite small talk, and she'd never picked up any vibes. Then again, he'd been a teen and probably used to hiding his feelings, as most teens did.

He'd had a crush on her. Hot damn.

The curtain pulled back and a nurse stepped out, saw her, and beckoned her forward. "Hey Cilla. Your young man's been waiting for you."

"Cilla, you came," Sergio said, sitting up straighter in bed, his brown eyes fixed on her like she was his lifeline.

Hospital boredom was the pits—she'd fractured her leg after falling in her garden three years ago, so she understood the yearning for visitors.

"Of course I came. We've got a rummy tournament to play."

"You better teach me right then," Sergio said, rubbing his bald head, an endearing habit. "I'm no good at card games."

The nurse smiled and slipped out of the room and Cilla pulled a chair up to the bed.

"You'll be the best by the time we've finished." She took a pack of cards from her bag, slipped them out of the packet and started shuffling. "Besides, I'm tired of you beating me at checkers."

He grinned, his missing front tooth adding to his adorability. "You were bad."

"Is that bad in a good way? Like how kids say something's wicked when it's good?"

He giggled. "You're funny."

"And don't you forget it," she said, giving his tummy a light tickle, well aware he bruised easily and not wanting to add to his pain. "Now, let me explain the rules."

However, Cilla never got around to the rules: Bryce sauntered into the room. He now wore a white coat and had a stethoscope hanging around his neck, adding to his attractiveness, damn the man.

"Hey, Sergio. I see you have a visitor." Bryce held up his hand for Sergio to high-five it.

"This is Cilla," Sergio said. "She's cool."

"I think so too." Bryce grinned when Cilla shot him a death glare. "We're old friends."

"Really?" Sergio's curious gaze swung between her and Bryce. "Did you go to school together?"

Cilla snorted. Maybe she should chat to Sergio's parents about an eye test.

"No," Bryce said, amusement lacing his tone. "But we've known each other a long time." He perched on the side of Sergio's bed. "Haven't seen each other for years though and I'm trying to make a time so we can catch up."

The ratbag. He was trying to use a child in coercing her to go out with him?

"You should have lunch," Sergio said, pronouncing it like the most natural thing in the world when the thought of dining with

Bryce at any time of day or night let loose an entire species of butterfly in her gut.

"Good idea, pal." Bryce stroked his chin, pretending to think. "But I work all day."

"Then go out to dinner," Sergio said, looking immensely proud of himself for coming up with a solution.

"That sounds doable." Bryce glanced at her with a faux innocence that would have made her laugh, if only she hadn't wanted to slap him silly.

"You should go, Cilla." Sergio tugged on her sleeve. "Doc Madden is your friend and you should have dinner with him. He's nice and you're nice. Dinner would be fun."

"Maybe I will."

"I don't like maybe," Sergio said, with surprising vehemence. "I hear that stupid word all the time. Maybe I'll get out of here by the end of summer vacation. Maybe I'll get a new room when I get home. Maybe my new medicine will fix me." He mimicked his mom's tone. "Maybe is dumb."

This time when Bryce met her gaze, he looked suitably chastised. So he should, roping Sergio into his underhanded plot to get her to agree. Which she now basically had to, if she didn't want to upset Sergio.

"Cilla, you need to pinkie-promise Doc Madden that you'll have dinner with him," Sergio said, his solemn expression tugging at her heartstrings. "Now."

With a resigned sigh, Cilla held up her little finger and glared at Bryce when he intertwined it with his.

"Yay." Sergio clapped. "You two will have dinner and tell me what you ate." His eyes brightened. "If you go to that cool burger place on Main Street, do you think you could bring me some fries? And a banana split? And one of those giant brownies?"

"I'm not sure where we're going yet, pal, but you know that stuff isn't good for you at the moment," Bryce said.

Sergio rolled his eyes. "Yeah, I know, because *maybe* I'll vomit."

Cilla knew Sergio enjoyed her plain butter cookies and they didn't disagree with his stomach, which was fragile from the chemo drugs. "How about I bring in some of those cookies you like instead?"

"You're the best," Sergio said, his grin infectious.

"I agree," Bryce said, and when their gazes locked, it was her stomach that roiled and tumbled and flipped.

She was going to have dinner with Bryce Madden.

She wasn't just crazy.

She was certifiably insane.

14.

Jake hadn't stayed long, thank goodness.

They'd had coffee on the back deck overlooking the garden that sloped away toward the back of the property. Made small talk mostly. Trivial stuff about the town and the weather.

Sara liked that he hadn't delved further. He hadn't asked about Lucy or her old job or her past. While curiosity had urged her to ask him about why he'd taken custody of Olly, and how he could take a few months off work to care for him, she hadn't.

If she wasn't willing to talk about her life, why should she expect that of him?

It had been oddly comfortable, sitting with him on the back porch. While their chatter had been inconsequential, his presence made her feel safe, in a way she hadn't in a long time.

She didn't need a guy to complete her life. Wouldn't go down the marriage path again. But for a brief time, allowing Jake's deep voice to wash over her, savoring his spontaneous laughter, she'd felt good having a man around.

As for the way he'd comforted her when she'd broken down over Olly's card, that had felt beyond good. She'd been mortified at first, but when her sobs had petered out, she'd become more aware of something more disturbing.

How good it felt to have a guy hold her.

His body had been hard. Strong. Muscular. And as he'd pulled away, she was pretty sure she felt his erection pressed against her hip.

Surprisingly, her body had reacted on a visceral level, a low persistent throb reminding her that while her head and heart weren't interested in anything remotely sexual, her body was having a hard time sticking with the program.

Ignoring the way her pulse raced at the memory of being pressed against him, she headed back inside, rinsed the coffee cups and stacked them on the sideboard.

Her gaze fell on Olly's card and she was instantly ashamed.

Olly was a kid and she'd hurt him. Not intentionally, but if he felt like he was responsible for making her sad and had made an apology card, she'd done wrong by him.

She had to get a better grip on her emotions. Had to be able to control her grief. It had been over twelve months since Lucy had gone and while she'd never get over it, she had to ensure that her emotional fragility didn't impact those around her. Especially other kids.

Maybe she'd done the wrong thing, deliberately shunning anything to do with children. And with Olly next door for the next few months, she couldn't keep avoiding him.

As she opened the card and glimpsed the sea pictures he'd drawn, her heart contracted. While the drawings were crude and rudimentary, he'd taken his time, painstakingly choosing colors and spacing.

He'd done this for her.

To cheer her up. To make her feel better. To apologize.

That was exactly what she would do for him.

Taking a seat at the table, she propped the open card against the box, chose a piece of beech wood and fired up her tool.

She hadn't touched it since replicating the photo of Lucy. It had been emotionally draining yet exhilarating to discover she could create again, but she'd wanted to treasure her first pyrography piece in years before continuing. So she'd hung it over the mirror in her bedroom, ensuring it was the first thing she saw every morning and the last thing each night.

Etching Olly's drawings into the beech would make a great present and hopefully reassure him that he hadn't upset her. No kid deserved to feel bad or to blame for an adult's pain.

It took an hour to complete and when she'd finished the last fin on the shark, Sara sat back and eyed her work critically. She'd always been able to do that, even as a teen—objectively assess and find room for improvement.

This piece, like the one she'd done of Lucy, appeared flawless. Better than anything she'd ever done before. But how was that possible, when she hadn't picked up a tool or touched a piece of wood creatively for so many years?

She should be rusty, tentative. Instead, when she scorched designs into the wood now, it felt natural, like she should've been doing this her entire life.

She found herself smiling at the thought of Greg trying to accept this as her career in the past. He'd been so driven to make partner at his firm and so proud to have a wife equally as motivated in the corporate world.

Not that Sara hadn't enjoyed her work. She had. But it was nothing compared to the rightness she felt when she etched strokes into wood.

Thankfully, she didn't have to worry about Greg's opinions anymore. The divorce papers had been finalized. They were no longer a couple, officially.

She should've been devastated. Disheartened. Yet all she felt was bone-deep sorrow that they hadn't been able to make their marriage work. In the end, Lucy had been the proverbial glue that held their marriage together and when she'd died, they had fallen apart.

Selling their home had been gut-wrenching, however, because it was where she'd brought Lucy home from the hospital, where they'd shared so many memories. Odd that Greg hadn't put up even a token protest when she'd moved out not long after the funeral, yet he'd made a last-ditch effort to save the marriage before the divorce went through.

He'd done as she'd asked and hadn't contacted her following that last videoconference call. It had saddened her, the way he'd asked her to come back more because they were a good "fit" than anything else.

He hadn't said he'd missed her or loved her or any other sentimental declarations. For him, having a second chance for their marriage would've been about appearances, maybe even prestige at his firm.

Whatever his rationale, she'd put it behind her. For a marriage that had held so much promise at the start, it had ended with an unimpressive fizzle.

But she didn't want to think about that now. She couldn't wait to see Olly's reaction when he saw his drawings embossed onto the beech wood. However, when she stood and picked up the piece, a momentary panic flared to life, fluttering in her chest like a caged bird.

Did she really want to seek out contact with a child? To potentially be exposed to that unique, addictive smell kids had? To hear his adorable chatter? To maybe receive a thank-you hug?

A hug from a child would undo her completely. Then again, hadn't she come to the realization after Jake left that she needed to get a grip and better handle her emotions around other people?

"You can do this," she muttered, cradling the piece in her hands as she headed for the door.

She didn't have to stay. She would deliver her work to Olly as a peace offering and cite some excuse to make a quick escape.

But that turned to crap when Olly spied her walking up Cilla's front path, flung open the door, raced out to meet her, and flung his arms around her waist.

She couldn't breathe, the memory of Lucy doing the same when she picked her up from preschool every day making her lungs seize.

But Sara took deep, steadying breaths, forcing the air down into her lungs. She wouldn't disappoint this child again. It wouldn't be right.

He squeezed tight for a second before stepping back. "Sara, did you like my card? Wasn't that shark the best ever? Are you happy now?" The questions tumbled out of Olly's mouth one after another and she swallowed the lump in her throat and forced a smile.

"The card was amazing, Olly, thank you." She held out the wood to him. "I loved it so much that I made something for you in return."

Olly's eyes widened to saucer-like proportions as he took the wood and studied it. "Those are my pictures. In the wood. Wow!" He jumped up and down on the spot, clutching the wood tight. "It's awesome! How did you do it?"

"It's called pyrography, where I use a special instrument to burn patterns into wood."

He traced the shark with his fingertip before fixing his pleading gaze on her. "Can I watch you do it one day? Pretty please?"

"Artists don't like being watched while they create," Jake said, stepping out onto the front porch, the impact of seeing him again more devastating than Sara had imagined.

It had little to do with his appearance, though the plain navy polo outlining his chest and the faded denim highlighting his legs weren't half bad. It had more to do with his eyes and the way he looked at her. Intense. Compelling. Mesmerizing.

Olly's face fell and the dislike in the glare he shot Jake made her wonder again about their relationship.

"This really is awesome," Olly said, brandishing the wood at her. "Thanks, Sara."

"You're welcome," she said, relieved when Olly clutched his present and ran inside.

A relief that was short-lived when she realized that left her alone with Jake.

"That was a really great thing you did," he said, and thrust his hands into his pockets. "Thanks."

"My pleasure." She shrugged, his scrutiny making her uncomfortable. "The least I could do after inadvertently making him feel bad because he thought he made me sad."

Jake nodded, thoughtful. "He's intuitive for his age."

"How old is he?"

"Six going on sixty."

They smiled in mutual understanding of what it was like to deal with precocious kids, an unexpected bonding moment that made Sara begin to like Jake more, even though she didn't want to.

"My sister Rose is going through a hard time at the moment so I'm looking after him." His declaration sounded almost defiant, like he expected her to judge him in some way and find him lacking.

"Have you two always been close?"

"Me and Olly, you mean?"

She nodded, though she was curious about his sister too, and about what was so terrible as to drag a mom away from her kid. Nothing had kept her away from Lucy. Except work on the odd occasion.

Tears burned the backs of her eyes but she wouldn't let them fall. Not this time. She had to toughen up. She had to.

Jake stared at her a moment longer than polite, as if he could almost see her anguish and the inner struggle she faced. Then he continued. "Rose and I have always been close so I try to be around for her and Olly when they need me."

There was a host of untold stories behind that one sentence. Jake was close to his sister, but only when she needed him? What about the other times? Did he keep his distance or did Rose not want him around? So many questions she had no right knowing the answers to.

"Cilla's husband and our dad were brothers. She's always been a good aunt." His brows knitted in consternation. "Barely batted an eyelid when I called her up after eighteen years and asked if I could visit."

"Eighteen years?"

Sheepish, Jake nodded. "Our family's pretty dysfunctional. Not Cilla's fault. More my dad's. When Cilla's husband killed himself, my dad blamed her and cut all ties." He glanced over his shoulder at the house, as if he expected her to materialize behind him. "Considering my mom died when I was eight, she was the only female relative we had and she was amazing. Still is."

As Sara absorbed the glut of info she hadn't been expecting, Jake blew out a breath.

"Sorry. No idea why I told you all that."

"Sometimes it helps to talk about stuff," she said, wishing she could take her own advice.

After Lucy died, she'd shunned any suggestion of therapy or grief counselling. She hadn't talked to Greg about her feelings, or to anyone for that matter. Which probably explained why her emotions were still on a hair-trigger over twelve months later.

As if he could read her mind, his enigmatic stare bore into her. "Yeah, it can help, if you talk to the right person."

Flattered that he was insinuating he felt comfortable talking to her, she blurted, "My door's always open if you want to talk anytime." Then second-guessed her impulsive invitation the second she'd issued it. Damn, why had she said that? Her stomach clenched at the thought of being his confidante when she had enough angst of her own to deal with.

"Likewise," he said, a moment before they heard a crash and the startled wail of a kid who has broken something. "Though it's kinda busy around here, so let's make it your place, not mine."

He hadn't made it sound remotely sexy but the cliché "Your place or mine?" immediately leaped into Sara's conscious and refused to budge.

"Sure," she said, confident he wouldn't take her up on the offer. What sort of guy wanted to unburden himself to a virtual stranger, especially a woman who'd already blubbered on him?

"Thanks again," he said, jerking his thumb over his shoulder. "I better go see what that was and whether I can salvage it before Cilla gets home."

She nodded and retraced her steps down the path, strangely discombobulated. A quick glance over her shoulder confirmed why. Jake hadn't moved from the top step as he watched her walk away.

With a quick wave, she continued down the path, all too aware of his heated gaze burning into her back.

She should never have issued that invitation for him to come chat anytime.

Worse, she shouldn't be looking forward to the prospect so darn much.

15.

Jake waited until Sara had reached the end of the drive and turned toward her place before heading inside.

He should've investigated the cause of that crash sooner but he hadn't heard any further distressed cries from Olly. And he hadn't been able to resist watching Sara's hips sway in those shorts.

Damn, that woman was hot.

Although she'd issued him an open invitation to drop by anytime, he'd be stupid to take her up on it, considering the way he'd blurted all that stuff about his family.

One minute she'd been asking about him and Olly, the next he was giving her an abbreviated version of Mathieson's Sordid Tales.

Yeah, like a woman he fancied wanted to hear more about his sad past.

He shook his head, trying to eradicate the vision of Sara's ass in those shorts. It didn't work and he sighed as he stepped into the hallway and saw Olly's handiwork.

He'd knocked one of Cilla's potpourri containers off a table. Thankfully, it was made of metal, but its contents lay scattered across the floor.

Olly was nowhere to be seen.

"Olly," he called out. "Come clean up, please."

"Don't want to," a voice said, from behind the sofa in the adjacent room.

Sensing he was in for a battle, Jake entered the living room and found Olly crouched behind the sofa, hugging his knees to his chest.

Jake squatted to his level. "Olly, you made that mess; you need to clean it up."

"No." Olly thrust his chin up, defiance darkening his eyes to black.

Completely out of his depth when it came to disciplining kids, Jake continued. "It's not fair on Aunt Cilla to come home and find that mess. Not when she's letting us stay here."

Jake only just heard Olly mutter, "I wanna go home."

"We can't do that for now, buddy, so why don't you come help me—"

"I'm not your buddy!" Olly scrambled to his feet and backed away. "Sara is, but you won't let me go watch her do that fire burning stuff."

Ah, so that's what this was about.

"We can talk about that another time but for now, you need to tackle that mess."

Olly rolled his eyes. "Big people always say that when they don't want to tell the truth." He mimicked, "We'll talk about it later."

Jake bit back a smile. This kid really was smart.

"How about you help me clean up and then we'll find a really good spot for your present from Sara?"

Jake hoped bribery would work because he was plain out of options on how to coerce Olly into cleaning up.

Interest sparked in Olly's eyes. "Can I keep it in my room?"

Jake nodded. "If you want."

"Fine," Olly spat out, making it sound far from fine.

But at least the kid followed him back to the hallway and carefully swept the dried rose petals and orange peel into a bag, then put it in the bin outside.

Jake had no idea why Olly blew hot and cold with him. He'd thought they'd been making progress, then an incident like this happened and they were back to square one.

Sure, the kid must've been scared, unsure how Jake would react to his knocking over one of Cilla's ornaments, but Jake had given him no reason to fear him. And he couldn't see Rose being the type of mom to rant and rave and punish.

So why was Olly okay with Cilla and not him? Even Sara, whom Olly hardly knew, seemed to have more success relating to his nephew than he did.

"Can I take this to my room now?" Olly clutched Sara's gift to his chest, glaring at Jake as if he would more than likely steal it.

"Sure, bud—" Jake bit back calling him *buddy*. He didn't want to ruin their tentative truce before it had begun. "Though perhaps Aunt Cilla might like to see it before you do?"

"Aunt Cilla might like to see what?" she called out from the kitchen and Jake breathed out a sigh of relief.

At last, someone who could handle Olly better than he could.

"Aunt Cilla, I've got a surprise to show you," Olly bellowed, all but skipping to the kitchen when a moment ago, he'd been the epitome of doom.

"Kids," Jake muttered, and set off after him. He found Cilla hanging her coat on the hook by the back door as she laughed at Olly, who was hopping excitedly from one foot to the other and brandishing the wood from side to side.

"Check this out," Olly said, finally coming to a stop when Cilla laid a hand on his shoulder. "I made a card for Sara, because I made her sad. Then she copied my card onto this wood." Olly turned adoring eyes to Cilla and handed her the picture. "Isn't it the coolest?"

Cilla's eyebrows rose as she studied the wood. "It sure is," she said, and then frowned as Olly snatched it back out of her hands.

"That's not polite," she said, her firm tone brooking no argument.

To Jake's surprise, Olly nodded meekly and said, "Sorry."

Jake had no idea how his aunt did it, but her skills as a child whisperer far exceeded his.

"Olly, why don't you go put that in your room?" Jake said, bracing for a potential rebuttal.

Thankfully, Olly shrugged. "Okay," he said, and ran from the kitchen with his prized possession.

Cilla eyed him speculatively. "Sounds like you've had a busy day."

"Yeah. Want a coffee?"

"No thanks. Drank my fill at the hospital." She toed off her shoes and sank into a chair. "But I'd kill for a brownie."

"Coming right up." Jake raided her brownie stash, piling several on a plate, and placing it on the table. "How did your visit at the hospital go?"

"Good." To his surprise, she blushed. "Actually, I want to talk to you about something, but first tell me about Sara and that amazing piece of art."

"You ain't seen nothing yet," he said, sitting alongside his aunt. "When I visited earlier to drop off Olly's card I saw her work. It's incredible."

"She invited you in?"

"Yeah, once I ditched my prison stripes," he said, and she chuckled at his dry response. "The house is filled with artwork like that, pieces that she did years ago. I'm surprised you didn't know."

Cilla shrugged. "Issy and I were friends, but the kind of neighbors who kept to ourselves, you know? We talked a lot over the fence, if we were gardening, but didn't invite each other in."

"I get it." Jake valued his privacy too. Fallout from not being able to invite friends home as a kid because of the mood his father might be in. "Anyway, her artwork is incredible. It belongs in a show."

"Does it now?" Cilla tapped her bottom lip, deep in thought. "It may tie in nicely with what I need to ask you."

Curious, he snaffled a brownie. "What's that?"

"There's a sick child at the hospital. Leukemia." Sadness clouded her eyes. "Sergio's the eldest of four kids and his parents don't have a lot of money, so I'm putting together a mini-fair to raise funds for him."

Impressed by his aunt's thoughtfulness, he said, "That's great. What can I do?"

"I'll need someone mechanical-minded to sort out the logistics. Placement of the stalls. Putting them all together. The general layout, that kind of thing. You up for it?"

"Absolutely." It would give him something to do so he wasn't spending every waking hour pondering his fraught relationship with Olly, worrying about Rose or, his latest mind-muddler, obsessing over Sara. "Whatever you need, let me know."

"Thanks." Cilla patted his hand. "It'll be good for you, getting out and about."

The hint of judgment in her tone surprised him. "Olly and I have been out exploring this week."

"I meant you." She gestured at the window. "It's been good, seeing you two spend time together outside most days, but you need some time to yourself. Head into town. Explore. Socialize." She pointed upstairs. "I'll look after Olly whenever you want."

"He's my responsibility," Jake said, knowing it sounded lame but not wanting to reveal his real reason for staying close to home.

He just wasn't up to facing people.

For the last six months, he'd been holed up in his apartment. Ordering take-out, watching movies, surfing the Internet and avoiding contact with people.

Because every time he saw anyone having fun with their friends or family, he remembered how he'd robbed eighty-nine people of having the same kind of fun.

"You don't have to be with the boy twenty-four-seven," Cilla said, staring at him with open curiosity. "You need to get out. It's healthy."

"Sara said I can pop by anytime, so maybe I'll go there to 'get out'." He made air quotes with his fingers.

Cilla barked out a laugh. "Yeah, that's what you need. To spend time with a woman who's as much of a hermit as you are."

"Didn't you just say you'd never been inside your friend's house in . . . how many years?"

"Touché," Cilla said. "Actually, I might pop next door and have a quick word with Sara."

"Yeah?"

Cilla nodded. "Maybe she'd consider selling some of her artwork at the fair."

"Good idea." Because, Jake thought, as one of the fair's newly appointed helpers, it would give him a legitimate excuse to see Sara again. Easier than taking her up on her invitation and feeling awkward if she regretted issuing it in the first place. "I think it would do her good to get involved in something. To have a goal."

Cilla pointed to the stove. "Pot. Meet kettle."

Jake grinned. "I have a goal. Helping with the fair." His first goal in a long time. His grin faded. "Seriously, I think she needs it. She's emotionally fragile."

"Did she tell you about her child's death?"

He nodded. "Not the details, but she did mention it. Considering how she freaked out in front of Olly, guess she felt like she owed me some kind of explanation."

"Yet she made an effort to come over and see him?" Cilla pushed her brownie plate away. "That's progress in itself for someone who must find being around kids incredibly painful."

"Olly likes her," Jake said, wondering if he was the only person in Olly's small world the kid didn't like. "Maybe it would do them good to spend some time together?"

"Whoa." Cilla held up her hands. "Don't go pushing them together. Give her time. As for Olly . . ." Cilla trailed off, appearing reluctant to continue.

"What about him?"

"Don't take this the wrong way, but you're too soft on the boy." Cilla steepled her fingers and rested them in her lap. "He needs boundaries. A male role model to look up to." Sadness downturned the corners of her mouth. "I don't know much about Rose's situation and how she's brought the boy up, but he's a good kid. He's respectful. He knows right from wrong. And he's affectionate. But having a strong man he can look up to is important for boys his age."

"Are you saying I haven't been around enough for him to respect me?"

Jake hated how defensive he sounded. He knew Cilla was trying to help, and God knew he needed it, but he could barely keep it together these days. How the hell could he be the role model Olly needed?

"That's not what I'm saying." She shook her head. "I just see the two of you around each other. At times, it's beautiful to watch. Others, it's like you're overcompensating by giving him a free rein." She tapped her temple. "Kids are smart. They're masters at manipulation and if Olly learns how to push your buttons, he'll do it."

Feeling increasingly incompetent, he sighed. "Guess I'm trying too hard. I see how he is with you, even Sara, who he hardly knows, and he's natural and spontaneous."

He pinched the bridge of his nose to ease the headache that was building. "With me, it feels stilted. One minute he's fine, the next he hates me." He eyeballed his aunt, wondering if she could see the silent plea for help in his eyes. "I'm lost."

"You're doing a great job." She squeezed his shoulder. "Just don't be afraid to be tough. Set barriers. Don't be a pushover."

She glanced away, stared out the window, as if lost in a memory. "Trust me, I wish I'd known all this with Tam."

Her bottom lip wobbled a fraction before pressing against the other, compressing in a thin line, effectively stopping him from asking any more.

"Thanks. I'll take your advice on board." He leaned across to kiss her cheek. "When do you want me to get started on the fair?"

Cilla took another moment to compose herself before turning back to face him. "I made a stack of notes while I was having coffee at the hospital. The folder's in my bag. I'll get it for you, then I'll go see Sara."

"Okay."

But as Cilla gathered her documentation and gave it to him, he couldn't help but wish he was the one seeing Sara again.

16.

Cilla usually liked her solitude but she'd never been so grateful to see Jake when she got home. Ironic, considering the reason she'd gone to the hospital in the first place was to escape Jake and Olly.

But talking with Jake meant she could focus on other things. The fair. Olly. Sara.

Anything but Bryce.

Even now, as she strolled down her driveway toward Sara's house, she couldn't believe she'd agreed to have dinner with him.

He was forty-two years old.

Eighteen years her junior.

And in the two times she'd seen him this week, he'd made her feel more aware as a woman than she had in decades.

The way he looked at her . . . Her skin pebbled at the recollection and her palms grew sweaty. If he made her feel this jittery by chatting, how the heck would she get through dinner? A few hours sitting across from him, watching him fork food into his mouth, watching those lips move . . .

Cilla stumbled and cursed. "Get a grip," she muttered, fanning her cheeks, which had automatically heated when she thought of the two of them alone.

Though technically, they wouldn't be alone at dinner. She'd see to it. Once he chose the place, she'd meet him there, so there would be no time together in a car. She'd bid him farewell in the restaurant too, avoiding any potential awkward goodbye outside.

Yes, that sounded like a plan. Now if only she could quell her nerves for the interminable few hours during which they'd be eating together.

She could back out of it. Fake an illness. Make up an excuse. But if Bryce was willing to go to the lengths of involving Sergio to ask her out, he'd be persistent.

As for the small part of her, buried deep, that responded to him on a level that involved attraction and flirting and sex . . . well, maybe that was the real reason she wouldn't pull out.

Because for the first time in a long time, she felt like a woman. A woman to be admired and charmed. A woman willing to revel in her sexuality rather than hide it away. A woman who didn't fade into the background because that's what she'd done her entire life.

When she reached Sara's, she'd mentally sorted her wardrobe and found it lacking in suitable attire for dinner with a suave younger man. And mentally kicked herself in the backside for caring.

She rapped on the door much louder than she'd intended, anger at herself making her hand shake. She'd been encouraging Jake to get out and about because he hibernated too much, yet the thought of her first dinner date with a man in forty-odd years was turning her into a wreck.

When the door opened and Sara stared at her, one eyebrow quirked, she forced a smile. "Hi. Hope I'm not interrupting?"

Sara shook her head. "You saved me from cleaning out the kitchen cupboards. Want to come in?"

"Sure." Cilla followed Sara inside, slightly ashamed that she'd never been inside until now.

Issy had been a lovely woman and while Cilla had valued her friendship, she'd deliberately kept her at arm's length. Cilla had spent so many years skulking in her own home, unable to have people over because of Vernon's moods, that she'd grown accustomed to her solitude as normal even after his death.

She'd treasured the peace of her home once Vernon had died, had protected it fiercely. Yet as she followed Sara toward the back of the house, and saw the artwork Jake had mentioned lining the hallway, she felt ashamed.

"Jake told me about your pyrography," Cilla said. "You made all these?"

Sara glanced over her shoulder and nodded. "I was obsessed. Whenever I visited Gran, I'd spend the entire time burning designs into wood."

Oddly enough, Cilla couldn't recall Issy's granddaughter visiting. Then again, she wouldn't have noticed back then, too busy protecting Tam from Vernon to bother about what was going on with her neighbors.

"Actually, that's what I've come to see you about," Cilla said, pausing on the kitchen threshold.

"Really?" Sara pushed a button on a fancy coffee machine, and Cilla didn't have the heart to tell her she was already wired from hospital caffeine—and a hospital doctor.

"I was wondering if you'd be willing to donate a few pieces to a fair I'm organizing?"

A tiny frown appeared on Sara's brow, not at all encouraging, so Cilla continued. "There's an eight-year-old boy, Sergio, with leukemia. He's the eldest of four kids and his folks are having a hard time with medical bills, so I'm trying to raise funds to help."

Sara's frown line softened. "He's eight? That's so sad."

Cilla agreed but now wasn't the time to debate the injustices of the world, especially with a woman who had lost her child so young. "He's a fighter, though. And has a good chance of beating the cancer. But his parents are finding it tough and I'd like to alleviate their stress any way I can. Provide funds they may need for further treatment."

"That's kind of you." Sara nodded, her expression pensive. "I would've given anything to have extra time with Lucy."

Cilla saw Sara swallow several times and she waited, giving the young woman time to compose herself.

After a few moments, Sara continued. "Whatever I can do to help, let me know."

"That's wonderful," Cilla said. "Your work is unique and I have no idea how much time goes into creating each piece, so whatever you want to donate will be fine." She hesitated, unsure whether to broach the subject of Olly or not, before deciding to take the plunge. "Olly loved what you made for him."

Sara's lips softened into a small smile. "He's a cute kid."

"Is it difficult for you, being around children?"

When Sara's eyes widened with surprise at her bluntness, Cilla said, "Jake mentioned that Olly upset you when you first met."

Sara gnawed on her bottom lip before nodding. "I've avoided kids since I lost Lucy. Even now, twelve months later, I can't go down to my work shed at the back of the property on the off-chance I'll hear them laughing or see them having fun."

Ah: the children's camp bordered the back of Sara's property. Cilla's heart ached for Sara's loss. She might not be close to Tam, but at least she could pick up the phone when she wanted and hear her voice.

"We all work through our grief in different ways," Cilla said, leaning forward to give Sara's arm a reassuring squeeze. "Don't rush it, but don't shut yourself off completely either."

"How did you cope when you lost your husband?" Sara managed to look sheepish. "Hope you don't mind but Jake mentioned he committed suicide."

"I don't mind." Cilla shrugged. "The whole town knows the story. Besides, it happened twenty years ago."

If Cilla's bluntness, bordering on callousness, surprised Sara, she didn't show it.

"How long did it take you to move on?"

"About a week, which was seven days too long," Cilla said, biting back a smile at Sara's round-eyed shock. "Vernon was abusive. Our marriage was a nightmare. And I lost my daughter's respect because I put up with it for so long." Sadness filtered through her bravado as it always did when she thought of how she'd inadvertently driven Tam away, when all she'd wanted to do was protect her. "Tamsin left for college and didn't come back, except for her father's funeral."

"I'm sorry," Sara said, looking like she wished she'd never brought up the topic. "For everything you had to go through."

"Likewise." Their gazes met and held, two women joined by memories of suffering and survival.

Cilla stood. "Anyway, I better be getting back. I've put Jake in charge of planning the fair layout and I'm sure he has a thousand questions."

"You sure you wouldn't like a coffee?"

"Thanks, but I'm fine."

However, as Cilla walked back to her home, and her thoughts returned to Bryce and their upcoming dinner, she knew she was far from fine.

Hopefully the restaurant Bryce booked served Valium-spiked shots for pre-dinner drinks.

17.

It had been a week since his aunt had advised Jake to take a firmer hand with Olly.

It hadn't helped.

When it came to his nephew, Jake couldn't do anything right.

He'd tried spending a lot of one-on-one time with the kid: had taken him to explore the town, taken him for ice creams, taken him to the park. While Olly seemed to enjoy hanging out with him, he reverted to angry and resentful when Jake least expected it. That was when the going got tough, because Jake didn't know how far to discipline Olly.

Cilla had said to take a firm stand, to set boundaries. But she hadn't told him how to handle a six-year-old whose eyes could fill with tears on cue as he stared at you with condemnation.

So after seven days of what he considered serious bonding time with his nephew, Jake needed a break. He lined up Cilla to mind Olly while he scouted the final locations for the fair. Hopefully, with a friend in tow.

He knocked on Sara's door, wondering if his physical reaction to her had cooled. He hadn't spotted her once in seven days, despite keeping an eye out for her in town, in her garden or even moving about inside her house. But the woman was like a ghost. Which was why he'd thought of her for this expedition. According to Cilla, Sara needed to get out of the house as much as he did.

This was his good deed for the day. It had absolutely nothing to do with the fact he couldn't wait to see her again. As she opened the door, wearing a white sundress covered in tiny daisies, held up by the thinnest straps he'd ever seen, and as heat surged through his body, he had an answer to whether he'd cooled physically toward her.

"Hi, Jake." She offered a tentative smile and dammit, a jolt shot directly to his groin.

"Hey, you busy?"

"Depends why you're asking." Her smile widened. "If you need me to help weed Cilla's extensive garden, I'm busy."

"Nothing like that." He found himself grinning like a loon right back at her. "I have to make a final decision on a location for the fair and thought you might like to tag along and offer an opinion?"

She hesitated, as if the thought of spending time with him alone was fraught with danger.

"Shouldn't take more than an hour," he added, slightly disappointed that she didn't seem interested in his company at all, when she hadn't been far from his mind over the past week.

"Okay." She grabbed her keys off the hall table near the door and closed it. "Actually, I've finished a few pieces for the fair. You can pick them up when we get back."

"Sounds good."

They drove around town, checking out the school's sports oval, the park near Main Square, the church grounds. None of them had particularly grabbed him so he left the best for last, hoping she'd like it as much as he did.

Crazy thing was, before the plane crash, he'd never second-guessed his decisions. Ever. In his occupation, he'd quickly assessed situations, weighed up facts and proceeded accordingly. That's what had ultimately cost him, and cost those innocent people their lives, because he'd ignored his gut instinct and stuck with the facts.

"You okay?" Sara half swiveled in her seat to face him. "You get this look on your face sometimes, like you're really down."

"It's nothing," he said, too quickly, and her face fell. "Sorry, I don't like talking about it."

"Tell me to shut up if you want, but is it Olly?"

"That too," Jake said drily, shaking his head. "Seriously, it's nothing."

"'Nothing' wouldn't make you look like this." She frowned, her eyes cross-eyed and her mouth pulled down in the corners.

He laughed. "I don't look like that."

"Yeah, you do."

He liked this teasing side of her, liked how it made him feel: like there could be lightness in the world again, despite the darkness that plagued him.

"I'll make a deal with you," she said. "One day we'll talk about our pasts, preferably over a dozen bottles of tequila, but that day's not today."

Nor would it be any day, considering he didn't drink and had no intention of divulging what he'd done.

"Okay." His abrupt agreement made it sound like hell would freeze over before they'd talk about their pasts.

She shrugged and returned to looking out the windshield, her blasé dismissal surprising him. Most women liked to pry. He hoped Sara's lack of curiosity didn't indicate disinterest too. "Where's this last place?"

"We're almost there." He pointed to the giant sign up ahead. "Here we are."

Sara made a weird half-choking sound, and he glanced across to find her as pale as her dress, her jaw clenched and her hands fisted.

"What's wrong?" When she didn't answer and her stare turned catatonic, he pulled the car over.

"Hey, tell me what's wrong." He had no idea whether she'd welcome a friendly touch on her hand or shoulder, so he waited.

She blinked, breaking that eerie stare. "Are there kids in that camp at the moment?"

Damn, so that was the reason behind her mini-freakout.

"No. It's booked for varying weeks over summer break but is empty at the moment." He quashed his reservations and reached for her hand, giving it a reassuring squeeze. "I saw how you reacted with Olly the first time. I wouldn't do that to you."

"Thanks," she said, her voice wobbly. "I know it's crazy but I can't face being around kids. Hearing their chatter and laughter. Seeing the excitement on their faces. It hits me right here."

She thumped her fist over her heart. "I know I need to get past losing Lucy but it's so damn tough."

He released her hand to prevent from following up on his urge to hug her. "Have you tried being around kids?"

She shook her head. "I can't even go down to my old work shed, which borders the camp, because I may see or hear them." Her teeth worried her bottom lip, drawing his attention to it, and damned if he didn't want to kiss her too. "How messed up is that?"

"We all deal with the hard stuff in our own way." Considering he hadn't been near an airport, let alone a plane, since the crash, he reckoned they were both ostriches, happy to avoid facing their terrors. "Would spending time with Olly help? Ease you into being around kids?"

Her rigid shoulders relaxed a little. "He seems like a good kid."

"So that's a yes?" There was more behind his offer and he made an instantaneous decision to come clean. "Actually, you'd be doing me a favor."

"How so?"

"I'm struggling," he said, hoping she wouldn't think less of him when she learned the extent of his incompetence. "Olly blows hot and cold with me. One minute he's fine, the next he hates me. Cilla said I need to take a tougher stand. I've tried that and while I value her opinion, her daughter moved out over twenty years ago and I need help from someone who was a parent more recently."

Hell, he was babbling, sounding like an idiot. He gritted his teeth and glanced out the driver's side window, wishing he'd never brought this up.

"Jake?"

Her voice sounded stronger and he turned to face her, glad when he saw acceptance and understanding rather than censure on her expressive face.

"I'd like to hang out with you and Olly."

"Thanks, I appreciate it," he said, suddenly eager to be out of the confines of the car before he followed that crazy impulse to kiss her. "Might do us all some good."

"Maybe." She smiled and pointed to the sign. "Shall we go check out this place?"

"You bet." He fired up the engine and drove the last hundred yards to the camp. "I left this for last because I think it's perfect for the fair, but I'd like to hear what you think."

"You value my opinion that much?" She'd reverted to teasing him again and he liked it. He liked it a lot.

"Depends if your opinion matches mine or not." He smirked. "If you disagree, I'll make you walk home."

"Considering I could hop over the back fence, that's an empty threat."

"Try me," he said, as he pulled over in front of the main entrance and killed the engine, enjoying their lighthearted banter a hell of a lot more than their previous conversation.

"Maybe I will," she said, her smile fading as her gaze fell to his mouth, and damned if he didn't want to haul her across the gearshift and kiss her until they were both breathless.

"I'll look forward to it."

With a wink, he flung open the door and all but tumbled out of the car in his haste to get away from the woman who tempted him more with every passing second.

She intrigued him on so many levels. Her vulnerability made him want to protect her. Her sweetness made him want to hold her. Her sexiness made him want to do things to her that he shouldn't contemplate.

The faster they scouted this place and he dropped her back at her place, the better.

18.

When Jake dropped Sara home, she handed over the pieces she'd done for the fair and cited an important phone call so he'd leave pronto.

She'd liked scouting around town with him, had enjoyed the company, but he made her feel discombobulated in a way she never had before.

Greg had never made her heart pound or her veins feel like viscous honey flowed through them. Even now, ten minutes later, she still felt the residual heat from being confined in a car with Jake.

When he'd flirted with her, she remembered what it felt like to trade banter with a guy. It felt good. A flicker of joy in an otherwise dull existence.

For that's what she was doing. Existing. She acknowledged it, accepted it, and at least in Redemption she could exist on a more acceptable level than in New York City.

She liked the solitude. Embraced it. Just as she'd embraced a return to her past with the pyrography. Her work continued to excel, like she was pouring out her grief through her creativity and healing in the process.

The pieces she'd done for the fair featured cartoon characters getting into mischief, the kind of doodles she'd done to make Lucy laugh. She hoped they sold for a reasonable price and added to the coffers for Sergio. If extra money could buy him better treatment, and ultimately save his life, she'd have done well. She'd give anything to have had extra time with Lucy and if she could gift those poor parents the same, she would.

She padded to the back window and stared at the work shed, a mere dot at the back of the property. With no kids at the camp, this was a perfect time to go explore her old stomping ground. But still she hesitated. Afraid.

Of what? Facing memories of the past and remembering happier times? Confronting the young woman she'd once been and finding herself lacking now?

Shaking her head at her foolishness, she slipped out the back door and strolled toward the shed. Bees buzzed in the background, their low hum soothing as she inhaled the heady blend of mint, rosemary and sage. That was another thing that was better out here than in the city: the freshness of everything. She'd lost a lot of weight after Lucy's death but having a profusion of herbs and vegetables on offer from Gran's garden meant she'd been experimenting with pastas and bakes. Her waistline thanked her.

When she reached the dilapidated shed, her breath caught. A vivid memory flashed across her mind of the last time she'd been down here. She'd been sixteen and Vera had been in Florida, chasing some strip club owner. Gran had been attending a church meeting and a delivery guy had dropped by with a parcel. He'd been late teens, cute, with shaggy blond hair, pale green eyes and long eyelashes. He'd asked her out. She'd said she'd think about it. Then bolted to the shed to recreate his likeness on a piece of cherry wood.

Smiling, she jiggled the handle on the door like she used to, until it gave and the door creaked open. Mustiness greeted her, along with a comforting smell that had been branded on her receptors a long time ago: dry wood.

Sunlight poured in through the east- and west-facing windows, highlighting the motes dancing in the air. Dust and cobwebs covered her old office chair, her worktable, and the box of tools stacked neatly to one side.

There, in the middle of the table, was Delivery Boy.

Feeling more lighthearted than she had in years, Sara entered the shed and picked up the wood. She swiped the years of dust off, revealed the burnt etching.

It was crude, rudimentary, done in the throes of a new crush and she smiled, remembering what it was like to be young and innocent with her whole life in front of her. Remembered the butterflies and anxiety of wondering if he really liked her or if he just asked all the girls out. If Gran would let her go. And if she did, what she should wear.

Sadly, Vera had turned up out of the blue the next day and taken her to Florida. Her crush on Delivery Boy never went beyond a few wishful daydreams. And she hadn't returned to Gran's until she'd finished college, had met Greg and was established in New York City.

Glancing around the shed, she realized something. She should never have given up who she was for Greg. Should never have hidden her hobbies. Should never have become the woman he wanted her to be for fear of being abandoned.

She had her mom to thank for that. That had been Vera's trademark, dumping her at Gran's whenever the wanderlust hit, which was often. But in becoming the corporate financial businesswoman, she'd left behind the part of her that liked to create and dream, the part of her that made her whole.

Maybe that was some of the attraction to Jake: he admired her work. It fostered her creativity. But she knew it was more than that and as she tucked Delivery Boy under her arm, she couldn't help but look forward to spending more time with him.

She'd keep Delivery Boy in a special place inside to remind herself to never lose sight of what she wanted. To be true to herself and no one else.

After all she'd been through she owed it to herself.

19.

I think I'm going to be sick," Cilla muttered, staring at herself in the mirror.

She had to meet Bryce in forty-five minutes at Buoy's in Dixon's Creek for their dinner date but all she could do was glare at her reflection.

She should never have gone to this much trouble.

She'd ditched her usual garb of leggings, kaftan tops and flip-flops for stockings, a fitted black dress and heels. Her, in heels! She'd probably fall flat on her face and it would serve her right for trying to get gussied up for a man young enough to be her son.

Not that the black dress was immodest. It had half-sleeves and a demure neckline, and ended at her knees. But paired with the sheer stockings and heels, it made her feel positively wanton. Or maybe that had more to do with the constant images of Bryce floating through her head.

While tonight terrified her, she shouldn't be looking forward to it this much. Because as her nerves increased, so did her anticipation.

Tonight would be her first date in over four decades.

No pressure on her or anything.

"Silly old fool," she said, poking her tongue out at her reflection as she spun away to grab her handbag.

Tonight would go exactly as she planned. She'd arrive on time at the restaurant, order the fastest things to cook on the menu, focus on eating and not talking, then make a quick getaway.

All up, she envisaged spending about ninety minutes in Bryce's company, with most of that time spent on eating and discussing mutual patients. Simple.

But forty minutes later, as she entered Buoy's ahead of schedule, her plan hit a snag. Bryce was in the foyer. Waiting for her. Looking like a model who'd stepped off the cover of a magazine.

Black pants. Black shirt. Black eyes that bored into her.

She couldn't breathe. Couldn't move. Desperately tried to quell the heat that rose from deep within to flood her body.

Oh heck.

"Cilla, you look lovely." He kissed her cheek, a soft, lingering brush of his lips that short-circuited what was left of her common sense. "Shall we go in?"

She managed a mute nod as his hand rested in the small of her back, gently guiding her forward. Acutely aware of the warmth of his hand seeping through her dress as they walked through the dimly lit restaurant, she focused on putting one foot in front of the other, mentally reciting a childish "left-right, left-right" to avoid chanting what she really wanted to: "Take me now, take me now."

When they reached the table, Cilla almost collapsed with relief into her chair, earning a raised eyebrow from Bryce.

"Shut up. I'm flustered," she said, not surprised that he grinned at her bluntness.

"If that's a compliment, thank you." He sat opposite, the light from the lone candle on the table casting flickering shadows, highlighting his chiseled cheekbones. "If it makes you feel any better, you're having the same effect on me."

She made a rude snorting sound and he laughed.

"How about we relax and enjoy each other's company tonight? No pressure, no expectations. What do you say?" He rested his forearms on the table and she couldn't help but stare at the way his shirt pulled across his shoulders, his biceps.

What should she say? What she was thinking couldn't be articulated out loud, not when decades worth of hormones were rioting through her body.

"I'm starving. Let's order," she said, snatching a menu and burying her nose in it.

If he found her boorish or rude, he didn't say. At least one of them had brought his manners along tonight. But as they discussed the various items on offer, Cilla found herself relaxing. She loved food and it looked like Bryce was a fellow aficionado. Only after ordering cured ocean trout with caper butter, spice-glazed duck breast and chocolate candied pecan tart did she remember her plan to eat fast and escape.

By the time they had three courses, it'd be close to midnight. What was she thinking?

She hadn't been—that was the problem.

Since the moment she'd caught sight of Bryce tonight and he'd kissed her cheek, she'd been drifting in some kind of alternate universe where average sixty-year-old women could actually be attractive to sexy forty-two-year-old men. A ludicrous, upside-down kind of place that didn't exist, but maybe, for tonight, she could delude herself into believing it could.

"That's a great thing you're doing, organizing the fair for Sergio," Bryce said, his admiration making her blush again. "It's all he talks about."

"His parents are really struggling; the money will help." She shrugged, uncomfortable with too much praise. Seeing Josephina and Paolo's relieved smiles when she'd told them a rough figure of how much she hoped to raise with the fair had been thanks enough.

"You're still doing it," he said, twirling a wine glass stem between his fingers.

"Doing what?"

"Downplaying how amazing you are." He stared at her, trying to convey a message she had no hope of understanding. "You used to do it when I was at your place with Tam. You'd whip up these amazing feasts and act like it was nothing. You'd help Tam with her assignments. You'd keep the house spotless. And you worked. You were like this super-mom . . ."

For the first time since he'd bowled back into her life, he appeared uncomfortable, his jaw clenched like he didn't want to say too much. "I'm not presuming to know anything about your marriage but Tam hated her father and you faded into the background deliberately when he was around, like you were invisible. So I'm guessing that's why you're so modest."

Cilla should be angry. She should rant and rally against Bryce's presumptuousness. Instead, she found herself nodding.

"Life with Vernon was hell. I stayed with him for Tam's sake and in the end she resented me for it. Lost all respect, because I put up with him for so long." A familiar sadness overwhelmed her, quickly replaced by annoyance that she'd allowed herself to wallow, even for a second. Her chin snapped up. "I'm proud of what I do these days. My naturopathy. Volunteering. Being a respected member of the community. But I guess the years of being invisible took their toll."

"An incredible woman like you should never be invisible." He glowered, suddenly fierce, as he reached across the table and snagged her hands. "I want you to know that I see you, Priscilla Prescott. I *see* you."

Cilla rarely cried but at that moment, with Bryce's strong, warm hands holding hers and the tenderness in his steady gaze more reassuring than anything she'd ever experienced from a man, she felt like bawling.

She cleared her throat and eased her hands out of his. "Want to know what I see?"

The corners of his mouth quirked. "Do I really want to hear this?"

"I'm going to tell you anyway. I see a smooth charmer who for some unfathomable reason has his sights set on an old woman—"

"Stop right there." His glower intensified, making her squirm a little. "There's a significant age gap between us. I get it—"

"Eighteen years to be exact."

"Eighteen years. Whatever." He blew out an exasperated huff. "The age difference is irrelevant to me. We're not talking marriage here, Cilla. We're dating." He rubbed the back of his neck. "At least, that's what I'd like to do. Date you."

She gaped at him, stunned he'd even contemplate dating her. One dinner together didn't constitute dating—far from it. A casual meal between friends. Nothing more. But he'd misconstrued her acceptance of his dinner invitation and had morphed it into *dating*?

"I'm not interested in having kids." He hesitated, his glance darting away before refocusing on her. "Truth is, I can't have kids and I reconciled myself to that fact years ago. So I get my kid fix by treating them. I lead a full life. I travel. I date women. But I've never met anyone I'd like to spend more than a few weeks with."

Yet he'd looked her up just a day after arriving in Redemption. Bizarre. As for his infertility, it saddened her to think an amazing man like him couldn't pass on his genes or didn't seem interested in other options. But it wasn't her place to question him. None of her business.

Before she could speak, he held up his hand. "And I don't need any trite apologies that I can't have kids. It doesn't bother me and frankly, I don't want them. So now that I've pre-empted another argument against us spending time together, and dispelled the age gap as irrelevant, what else can you come up with?"

Annoyed that he had circumvented her next argument, the one citing that time spent with her would be wasted when he could be dating someone his own age with a view to children, she reached for a little white lie.

"Has it occurred to you that maybe I'm not interested in dating anyone? That maybe I don't like you that way?"

"Liar," he murmured, reaching across the table to place his fingertips over her wrist pulse. "And the way your heart's beating proves it."

She snatched her hand away and he laughed.

"Come on, Cilla. Let's have some fun while I'm in town."

"I haven't had fun in two decades, so trust me, you'll be disappointed."

Damn. She hadn't meant to blurt that out. His eyes widened in surprise.

"You haven't dated at all since Vernon died?"

She shook her head, embarrassment flushing her cheeks. "After what I put up with, I like being alone."

"So you haven't . . . I mean . . . Crap." It was his turn to blush and he looked so awkward she took pity on him.

"No, I haven't," she said, unable to comprehend they were actually discussing her non-existent sex life. "Bet that douses your interest."

He tilted his head, as if studying her. "On the contrary, I see it as my duty to reintroduce you to fun."

"So you see me as a duty now. Nice."

How could one word, *fun*, be laced with so much promise?

A bolt of potent longing shot through her, making her rub her arms.

"I'm teasing," he said, his slow, sexy smile intensifying her longing. "I'd like to spend time with you. No pressure, no expectations. For the simple reason I like you and I'm attracted to you."

There was nothing simple about having a guy like Bryce fancy a woman like her. But in that moment, with sincerity radiating from his steady stare, she decided to throw caution to the wind for the first time in her life.

"Let's see how this goes," she said, remaining noncommittal while inwardly yearning for him to say "Let's ditch the restaurant and head back to my place."

It had been so long, though, that she wouldn't know what to do. Sex with Vernon had been as awful as the rest of their marriage. No satisfaction for her. A few rough thrusts from him, leaving her feeling empty and used. She'd considered sex yet another marital duty she had to fulfill, like cooking and cleaning and raising Tam. As lackluster and miserable as the rest of her life had been with Vernon.

She couldn't contemplate sex with Bryce. Despite the way her body reacted to the timbre of his voice and the power of his glances, her long dry spell ensured that she'd make a fool of herself before they'd begun.

"I can live with that," he said, with not a hint of smugness. He raised a wine glass. "To us and seeing how it goes."

Emboldened by her decision to allow their relationship to unfold, she picked up her glass and clinked it against his. "To seeing how it goes."

The rest of her toast, which went something like "Here's to senile old women who start fantasizing late in life and need to be committed," she kept to herself.

Over the next few hours, and three exquisite courses that tantalized her palate almost as much as Bryce tantalized her, they talked. Laughed. Flirted.

And for the first time in her life, Cilla felt appreciated. Like her opinions mattered. Like she could entertain. Like she was worthy of attention.

She'd known Vernon had battered her self-esteem until it didn't matter. She'd blamed herself, too, for tolerating it. Had deluded herself into believing all these years, even the last twenty without him, that she was okay. She was a survivor. A strong woman capable of anything.

But as she sipped her peppermint tea and listened to Bryce wax lyrical about the sights and smells and tastes of India during a locum stint in Bangalore, she realized something.

In keeping her solitude, she'd shut herself off from emotions.

She didn't *feel* anymore.

Sure, she loved Tam, but that was more an obligatory kind of love a mother had for her child. They rarely conversed and Cilla didn't push. She assumed Tam knew how much she loved her and that she was here for her if needed. Maintaining the status quo was easier than confronting the real issue: that they weren't close and never would be.

She cared about the kids at the hospital and the townsfolk she helped, but caring didn't constitute any deep bond.

Her parents had died in a car crash a month after she'd met Vernon; she'd married him soon after and had Tam at eighteen. Her capacity for love had dwindled since.

Yet in one evening, Bryce had opened her up to the possibility of feeling again. Of taking a risk. Of moving out of her comfort zone. Of being a woman.

"So you're up for checking out my Kama Sutra swing then?"

Bryce's question jolted her out of her musings and she choked on her tea. Blushing, she had to clear her throat several times before answering. "Sorry, was thinking about something else for a moment."

"Several moments, judging by that faraway look in your eyes," he said, smiling. "So the swing's out?"

"Behave," she said, loving how lighthearted his teasing made her feel.

"Never." He leaned forward, the light lemony tang of his aftershave washing over her in a welcoming wave. "For all your protestations, I think you enjoy flirting."

"I'm woefully out of practice," she said, hiding behind her peppermint tea before she blurted out exactly how much she enjoyed his flirting.

"Only one way to perfect it and that's *lots* of practice." His hand snaked across the table toward hers. "I've heard touching is an integral part of flirting too."

"Is that right?" She allowed him to intertwine his fingers with hers.

"Kissing too." He raised her hand to his lips and brushed a feather-light kiss across the back of it, setting her arm alight. And a few other choice places.

"You're a born charmer," she said, stifling a sigh of regret as he released her hand. "You must've left a swathe of broken hearts in your wake over the years."

A playful smile lit his face. "Why, Cilla, are you fishing for details about my dating history?"

"Call it natural curiosity."

"Okay, let me think." He drummed his fingers on the table. "Didn't have a steady girlfriend in college. Played the field a bit, concentrated on getting good grades mostly. Did an internship stint in LA. Been working in New York City since graduation, had a three-month relationship with a nurse. Did locum stints in India, Australia and New Zealand. Casually dated over there."

He counted his dating history on his fingers and pinned her with a meaningful stare. "Now I'm here, trying to figure out if the first woman I fell in love with is the real reason I've been spoiled for all other women."

Cilla's jaw fell open as she stared at him in disbelief.

"Yeah, that crush I mentioned I had on you? Kinda blossomed into first love." He grimaced, utterly adorable in his mortification. "And it was damn painful, lusting after an older woman I thought I could never have."

He paused, reached across to place a fingertip under her chin and closed her jaw. "Until now."

Cilla wanted to tell Bryce he was crazy. That he may have held a torch for her back then but first loves in the teenage years were always blown out of all proportion. Larger than life. Dramatic. Totally implausible.

But the serious glint in his eyes told her he wouldn't take kindly to her making light of his declaration, so she settled for silence.

"You're surprised," he said.

"Stunned, more like it." She sat on her hands to stop her fingers fiddling with the edge of the tablecloth. "And undeservedly flattered."

"You shouldn't be surprised. And you definitely deserve flattery. You're beautiful."

With his adoring gaze fixed on her face, she almost believed him.

A waiter appeared, hovering nearby, and the irrational spell that Bryce held over Cilla broke. She should be grateful. Instead, all she could think was how incredible this man had made her feel in a few hours, more cherished than she had in decades, if ever.

"Sorry to interrupt, but we're closing up, folks." The waiter slid the bill folder onto the table and disappeared as quickly as he'd appeared.

When Cilla reached for the bill, Bryce covered her hand with his.

"My treat," he said, his tone brooking no argument.

She nodded. "Thank you. Dinner was lovely."

"Dinner was delicious," he said, sliding notes into the folder. "You are lovely."

Unused to compliments, she made a weird face, somewhere between grateful and uncomfortable, and he laughed.

"You better get used to compliments because there are plenty more where that came from."

"I'll try," she said, and meant it.

Bryce had summed up the situation between them pretty darn well at the start of the evening. They weren't considering marriage. They weren't headed for a heavy relationship. They would be dating. Enjoying each other's company. Having fun. For the short time he was in town. Where was the harm in that?

"Cilla, is that you?"

Cilla froze as a shadow fell over the table and she glanced up into the face of Willow Ziebell, Tam's BFF.

Cilla had no idea if Willow and her daughter were still in touch but running into her before she'd had a chance to discuss Bryce with Tam didn't bode well.

Even if Willow and Tam didn't see each other these days, there was the dreaded social media, where young people reveled in revealing every nitty-gritty detail of their lives. So if Willow and Tam were friends on social media and Willow let slip that she'd run into Cilla with a much younger man . . .

Damn.

"Hi, Willow. How are you?" Cilla held out her hand and Willow shook it briefly, her interest more focused on Bryce, whom she eyed with open speculation.

"I'm good. Still running life coach seminars for the region," Willow recited almost by rote, now openly gawking at Bryce.

"This is Dr. Bryce Madden—"

"Bryce. Oh wow, I thought it was you." Willow squealed and clapped her hands like a little girl. "You look great."

"Nice to see you, too," Bryce said, his tone flat and sounding nothing like the sweet, animated guy Cilla had been listening to with rapt attention.

Willow's knowing glance flicked between the two of them and Cilla struggled not to squirm.

"What are you doing here?" Willow made it sound like she'd found Bryce floating through space rather than dining with Cilla in Dixon's Creek.

"I'm doing a three-month locum in Redemption," he said, making a grand show of glancing at his watch. "Actually, I've got a stack of reports to finish, so we need to get back."

"Sure," Willow said, sounding a tad put out. "I think it's lovely you're taking Tam's mom out for dinner while you're in town."

Willow leaned forward, giving Bryce a decent eyeful of fake-tanned cleavage. "Tam says she never gets out much and could do with more friends," she said, flicking her eyes meaningfully at Cilla.

Embarrassment flushed Cilla's cheeks. Guess that answered the question of whether Tam and Willow were still in touch. She needed to call Tam ASAP before her daughter heard the news secondhand. But the thought of her daughter pronouncing judgment on her lack of social life sparked a tsunami of humiliation. Her cheeks flushed hotter and she lowered her head.

"Cilla and I aren't just friends." Bryce stood and moved around to her side of the table with purpose, pulling out her chair so she could stand. "We're much more than that."

He slid his arm around her waist. A good thing, considering she would've slid to the floor in mortification otherwise.

Willow's red-glossed mouth made a perfect O and Cilla had an insane urge to laugh.

"See you later, Willow," he said, giving Cilla's waist a squeeze that sent a very pleasant zap lower.

Cilla managed a brief "bye" before Bryce guided her through the tables and out the door. Where she proceeded to collapse into giggles. The type of insane laughter that refused to be quelled and only spilled out more the harder she tried.

"Oh my goodness, did you see her face?" Cilla wrapped her arms around her middle. It did little for the stitch that twanged with every guffaw. "You're bad."

"You're only realizing this now?" His hand splayed across her lower back, his fingertips grazing the top of her butt, and Cilla almost died on the spot. "I remember Willow from high school and she's still bitchy."

Cilla's laughter petered out as the reality of the situation hit. "You can't blame her for thinking you were taking pity on her friend's mother."

"I hate people making assumptions." A frown creased Bryce's brow, making him attractively formidable. "They should get their facts straight before opening their big mouths."

Heartened by his defensiveness, she nodded. "True, but it's going to happen a lot if we're seen together."

"That bothers you?"

"Usually it would, but tonight has taught me something."

"What's that?"

Having no clue whether she was doing the right thing in telling him exactly what she was feeling, Cilla blurted, "I've shut myself off emotionally for years and being with you makes me feel good."

"The feeling's entirely mutual." His expression softened as he cupped her face in his warm hands. "You're not going to freak out if I kiss you, right?"

"I might," she said, caught in the intensity of his eyes, unable to look away.

She might not freak out but she might die of a heart attack. For that's what it felt like the longer he stared at her—like her heart might explode from her chest. It pounded that hard, making her breathless and anxious. With cardiac arrest imminent, lucky for her Bryce was a doctor.

His thumb brushed her bottom lip softly, and she swayed toward him. "Cilla, I've wanted to do this for so long . . ."

The next few moments happened in slow motion. Bryce lowered his head. Pressed his lips to hers. Once. Twice. Barely-there kisses. Butterfly kisses. Light and heady and intoxicating.

The third time, he increased the pressure, more demanding. Challenging her to give in to the questionable attraction between them.

For the first time in decades, she did.

Cilla relaxed her lips, giving Bryce entrance. When his tongue touched hers, she wanted to cry, the jolt down below was that powerful.

She'd sacrificed her sexuality along with her self-esteem to Vernon and she'd never expected to feel like this, ever.

But as she was ready to give herself over to the best kiss of her life, Bryce eased away.

Oh no. Was she bad at this?

"Too much, too soon, huh?" He released her but didn't look unhappy. "I've been imagining that for so long, but then when you said all that stuff over dinner I vowed to take it slow—but Cilla, you have no idea what you do to me." He took a step back, his grin rueful. "Actually, if we'd kept kissing, you would've had a fair idea. But I sensed you weren't in the moment?"

Embarrassed, she winced. "Sorry. My first kiss in decades, so I was over-analyzing."

Rather than laughing at her, he nodded. "So that means the next time I need to sweep you off your feet so spectacularly that you can't think of anything else?"

His understanding touched her. "I don't need bells and whistles. I just need . . . time."

"That your way of saying don't rush you?"

"It's my way of saying we do need to take things slow, because I have no idea whether I'm up for this or not."

She couldn't be any more honest, and if it drove him away, despite her yearning for a repeat of that kiss, so be it.

He smiled and the tension kinking her neck dissolved. "Haven't you heard? Slow and steady wins the race."

"I've also heard clichés are mood killers."

They laughed and Cilla wondered how on earth, after so many years of being satisfied with her own company, she could look forward to their next meeting so much.

20.

elieved that it was still summer vacation, Sara entered Redemption Elementary.

It was her first time anywhere near a school since Lucy's death and it made her throat tighten stepping inside the main building.

But the art teacher had seen her pyrography pieces for the fair and wanted to discuss further work with her. When Andy Symes had first called and asked her to come in for a meeting, she'd been inclined to blow him off with some lame excuse.

Then she'd remembered why she'd done those pieces, for a little boy who deserved a fighting chance to live, and she'd agreed.

However, as she neared the art room, courtesy of the directions Mr. Symes had given her over the phone, her feet slowed.

She could hear voices. Chatter. Giggles.

When she peered through the door's glass panel, her stomach somersaulted.

The room was filled with kids. Ranging in age from five to ten, all wearing art smocks and holding paintbrushes, standing behind easels.

Damn. Andy Symes was teaching summer art classes.

She had to escape. Had to get outside where she could breathe again.

But as she forced herself to look at the kids' happy faces, a strange thing happened.

The pain of loss, the ache of bitterness that seemed permanently lodged in her chest, eased. It didn't vanish completely, the sharp stab reminding her of all she'd lost, but the longer she looked at those kids, the easier it became to breathe again.

One of the kids, a freckle-faced boy with red curls, caught sight of her and said something, presumably to Mr. Symes, standing behind a supplies cupboard out of sight.

When all the kids turned to look at the door, she forced a smile and waved. Baby steps. Progress. Such a minor advance but with her labored breathing it felt like she'd run a marathon.

The door opened and she stepped back to allow the teacher out. When he smiled at her, her heart stopped all over again.

Andy Symes was Delivery Boy. All grown up.

"Hi. You must be Sara?" He held out his hand. "I'm Andy."

"Pleased to meet you," she said, shaking his hand and trying not to giggle like the teenager she'd once been.

His eyes crinkled a little, as if he was thinking. "Have we met before? You look awfully familiar."

"Don't think so," she said, not wanting to embarrass herself by divulging the ludicrous fact that she remembered who he was from a parcel delivery over fifteen years ago. "What did you want to talk to me about?"

"Your work, and other things," he said, staring at her like he was trying to place her. "Come into my office so we can chat."

He opened the door to a small cubicle next to the art room and she glanced back at the kids.

"Will they be okay?"

He waved away her concern. "Kids who attend art programs during summer vacation want to be here. They won't mess up."

Impressed, Sara followed him into the small office and took a seat opposite his. Several of the pyrography pieces she'd donated to Cilla's fair were on his desk.

"These are amazing," he said, picking up the top one and studying it. "You're very talented."

"Thanks."

"Do you create in other media besides wood?"

"Leather."

"No painting or sculpting?"

Feeling like a prospective assistant being interviewed for a job, she shook her head. "Pyrography's always been my passion."

"I was hoping you'd say that." He smiled, catapulting her right back to that day he'd stood on her doorstep, parcel in hand, asking her out on a date. "How would you feel about teaching the kids a few basics?"

Uh-oh. Sara couldn't have heard right. She resisted the urge to slap her palms over her ears.

"I know you've only moved to town recently and are probably getting settled in, but it would be great for the kids who are genuinely interested in art to get a well-rounded education while they're doing the vacation program."

He made it sound so easy, so logical. Her first reaction, to throw up, was far from that.

Clueless how to extricate herself from the situation without sounding mean and heartless, she said, "But I'm not a teacher. I wouldn't know where to start."

"Doesn't have to be a big deal," he said, replacing her piece on his desk. "A demonstration or two. Maybe a mini-lecture on the history of pyrography, that kind of thing."

She'd done a hundred presentations in her old job. Public speaking didn't intimidate her. But standing in front of a roomful of kids? That terrified her.

"We can't pay you, but the kids would really love it." He leaned back in his chair, fixing her with a quizzical look, like he couldn't believe she wouldn't jump at the chance. "What do you say?"

Sara waited for the panic to set in. Waited for the familiar sick rolling of her gut when she envisaged being around kids again.

But it didn't come, and in that moment, she knew she had to take the next step. A giant leap, more like it, but it was time.

She remembered drawing with Lucy. Using chalk and crayons and pencils. The joy of seeing a little person create. The wonder in her child's eyes as she traced one of Sara's doodles.

She could do this. In Lucy's memory. For her.

"Sure, I'd be happy to help out," she said, surprised by how lighthearted she suddenly felt. "Just let me know convenient days and times and I'll work around it."

"Thanks, Sara. The kids will love it." He stood up, staring at her with intent bordering on confusion, before his expression suddenly cleared. He snapped his fingers. "I remember you. You lived at Issy's place on the outskirts of town."

Sara blushed. "Yeah."

Andy chuckled. "Did I hit on you?"

Dying from embarrassment, Sara nodded.

"Sorry. I asked out a lot of girls back then. Being a delivery boy was the best job ever." Andy laughed louder and Sara joined in. "Would you believe that's how I met my wife?"

"Then it was meant to be," Sara said, glad that Delivery Boy had found his happily ever after. If only they could all be so lucky. "I'll talk to you soon, Andy."

She let herself out and strode down the hall, unable to stop smiling.

In agreeing to work with Andy's art class, she hadn't just taken a giant leap forward.

She'd taken a running jump into a massive chasm.

It felt great.

A major part of Sara had died along with Lucy and now, for the first time in a long, painful twelve months, Sara felt like she was finally living again.

21.

Jake knocked twice on Olly's door and entered. If he waited for Olly's approval to come in, he'd be waiting all day.

"Hey there, time for lunch." Jake hovered in the doorway, hating how gauche he felt around his nephew.

Three weeks later and their relationship was still fraught with an unspoken tension that nothing he said or did could break.

"Not hungry," Olly muttered, not looking up from a hand-held computer game Jake had bought him not long after they'd first arrived.

"It's your favorite, macaroni and cheese." Jake had learned to perfect it in the hope it would impress Olly. It hadn't. Nothing he did worked.

"I'll have it for dinner," Olly said, his thumbs flying over the game console, the tapping annoying Jake as much as the rudeness.

"No, you'll have it now." Jake never raised his voice. He hated it, memories of his father's yelling ensuring he never wanted to be like that.

But Olly must've heard the frustration in his tone because he glanced up from his game with a frown.

"Come on, Olly, your food's getting cold—"

"Don't wanna." Olly returned to his game and flopped onto his stomach, knees bent, kicking his feet, effectively dismissing him.

In that moment, Jake knew they couldn't go on like this.

He'd tried the soft approach; it hadn't worked. Cilla was right. Time to get tough.

"Sit up and look at me when I talk to you," Jake said, his tone so firm that Olly startled.

To his surprise, Olly obeyed.

"It's bad manners to ignore someone when they're talking to you." Jake folded his arms then realized how defensive it looked, so he lowered them and tried like hell to keep his tone even and non-confrontational. "We have rules in this family and respecting each other is one of them. I've cooked a meal for you. We're going to sit down together and eat. Now wash up and let's go downstairs before it gets cold."

Olly stared at him in wide-eyed wonder before scrambling to his feet and bolting for the ensuite attached to his room.

"Well I'll be," Jake murmured, wondering how on earth his sister did it, raising a little person.

The best decision he'd made since taking custody of Olly was asking Cilla if they could stay. If he hadn't, he would've barely lasted a week. Which made him re-evaluate the stress Rose must be under. Not only was she raising Olly, she was holding down a job and trying to make ends meet while doing it.

While he did his best to support her, he'd been AWOL the last six months, dealing with his own demons. That made him feel guiltier, the possibility that Rose's increased alcohol consumption could've been a coping mechanism because he hadn't been around.

"I'm ready," Olly said, holding up his hands for inspection. "All clean."

"Great. Let's go eat." Jake's fingers curled into his palm as Olly passed, resisting the urge to ruffle his curls.

The kid was so darn cute. He was a good kid too. But Jake couldn't seem to get through to him and he hoped what had just happened would be the breakthrough they needed.

However, they'd barely finished forking the last macaroni into their mouths when Olly fixed him with a baleful glare. "When can I go home?"

It seemed like Jake had answered this question a thousand times over the last few weeks. He hated how trite his answer sounded, even to his own ears.

"When your mom's better," he said. "You saw her email. She's doing really well."

But not well enough for visitors yet, apparently. Jake had no idea if taking Olly to see Rose would be a good idea, but it couldn't be any worse than this. A kid needed his mom and he hoped that when Olly did see Rose, it would help him cope with their enforced absence from each other.

"When can I see her?" Olly's bottom lip thrust out. "I really want to see her."

"I know you do, buddy. It'll be soon—I promise." The moment the platitude slipped from his lips he wished he could take it back.

He wasn't in a position to make promises, not when he had no idea if Rose could relapse at any time or her privileges could be revoked.

When Olly's face lit up, he wished he'd kept his big mouth shut. The fact that the kid had not objected to being called *buddy* proved how keen he was on the idea of seeing his mom.

"I miss her," Olly whispered, and Jake had to lean down to hear him.

"Me too," Jake said, meaning it.

He'd shut himself off from everyone since the crash: his colleagues, his friends, his sister. In the weeks since he'd been here, bonding with Cilla again, meeting Sara, spending time with Olly, he had realized how much he'd been missing out on.

He usually liked socializing. Liked having a few beers with the boys after work. Taking women out to dinner and a movie. Doing handiwork around Rose's apartment.

Yet for six months he'd done nothing but wallow. Maybe having Olly thrust upon him had been the best thing that could've happened. He'd been forced out of his solitude. Been awakened to other people's problems, not just his own. Been made to acknowledge that being swamped by guilt wasn't the solution if he wanted to move forward with his life.

"Do you cry sometimes, Uncle Jake?"

Crap. He didn't usually but he sure felt like bawling now. They'd already had this conversation in the early days, so for Olly to ask again meant it must be playing on his mind.

"Sometimes, when I'm really sad about something." Like when his incompetence caused a plane crash that killed eighty-nine people.

That was the last time he'd cried, the night of the crash. He'd sobbed his heart out in the privacy of his apartment, after flinging the TV remote against the wall so he wouldn't watch any more news reports.

He'd hit rock-bottom that night, had knocked back four whiskey shots in a row before his vision blurred and he was reminded of his father.

Jake didn't drink because he didn't want to be like Ray and that night, despite feeling like his life had been flushed down the toilet, he'd re-capped the bottle and put it away. That's where he differed from his dad: Jake had limits.

"Are you going to cry now?" Olly laid a hand on his forearm. "Because you look really sad."

Jeez, this kid was breaking his heart.

"We all get sad sometimes." He patted Olly's hand. "But you know what I do?"

Olly's eyes widened. "What?"

"I think about my favorite thing in the world and it helps."

Damn, Jake had inadvertently said the wrong thing again as Olly seemed to shrink in on himself. His shoulders slumped, he hunched over and his head hung low.

"Mom's my favorite thing in the world."

Jake heard a sniffle, another, before Olly flung himself into his arms and sobbed.

Blinking back tears, Jake hugged his nephew tight, rested his chin on top of his head, and hoped to God that Rose recovered fast.

22.

It took three days for Cilla to come down from her post-date high. Three days of acting like everything was completely normal in front of Jake and Olly, only to have them both bust her on separate occasions for grinning at nothing.

Three days of burying herself in her garden and stocking up on her remedies. Three days of avoiding town on the off chance she'd run into Bryce. Three days of not answering the phone in case it was him.

Crazy behavior, considering she'd vowed to see how things went between them. But whenever she thought about the possibility of them dating, she'd remember that kiss and what it had done to her. Or more precisely, how it had undone her completely.

She'd driven back to Redemption in a mental fog that night, grateful he'd been behind her to see her safely home. Otherwise she might have been tempted to pull over on the side of the road, close her eyes and replay the kiss in minute detail.

When she'd got home, she'd made some hot milk and taken a valerian tablet to foster sleep. Neither had worked. She'd lain in bed staring at the ceiling all night, sporting a grin bigger than the town itself.

She couldn't think of the last time she'd been this happy. Marrying Vernon so quickly in her teens had been a rebound reaction while dealing with the sudden death of her folks. She'd liked him; he'd made her feel secure in a world turned topsy-turvy, so they'd got hitched. But she'd never had the euphoric dating bliss with Vernon, so to feel this carefree now, at her age, seemed plain wrong.

Until she remembered her motto since Vernon had died: she deserved to feel good about herself. If Bryce made her feel good, she'd be a fool to deny it.

Which meant one thing: she'd have to call Tam.

She'd been putting it off, hoping she could talk herself out of this ridiculous situation and avoid having to tell her daughter altogether. But with her mind made up to see Bryce again, she had to do it.

After the awkward run-in with Willow at the restaurant, she'd half expected Tam to call her, abuzz with the gossip. But her phone had remained silent and she knew it was time.

Swiping her sweaty palms against her pants, she mentally recited what she would say.

Hey Tam, remember Bryce? Turns out we like each other.

Tam, I'm dating your high-school crush.

How would you feel about your mother and Bryce getting it on?

Cilla grimaced. Nothing she could say would sound remotely plausible. Ugh. How had she got herself into this situation?

The phone rang and she jumped. Darn, she was so not ready for this.

She picked it up, holding the receiver like it was radioactive. "Hello?"

"Hey Cilla, remember me? The guy who has been sitting by the phone for the last three days hoping you'd call."

Cilla released the breath she'd been inadvertently holding. Bryce, not Tam. She wasn't sure if he was the lesser of two evils.

"I'm an old-fashioned gal. Actually, I'm plain old. Which means I expect the men to do the calling."

He chuckled. "I was trying to stick to your 'let's see how this goes' plan and not push you."

She liked the fact he'd listened to her and respected her enough not to push. She didn't like how she throbbed with longing at the sound of his voice.

"I appreciate that," she said, squeezing her legs together. "How are you?"

"Busy at the clinic and the hospital." He paused. "I haven't seen you around there the last few days either. You're not avoiding me?"

"No," she said, crossing the fingers of her free hand for her little white lie. "Been busy making up new batches of my remedies."

"Do you have a remedy for a broken heart? Because I'm pining away for you."

She snorted. "Your heart's just fine."

"Maybe you should visit tonight and check it out?"

Cilla's legs wobbled, then gave out, and she sank into the nearest chair. The thought of seeing Bryce's bare chest, which looked hard and broad beneath his clothes, was enough to make her lightheaded.

"Cilla, you still there?"

She fanned her face. "Yeah."

"Do you want to come over tonight? I'll cook."

The thought of having a man cook dinner for her was as foreign an idea as seeing said man naked. Not naked. Bare-chested. Yeah, like that's what he meant with his flirting.

Get a grip.

Which unfortunately only served to make her hotter, the thought of gripping anything anywhere on Bryce's body.

"I make a mean pasta carbonara."

Carbs. Cream. Cheese. The man sure was playing hardball.

She found herself nodding. "That sounds lovely. What time and where?"

"Eight. I'm at 8132 Honeysuckle Lane."

She knew the place, a cozy cottage on a dead-end road not far from the hospital.

"See you then." She was about to hang up—considering the man was cooking for her tonight, she definitely had to call Tam ASAP—when Bryce said, "Cilla?"

"Yeah?"

"Dessert's going to blow your mind."

He hung up, the dial tone loud in her ears as she tried to decipher whether he'd meant he could satisfy her sweet tooth or would satisfy her craving for *dessert*.

In desperate need of a cool-down, she drank two glasses of water. Steadying her resolve, she picked up the phone and pressed 1 on speed dial.

As usual, Tam let it ring for an eternity and Cilla hoped she wouldn't get the answering machine. What she had to say couldn't be left as a garbled recorded message.

When the phone picked up, Cilla didn't know whether to be relieved or sorry.

"Tamsin Mathieson speaking."

Her heart gave a little buck as it always did at the sound of her daughter's voice. She missed her so much and hated that their relationship had waned to the point of the occasional brief phone call only.

"Tam, it's Mom." Cilla always added that, knowing it was stupid, but terrified if she said "It's me," one day her daughter might say "Who?"

"Hey Mom, everything okay?"

Another thing Cilla hated: the guarded tone that crept into her daughter's voice whenever she discovered her mother on the other end of the phone.

"Fine. I just wanted to touch base."

A lie Tam would definitely pick up on, considering they only called each other on birthdays or holidays.

"I'm actually in the middle of something, Mom."

Tam was always in the middle of something at the busy law practice on Wall Street. She was the youngest senior associate at the firm and worked eighty-hour weeks. She had no boyfriend, no kids and no life beyond work as far as Cilla knew. Then again, she doubted Tam would tell her if she was seeing someone.

"I'll make this quick," Cilla said, gripping the cordless phone tighter as she paced. "You remember Bryce?"

Tam made a rude scoffing sound. "Is this about Willow? Don't worry about it, Mom. Like I'd believe the crap she was implying about you and Bryce."

Cilla stilled, a chill sweeping through her body and making her shiver. So her suspicions had been correct: Willow had blabbed to Tam before she'd had a chance to tell her daughter. But what made her cold, now, was Tam's dismissive tone, like she found the thought of her mother and Bryce as a couple ludicrous.

Which it was, but to have Tam articulate her innermost doubts made Cilla question her own sanity.

"What did Willow say?"

"That she saw you and Bryce having dinner at a restaurant in Dixon's Creek, and that Bryce implied you were dating." Tam snorted. "As if."

"What if we were?"

Silence greeted her murmured question and Cilla mentally counted to ten, hoping her daughter would understand.

"You can't be serious?" Tam sniggered. "I mean, come on, Mom. You and *Bryce*? He's eighteen years younger than you."

"A fact I'm well aware of," she said, a slow-burning anger she hadn't known she possessed taking hold.

She was sixty years old and telling her daughter out of courtesy, because Bryce had been Tam's teenage crush. But she hadn't seen Tam in years; they weren't as close as she would like and she didn't owe her any explanations.

"Bryce is working as a locum in town for a few months. He asked me out. We're enjoying each other's company."

"Well, when you put it like that, it's so much easier to understand." Sarcasm dripped from every word and Cilla gripped the phone so hard she thought it'd crack.

"Look, I just wanted you to know—"

"Why, Mom? So you can feel better about the fact you're making a fool of yourself? So you can get my approval?"

That's when Cilla's anger really lit. "I don't need your approval, Tam. In fact, I don't need anything from you. I thought that, for once, my daughter might actually care what's happening in my life rather than acting like I don't exist."

Cilla's chest ached and she blinked back tears, surprised at how much Tam's judgment hurt.

She was right. She didn't need her daughter's approval, but it would've been nice to have her support rather than be ridiculed.

"I'm sorry, Mom. I know you had a hard life with Dad. And I know you've been single a long time. But wouldn't you be more comfortable dating someone your own age?"

Tam's contrite tone did little to soothe her.

"Don't you mean it'd make *you* more comfortable?" Cilla swiped at her eyes as a lone tear escaped. "You're right, Tam, I had a *hard* life with your father. He wrecked my self-esteem, my ability to trust and my relationship with you. He took away my belief in

152

happiness. And now that I have a chance to feel good for the first time in a long time, you want to shit all over it?"

Cilla never swore. She felt ashamed.

"Whatever, Mom. Just don't be surprised when I say I told you so when this farce goes pear-shaped and you're left broken-hearted again."

Tam hung up, leaving Cilla staring at the phone, fury making her hand shake. She'd accepted long ago that they would never have a normal mother–daughter relationship, had come to terms with their irreversible rift.

But to have Tam berate her like that, to hear her derision . . .

Cilla slipped the receiver back into its holder. She'd given up depending on anyone for happiness a long time ago.

Time to start making her own.

❦

Jake found her in the kitchen an hour later, freeze-dried herbs scattered on the bench, an empty pot on the stove, as she continued to replay Tam's conversation in her head.

"I'm thinking of taking Olly to visit Sara." He stared at her, concern creasing his brow. "You okay?"

Cilla gritted her teeth against the urge to unburden her soul and nodded. "I had an argument with Tam."

"Want to talk about it?"

Usually, Cilla would shake her head and give Jake the brush-off. Her nephew had enough problems without listening to hers, which were trivial in the grand scheme of things.

But the ache in her chest hadn't eased and despite her self-talk that she'd go to Bryce's tonight and enjoy herself if it killed her, she couldn't seem to move from standing on this spot in the kitchen.

"Sure you want to hear this?"

Jake nodded and propped against the island bench. "Olly's playing upstairs. I didn't want to get his hopes up about visiting Sara so thought it'd be easier if he wasn't around when I called her."

"Good idea." Cilla sighed. She paused for a moment and then took a deep breath. "One of Tam's high school friends, a guy she had a crush on, is back in town and wants to date me."

Jake's eyebrows shot so high they almost reached his hairline.

Cilla managed a rueful chuckle. "I know, it's crazy. That's what I told Bryce. Eighteen years between us is laughable. But he's genuine and sweet and makes me feel good for the first time in forever."

"Then there's no problem. You date him." Jake reached out to grip her upper arms. "If anyone deserves happiness, you do, Aunt Cilla. Don't worry about what society or Tam thinks. You go for it."

"You're a sweet boy." She stood on tiptoes to kiss his cheek. "But Tam and I aren't close, and this seems like yet another insurmountable obstacle between us."

He hesitated, before continuing. "We hadn't spoken in eighteen years, yet here we are. Honestly? Family can repair relationships when the time is right. Maybe you and Tam need to have it out face to face one day, but in the meantime, you need to do what's right for you."

Problem was, Cilla didn't know what was right for her. She'd thought sticking it out in an abusive marriage was right at the time. She'd thought being fiercely independent for the last two decades was right.

Now Bryce had breezed into town, made a few heartfelt declarations to charm her, and she thought dating him was right.

What if her inner radar was all wrong?

"Uncle Jake, wanna come play with me?" Olly yelled from upstairs and Cilla gave Jake a gentle shove.

"Go call Sara," she said. "I'm fine."

"Sure?"

Cilla nodded and forced a smile. "Thanks for the advice."

"Make sure you take it, okay?" He hugged her, before heading out of the kitchen.

Jake thought she should date Bryce. She did too.

So why the prevaricating that wouldn't quit?

23.

Sara had spent hours poring over art textbooks, hoping she could make the history of pyrography fun for the vacation program kids, when her cell rang.

A quick glance at the caller ID made her pulse speed up a tad.

She stabbed at the answer button after five rings, not wanting to appear too eager. "Hey Jake, how are you?"

"Not bad. Hope I'm not interrupting anything?"

His deep voice sent a delightful shiver through her, an irrational reaction that made her wonder if she'd had her head stuck in those books too long and would welcome any intrusion.

"No, I'm just reading."

"In that case, do you mind if I bring Olly over for a visit?" He hesitated and she heard a muffled bang in the background. "He's a little stir-crazy today."

Sounded like Olly wasn't the only one. Jake's tone held a hint of desperation.

While she didn't want to encourage Jake, she admired him for taking on the care of his nephew. Plus a small part of her wanted to see if the progress she'd made last week at Redemption Elementary would affect how she dealt one-on-one with Olly, whom she hadn't seen for a few weeks.

"Sure. Come on over."

"Thanks, be there soon."

Resisting the urge to check her hair in the mirror after he hung up, she tidied up the textbooks. Prepping for her art classes with the kids in the vacation program had been interesting and she was actually looking forward to them. Resuming pyrography had infused her with excitement for the first time in a long time and it looked like these classes were doing the same.

A few months ago, the thought of being surrounded by kids only a few years older than Lucy would've made her hibernate for a week. Now, she almost looked forward to being surrounded by innocent laughter again.

Lucy had been a great laugher. She'd laughed a hundred times a day, at the most innocuous of things. From a butterfly landing on her arm to a graffiti tag on a building, Lucy had smiled and giggled and made Sara want to laugh with her. She'd been the shining light in Sara's life; her death had plunged Sara into darkness, but at last, a flicker of hope made Sara want to do more than nurse her grief in peace.

There was a knock on the front door, and she hastily gathered her notes for the art classes and stuffed them into a portfolio. She'd tell Jake about the classes, had thought about inviting Olly to participate if he was interested, but that might mean Jake tagged along too and she was nervous enough standing in front of a roomful of kids without worrying about his overwhelming presence too. Then again, he wouldn't be sticking around in the classroom and she knew it would be good for Olly.

She padded to the front door and opened it, to find Jake smiling in relief and Olly half hiding behind his uncle. Wow, she'd really done a number on the kid if he was apprehensive about seeing her.

"Hey Olly, I'm so glad you've come to visit," she said, squatting down to his level. "I've got some new art to show you if you're interested?"

"That'd be awesome," Olly said, stepping out from behind Jake, who hadn't stopped staring at her like she was his savior. "Can I look at it now?"

"You bet. It's in the kitchen. Follow the hallway to the end."

As she stepped aside to let them in, Jake lowered his head to murmur in her ear, "Thanks for this."

"Everything okay?"

"Yeah, mostly." He rubbed a hand over his face. It did little to eradicate the weariness etching deeper lines around his eyes. "Still floundering a little, you know?"

His sincerity impressed her and she touched his arm in reassurance. "Parenting is hard. Don't let it get you down."

"I don't think I'm doing it right."

He sounded so forlorn she wanted to hug him.

"There's no manual, so you pretty much have to wing it." God knows she'd felt that way most days with Lucy.

"I'm a winging it kind of guy but I'm not sure it's cutting it with Olly."

"You're doing great," she said, wondering what it was about this guy that made her resistance waver.

She wasn't interested in dating or a relationship of any kind, but whenever she chatted with Jake, she felt strangely comfortable, like they could talk about anything.

Their brief thirty-second interlude discussing parenting was more than she'd done with Greg during the three years they'd been parents.

Greg had been an absentee dad who believed providing financially for his family was enough. He worked long hours and when he was home, he didn't want to be disturbed. Lucy had loved her dad but had barely known him. It had made Sara resent him all the more.

"He's missing his mom something fierce and I'm not enough," he said, his voice filled with pain and resignation.

"You're more than enough." She slipped her hand into his and squeezed, hoping he wouldn't misread the bold gesture but needing to convey that she understood.

She'd have given anything to have a simple hand squeeze after she'd lost Lucy. Not the tiptoeing Greg had done around her, casting furtive glances when he thought she wasn't looking. Not the overbearing false platitudes from co-workers who she'd never been close to anyway. Not the awkward silences from her neighbors, who'd often complained about Lucy's colicky crying when she'd been a baby.

Sometimes a touch conveyed so much and when Jake stared at their joined hands, then raised his gaze to meet hers, his obvious gratitude allayed her fear that she'd overstepped an invisible boundary in their tentative friendship.

"You're amazing. You know that, right?" He squeezed her hand in return and something in her chest did an embarrassing backflip.

"I try," she said, aiming for flippant, hoping he didn't see right through her. Time to change the subject pronto. "What's Olly's favorite snack?"

"Cookies and milk." Some of the tension bracketing Jake's mouth dissolved. "For a little guy, he sure can pack away the food."

"Boys have bottomless pits, though Lucy seemed to consume more than her weight in fruit and yoghurt."

"I like it when you talk about her," he said. "You get this faraway look in your eyes and your lips curve into a soft smile."

"Really?"

Whenever she thought about Lucy, let alone mentioned her name, it felt like Sara's intestines twisted into pretzels and her chest caved in on itself.

"Yeah, it's sweet." He paused on the threshold. "Anytime you'd like to tell me about her, I'd love to hear it."

"Thanks," she said, not quite sure if she was ready to discuss the love of her life without dissolving into tears. But the fact he wanted to be there for her if she did meant a lot. "Now let's go ply that cute nephew of yours with treats."

When they reached the kitchen, Olly folded his arms and frowned. "Where have you guys been? I'm starving."

Sara bit back a grin when Jake shot her a helpless glance. Nothing like kids to get straight to the point.

"Grownups like talking, Olly," Jake said. "Sometimes we have a lot to say."

Olly pondered this answer, and eventually nodded. "Kids like talking too. But we mostly do it after we have snacks, like milk and cookies, so we have more energy to do it."

"Good point," Sara said, taking three glasses from a cupboard and loading a plate with chocolate chip cookies. "Let's stock up on some energy."

Olly pointed to her work, which was spread across the table. "You must've had a lot of energy to do all this, Sara. It's really good."

"Thanks. I love doing it." Sara poured milk into the glasses, mentally reminding herself she had to ask Jake about the art classes for Olly. "Do you like drawing and painting?"

"It's awesome," Olly said, suddenly solemn. "When Mommy's tired and lying down a lot, she says I have to draw and keep quiet."

Jake stiffened and glanced at her, a silent plea for help in his eyes.

Only too happy to oblige, Sara placed the milk and cookies in front of Olly and slid onto the seat beside him. "That's the best bit for me when I make these pictures, the quiet. I get to listen to the ideas that bounce around my head and it helps me do better work."

"You have stuff bouncing around your head?" Olly stared at her head, a quizzical frown wrinkling his forehead. "That sounds weird."

"It's okay for artists to be weird. It's how we do really great work."

He shrugged. "My work is okay, I guess. Maybe I don't have enough stuff bouncing in my head?"

"I think you have plenty of ideas; you just need to be really quiet to hear them."

Sara reached out to lay a hand on Olly's shoulder, then hesitated. She'd barely got used to talking to a child again. Could she face the warmth of a touch?

When Olly looked at her funny, she gave his shoulder a brief pat then reached for a cookie. "The card you made for me had amazing drawings on it."

"They were okay." Olly crammed half a cookie into his mouth and almost demolished it in two chews. "Maybe we could draw together sometime?"

Sara wasn't sure how much time Olly had left in Redemption so she glanced across at Jake for confirmation. When he gave a slight nod, she said, "I'd really like that, Olly."

"Yay." He clapped his hands, before reaching for another cookie. "Uncle Jake's not very good at it, you know."

Jake guffawed. "Hey, I tried really hard to draw those trees."

Olly leaned across and cupped his hand to his mouth. "They looked like sticks. Really bad." His whisper was so loud Cilla could've heard it and Sara laughed.

"Not everyone can be an artist," Sara said, experiencing another pang at the thought of never seeing if Lucy had inherited any of her artistic talent.

Olly nodded. "If you're no good at art, Uncle Jake, what are you good at?"

In the short time Sara had known him, she could list a few things Jake was good at: honesty, understanding, comfort. And he excelled at filling out a pair of denim jeans.

"Fixing things," Jake said, shooting her a loaded glance, like he could read her mind.

"That sounds boring." Olly drank his milk without stopping, then wiped his milk moustache off on his sleeve, catapulting Sara back to the many times Lucy had done the same thing.

Her throat tightened and she swallowed. She wouldn't freak out this poor kid; he'd been through enough.

Intuitive as ever, Jake picked up on her silent distress. "Hey Olly, want to check out Sara's backyard?"

"Yeah." Olly didn't have to be asked twice. He pushed back his chair and bolted for the back door, where he stopped, like he'd forgotten something. "Thanks for the snacks, Sara. And for letting me see your great art work."

Touched, Sara managed a wobbly smile. "You're welcome, sweetie."

The happiness on Olly's face faded. "Mom calls me that sometimes."

Before Sara could move, Olly ran across the kitchen, flung his arms around her neck and snuggled into her.

Sara froze, bombarded with too many memories, too many sensations. But as Olly held on for dear life, she knew this child needed her far more than she needed to hold on to her grief.

With infinite slowness, she slid her arms around Olly and hugged him tight. Tears clogged her throat again but this time she didn't care, as she rested her cheek on the top of his head and inhaled the fruity fragrance of his shampoo.

When Olly disengaged as suddenly as he'd hugged her and ran outside, Sara finally risked a glance at Jake.

He looked shell-shocked and she belatedly hoped she hadn't overstepped the mark, not when he'd articulated the problems he'd been having with Olly.

"I hope that was okay?"

He nodded and swallowed several times, his Adam's apple bobbing. "I'm a stoic guy most of the time but seeing that made me want to bawl like a baby."

"Me too," she said, stifling a sniffle. "In fact, you better say something outrageous to distract me right this minute before I start blubbering."

"Cilla's a cougar."

"What?" Confused but pleased he'd changed the subject, Sara beckoned to the chair next to her.

"Cilla's dating a much younger guy." He sat and crossed his legs at the ankles, looking way too comfortable and way too appealing in her kitchen. "Eighteen years younger."

"Good for her," Sara said, sufficiently surprised and distracted. "How old is she?"

"Sixty. And loving it, apparently," Jake said, with a wry grin.

"She doesn't look that old."

In fact, Sara had pegged her for nearer fifty with her trim figure, barely lined face and spritely step. Not to mention her standard dress of leggings, spangly flip-flops and paisley kaftan tops.

"She deserves happiness, whatever her age." Jake looked like he wanted to say more before his lips compressed and he glanced away.

"We all do," she said, wishing she could take her own advice. Most days, she accepted the fact she'd never be happy again.

"Maybe," Jake said, the doubt clouding his eyes implying he didn't believe her.

Wanting to get their conversation back on lighter ground, she tapped the portfolio in front of her. "Speaking of being happy, do you think Olly would enjoy art classes?"

"I'm not sure. What did you have in mind?"

"When you rang, I was planning a few classes I'm teaching at the elementary school. The art teacher approached me after seeing the pyrography pieces I donated for the fair and asked if I could run a few informal sessions for the kids doing the vacation program."

"That sounds great," he said, staring at her with frank admiration. "If you don't mind me saying, I think it's fantastic you're willing to surround yourself with kids after you confided in me about how hard it was for you to even approach the camp."

"It's time," she said, meaning it. "And I think I have you to thank for that."

"What did I do?"

"Well, you and Olly." She gestured at the backyard. "That first day, when I freaked out, you were understanding rather than judgmental." She sucked in a breath and blew it out again. "In a way, you made me confront my greatest fear, being around a child again, and realize I could get through it without falling apart."

"You did that all on your own. Olly was the catalyst." His gentle smile made her want to do what Olly had done to her five minutes earlier: fling herself into his arms and hold on tight. "I'm just the bozo uncle along for the ride."

He leaned forward and rested his elbows on his knees. "The nefarious uncle who's not ashamed to admit he's thrilled you like Olly so he can tag along to see you."

She chuckled, his frankness utterly charming. "I like a guy who admits to nefarious methods."

"And I like you back," he said, his low tone rippling over her like a balmy breeze, raising goose bumps across her skin.

Sara resisted the urge to rub her bare arms as their gazes locked, neither of them moving a muscle as she tried to decipher if he'd answered in jest as she had, or if he'd meant more.

She might not be ready for any guy to like her, let alone a guy like Jake, but in that long, loaded moment, she wondered if she could be.

24.

Cilla hit the play button on her answering machine for the third time.

"Hey Mom, it's me. Sorry for being such a bitch before. If you want to date Bryce, it's none of my business. Maybe I was jealous. Not because of that teenage crush I had on him, but because my own love life is non-existent and I took my frustrations out on you. Anyway, have a great time. From what I remember, Bryce is a really nice guy. You know, I caught him staring at you a few times back then and I teased him about it. Guess I was pretty close to the mark, huh? Let me know how you get on. Love you. Bye."

When Cilla had heard Tam's message for the first time, it had floored her. And it hadn't lost any impact on subsequent listens.

Tam never admitted to any weakness. Never showed a flaw. She was tough, resilient and fiercely independent. A ballbreaker, she'd said they called her at work, and Tam was proud of it.

So for her to admit to jealousy . . . Cilla had heard the loneliness in her daughter's voice and it made her want to jump in her car and drive to New York City.

Neither had ever tried to breach the yawning gap between them. The fact Tam had called back to apologize was huge and gave Cilla renewed hope they could mend their fractured relationship.

In the meantime, she had a handsome young man cooking her dinner tonight and she'd dithered long enough. Her makeup application took forever. She'd spent an inordinate amount of time on her hair and had changed outfits four times, eventually settling on a beaded black skirt that skimmed her calves, a silky cobalt top and suede ebony ankle boots.

Time to pull up her big-girl panties and see where this thing she'd started with Bryce could go.

As she stepped out onto the back porch, Olly came tearing around the corner, Jake in tow.

"Aunt Cilla, guess what? Sara invited me to do art classes with her at the school. And she let me look at her stuff. And I explored her backyard. It was awesome!" Olly hopped from one foot to another, his enthusiasm endearing. "But Uncle Jake's no good at art—he can only fix things. But he said he'll take me. Isn't that cool?"

"Very," Cilla said, locking gazes with a bemused Jake over Olly's head. "I'm heading out now so you can tell me all about it tomorrow."

"Okay. I have to go inside and wash up because Uncle Jake's making me sausages for dinner. Yum." Olly tore inside and Cilla waited until the screen door slammed before approaching Jake.

"That's one excited little boy," she said, observing that Olly wasn't the only one who had benefitted from Sara's company.

She'd never seen Jake look so relaxed. Gone was the tension that raised his shoulders slightly and made his neck muscles bulge. Gone was the perpetual frown that, while faint, was ever-present.

"He likes Sara." Jake shrugged. "He's having a good effect on her too."

"And you."

Jake glanced away, but not before she saw a tell-tale flare of awareness.

"I've already said this, Jake, but be careful." She touched his forearm. "You're all vulnerable right now. Getting too attached may end in heartache."

His frown returned and Cilla silently cursed her bluntness.

"Did it ever occur to you we all need to heal, and that spending time together could facilitate that?"

With that, Jake stalked inside, leaving her feeling like an ogre.

Maybe Jake was right. She'd lectured Tam on the phone about needing to find happiness after her past. Jake and Sara and Olly needed the same.

She poked her head back inside and saw Jake braced at the sink, his back slumped like he struggled with some huge invisible weight. "Sorry."

He glanced over his shoulder, stony-faced. "Don't worry about it."

When he didn't seem inclined to speak further, she managed a terse nod and backed away, wishing she'd kept her big mouth shut before.

Wanting to put things right between her and Jake, she decided to make a stop before heading to Bryce's.

Less than a minute later, she knocked on Sara's door, hoping she was doing the right thing. When it opened, she knew she was.

Sara looked years younger, like a weight had shifted from her shoulders. Her expression was softer, more relaxed, than the other times Cilla had seen her.

"Hi, Cilla." Sara's gaze swept her from head to foot. "You look lovely."

"Thanks. I have a date," Cilla blurted, feeling like a fool.

"That's wonderful. Hope you have a good time."

"I'll try."

"Did you want something?"

Cilla sent a silent prayer to the karma gods that pushing Jake and Sara together was a good thing. "Would you like to come over for dinner tomorrow night? Nothing fancy."

Sara smiled. "I'd love to. Thanks. Can I bring anything?"

"Just yourself. See you then." Cilla waved and headed back to her car.

If spending an hour or two together could make Jake and Sara look like that, and infuse Olly with excitement, she should be all for it.

Thirty minutes later, she hoped those karma gods were still looking down on her as she fiddled with her handbag strap outside Bryce's door, stalling.

What on earth was she doing here?

A minute later, after she'd plucked up the courage to finally knock and Bryce opened the door, looking incredible in khaki slacks and a white polo top, she knew.

She wanted to feel good about herself and this man had the power to do that for her.

"Hey, Gorgeous." He snagged her hand, pulled her inside and shut the door with a kick. "You look sensational."

She didn't get a chance to thank him because he kissed her. On the lips. It didn't last beyond a few seconds, but long enough to addle her wits.

That was the only explanation for her total capitulation when he tugged her into his arms and hugged her so tight she could feel exactly how glad he was to see her.

Her first instinct was to pull back but when he nuzzled her neck and inhaled her fragrance, she gave herself over to the pleasure of being embraced by a man.

When he released her, he appeared unfazed by his obviously aroused state, whereas she could've fried eggs on her burning cheeks.

"Hope you're hungry," he said over his shoulder as he strode toward the kitchen.

"Starving," Cilla said, staring at his taut butt, knowing it wasn't for food and feeling foolish because of it.

"Good. Take a seat at the table and I'll dish up."

"Need a hand?"

"Thanks, but I'm good." He moved about the kitchen with the confidence of a man used to cooking.

Considering the only time Vernon had entered the kitchen was to grab a beer from the fridge, Bryce's culinary capabilities turned her on even more.

"Wine?" He placed a pasta dish piled high with steaming fettuccini carbonara in the middle of the table and she didn't know what made her mouth water more: the delicious aroma of the food or the smell of his clean skin, fresh from the shower.

"No thanks." She needed to keep her wits about her—what little of them was left.

Wine always made her mellow. She hadn't minded having a glass when they were eating together at the restaurant, but in the intimacy of his home, she couldn't afford to let down her guard too much. Not when she had no idea how far she wanted to take this.

"You don't have to drive home, you know." He pulled his chair closer to hers and she silently cursed the small table for two. "You're welcome to stay over."

He placed his hand over hers, and for one insane moment she considered it.

What would it be like to feel his firm body against hers? To run her hands over his skin, his muscles? To have sex for the first time in decades? To wake up in his arms, to find herself naked and vulnerable and feeling every one of her sixty years?

No, she couldn't go there yet.

Maybe not ever.

"No pressure," he said, removing his hand and reaching for the pasta.

Easy for him to say. That's all Cilla felt whenever she was in his company: pressure. The pressure of expectation. The pressure of not living up to his expectations. Considering she'd reveled in not having to meet anyone's expectations since Vernon died, she didn't want or need that kind of pressure. It made her a little crazy.

She blamed him. This forty-two-year-old suave charmer who'd breezed into her life and turned it upside down.

"You're awfully quiet," he said, heaping a healthy serving of pasta onto her plate. "Is being here making you uncomfortable?"

"Partially," she admitted, reaching for her fork. She figured if she stuffed her mouth with pasta, she wouldn't have to talk. Or admit how much she liked his intuitiveness.

"Don't be. I didn't invite you here to jump your bones." He winked. "Not 'til later."

"Stop it." She swatted his arm, her fingers lingering on his biceps a few seconds longer than necessary.

"Do you really want me to?" He glanced at her hand, still on his arm, and she snatched it away.

"I'm out of my depth," she said, her appetite vanishing as she realized they'd need to have this conversation at some point and it had come around sooner rather than later. "So far out it's not funny."

"How about we eat dinner and leave the hard stuff 'til later?"

Cilla looked into his guileless dark eyes, knowing that later might never come if it were up to her.

But she found herself nodding and devouring the delicious pasta with renewed gusto. They made small talk. About the hospital mostly. The upcoming fair she was organizing for Sergio. A whole range of innocuous topics that did little to settle her rampaging nerves.

Because all she could think about throughout the entire dinner was what she would do if Bryce put the moves on her.

Ludicrous for a woman her age to feel so jittery, but Bryce was confident and gorgeous and skilled, three things she wasn't in the bedroom.

If she could remember back that far.

"Was there something wrong with my cooking?" His eyes twinkled with amusement as if he could see straight through her. "You've got a funny look on your face."

"No, I'm just nervous," she blurted, feeling like a fool as she bustled about, cleaning the table, rinsing plates and stacking the dishwasher.

"Stop." He came up behind her and placed his hands on her waist.

She yelped and spun around, dislodging his hands.

"Cilla, this is ridiculous. I said I wouldn't pressure you and I won't." He propped against the island bench. "We've had a lovely dinner, and I've just engaged in the most interesting conversation I've had with a woman in years."

He took a step closer and gripped her upper arms. "I've been completely honest with you right from the beginning. I like you. I want you. But we don't have to do anything you don't want to."

Cilla sighed. That was the problem. She did want to, but had no idea how to go about it.

"I don't want to disappoint you," she said, so softly it almost came out a whisper.

He swore. "You could never do that."

Their gazes locked and the blazing lust in his made her knees go weak, a second before his mouth slammed onto hers. Commanding and demanding. Compelling and challenging. All she could do was go along for the ride, clinging to his shirt in a world turned topsy-turvy.

He tasted divine, a heady combination of the pinot noir and spicy undertones of the chilies he'd liberally sprinkled on his pasta. His hands skimmed her back, caressed her hips, grabbed her butt.

When he started grinding against her, she whimpered, his hardness pressing against her sweet spot. She wanted more. Craved it with every cell in her long-neglected body.

But when Bryce's hand slid between their bodies to palm her breast, his fingers rolling her nipple, she froze. Pushed him away.

And lost it.

"I can't do this. I don't ever think I'll be able to do this. And having you sweet-talk me over dinners and pay me compliments and pretend like our age difference is irrelevant isn't helping." She was shrieking now and didn't care. She had to get through to him. Had to get him to leave her alone.

"See this?" She gestured at her body. "Closed up shop over twenty years ago. I don't need sex. I don't want sex. And I sure as hell don't need some young guy pressuring me into feeling worse about myself than I already do."

Stricken, he stared at her in wide-eyed shock. "Cilla, please—"

"Please what? Please don't go? Please don't speak the truth?" She held up her hands and backed away. "Just leave me alone."

She snagged her bag and made it to the door. "I don't want to see you again. It's not you, it's me. And that's not some trite line from a rom-com, it's the sad truth."

He didn't stop her when she flung open the door and made a run for her car.

He didn't come after her.

After the monumental fool she'd just made of herself, she should be thankful for small mercies.

Instead, she cried the whole way home.

25.

Sara stood at the front of the classroom, trying to quell the rising dread that was making her gut burn.

She should never have agreed to this.

She risked a glance in the direction of Andy, who stood to the right of the class alongside the windows. His thumbs-up sign of approval did little for her riotous nerves.

Twenty pairs of curious eyes were fixed on her, like she was about to impart the secret of the perfect artwork.

She swallowed, wondering what she could say now that she'd already introduced herself, when a hand shot up in the back row.

"Ms. Hardy, is working with fire and wood dangerous?"

Just like that, her first art class at Redemption Elementary started.

The next hour flew by in a blur of questions and demonstrations. She didn't have time to doubt herself; the kids didn't let her. They bombarded her with insightful questions and were patient when lining up to try their hand at pyrography. They were polite and sweet and genuinely lovely. And for the first time since Lucy's death, she found the sound of children's laughter comforting rather than appalling.

When the last child filed out of the classroom, Andy perched on the desk she was tidying up.

"They loved you," he said, crossing his arms, a speculative gleam in his stare. "Which was great, considering you looked like you were ready to bolt before the class started."

"My three-year-old daughter died fourteen months ago and I've avoided kids ever since," she blurted, not to make him feel bad, but because she could finally articulate the truth without it choking her.

"Hell. I'm sorry." Bug-eyed, Andy covered his shock with a nervous step forward, like he was about to hug her, before resuming his seat on the edge of the desk. "Just tell me to shut up."

"It's okay."

And it was. Because she'd faced one of her greatest fears over the last hour and had come out unscathed. Being around happy children didn't make her resent them as she'd been afraid it would. Her initial fear of being around kids—how dare they be happy and alive when Lucy wasn't?—had been replaced with a sense of joy, as though their warmth and vitality could help heal her.

"If these classes are too tough, we can cancel the rest and—"

"No, I want to do them," she said, surprised by how much she meant it. "I enjoyed it and I think the kids did too."

He nodded. "I've never seen them so animated."

"I'm glad." She continued packing her tools. "I may have another candidate for the class. A six-year-old who's had a rough time being separated from his mom, and is in town for the summer. Can he join?"

"Sure. Get his guardian to call me and I'll email the forms."

"Thanks." Sara slung her portfolio bag over her shoulder and grabbed the handle of her wheelie suitcase. "I'll see you next class."

"See you then."

Sara felt Andy's curious gaze boring into her back as she left. He'd been more circumspect than most, not asking how Lucy had died. She'd never gotten used to that, people's blatant curiosity for the macabre. Apparently no question was off-limits, even for a grieving mother.

Buoyed by the success of her first art class, she spent the afternoon working on new pieces, losing track of time until she happened to glance at the clock and realized she was due at Cilla's for dinner in ten minutes.

After the quickest shower on record, she donned jeans, a pink sweater set and beaded flip-flops. A dash of mascara and a slick of gloss added color to her face, but she didn't have time to do anything with her hair so she snagged it into a ponytail and pinned it loosely at the nape of her neck.

As she glanced in the hallway mirror on the way out, she halted briefly in surprise. For the first time in a long time, she looked . . . carefree. Young. Stress-free.

She could attribute her glow to Redemption's fresh air and organic produce but she knew better. Coming to terms with Lucy's death, being around children again without falling apart, had done more for her today than anything else.

Or the faint pink coloring in her cheeks could have something to do with her excitement at seeing Jake over a dinner table, but she preferred her first explanation.

Humming a song that one of the kids had been singing today, she strolled along her driveway and up Cilla's, the light spilling from every window in the cottage a welcome sight.

She liked the peace of the country and the inky darkness that would descend in a few hours. New York City had never been dark, the constant glow lighting the roof of her apartment even when she'd lain in bed, listening to Lucy's soft snores through the monitor.

She hadn't minded it so much then, but not until she'd moved out here did Sara relish nightfall and the certainty that when she closed her eyes, darkness would prevail and the glow of city lights wouldn't be yet another contributor to her often sleepless nights.

Wondering if she should've brought more than a bottle of wine, she knocked on the door, smiling when she heard the stampede of footsteps signaling an excited kid.

When the door flung open, Olly grinned at her. "Hi, Sara. Guess what? Aunt Cilla's made pot roast and veggies." He screwed up his nose. "I don't like the veggies so much but I have to eat them or I don't get any dessert."

She adored this little boy with his big brown eyes so earnestly fixed on her. "Want to hear a secret?"

His eyes widened as he nodded. "What is it?"

She crooked a finger, smiling when he came closer. "I like dessert much better than veggies too, but if Cilla's gone to the trouble of cooking for us, we should eat everything on our plates."

"Guess you're right," he said, snagging her hand, tugging her inside and slamming the door. "She won't tell me what dessert is. Said it's a surprise."

"I love surprises." She allowed herself to be tugged toward the kitchen, making a mockery of her statement when she caught sight of Jake elbow-deep in suds at the kitchen sink.

Now there was a surprise she didn't dare love.

He looked incredible in black cargo shorts, a loose olive T and sneakers. Relaxed, at home, a guy at ease in his own skin. Throw in the way he scrubbed a pan, making his back muscles shift and bunch beneath cotton, and she seriously doubted her heart could stand a surprise of that magnitude.

"Hey," she said, her stomach doing a weird fluttering thing when he glanced over his shoulder, caught sight of her and smiled.

With day-old stubble covering his jaw and his eyes alight with genuine happiness at seeing her, he certainly packed a punch.

"Hey yourself," he said, rinsing the pan and stacking it on the sideboard to dry. "You've caught me at my domesticated best."

"I'm impressed," she said, meaning it.

"I can wash dishes too." Olly frowned at Jake. "But I'm better at drying."

Surprised by the hint of animosity in Olly's tone, she laid a hand on his shoulder. "Maybe we should do the washing up later. What do you say?"

"Maybe." Olly shrugged her hand off and ran into the other room. "Aunt Cilla, Sara is here. Can we eat now? I'm starving."

"Is he okay?" Sara mouthed to Jake, who nodded, but the groove between his brows deepened.

"I brought a Napa Riesling," she said, placing it on the table.

"Thanks." Jake crossed the kitchen to stand close. Too close. Not close enough. "Thought I'd warn you: Cilla's been in a bit of a mood all day. She won't tell me what's wrong but maybe you can talk to her?"

"Uh-oh. When she dropped by last night to invite me to dinner, she was on her way to a date."

Jake groaned. "I'm such a putz. That must be it."

"I don't think I'm close enough to Cilla to interrogate her about how her date went."

"Maybe sound her out a little?" Jake held his hands out in a silent plea. "She'll probably talk to you, woman to woman, whereas I'll put my big foot in my mouth if I try."

"Okay," Sara said, increasingly doubtful. The last thing she felt like doing was sticking her nose into Cilla's business, especially if her date hadn't gone well.

"You're the best." Jake slipped an arm around her waist and gave a gentle squeeze, setting off a chain reaction starting in the vicinity of her chest and spreading outward, like warm treacle flowing through her veins.

Olly bowled into the kitchen and skidded to a stop when he saw Jake semi-hugging her, his frown returning. "Aunt Cilla is coming."

Sara gently slipped out of Jake's embrace and Olly brightened. Could the child be jealous of her, thinking she was vying for Jake's attention? It would make sense if he resented her but he seemed happy to see her tonight. She'd have to tread carefully, because the last thing she wanted was to ruin the fragile relationship developing between Jake and his nephew.

"She looks sad," Olly said, taking his place at the table. "Mommy used to look sad all the time, so that's how I know."

Sara only just heard Jake's muffled curse as he strode to the table and sat next to Olly.

"Listen, buddy, we all have sad days. But grownups don't like it when kids talk about it, so maybe we shouldn't say anything about Aunt Cilla at dinner, okay?"

Olly tilted his head to one side, pondering, before eventually nodding. "Okay. I'll eat my dinner and won't say anything about Aunt Cilla looking sad or you looking really happy to see Sara."

Sara bit back a guffaw as Jake shot her a rueful grin.

"Sounds like a plan." Jake stood and headed for the stove. "I'll start to dish up while we wait for her."

At that moment, Cilla slipped into the kitchen and Sara had to agree with Olly's astute assessment of the situation: Cilla looked miserable. Like a light had been switched off behind her eyes.

It made her mad, to think a vibrant woman like Cilla could be this affected by some guy who'd obviously hurt her.

"Dinner smells wonderful, Cilla." She gave the older woman an impulsive peck on the cheek. "Thanks so much for inviting me."

"My pleasure." Cilla waved her toward the table. "Take a seat and we'll dish up."

"Anything I can do to help?" Sara had meant with dinner, but when Cilla's startled gaze flew to hers, she knew Jake was right. Cilla might need a woman to talk to.

"We're fine," Jake said, sending her some weird eye signals to relay that he'd noticed Cilla's reaction too. "We don't put our guests to work."

"But I'm a guest and I work," Olly piped up, with a cheeky grin.

"You're family," Cilla said, some of her moroseness alleviated when she glanced fondly at Olly, who puffed up with pride at being labeled family.

In that instant, Sara realized why they all seemed to get on so well. A band of misfits in their own way, they were all craving a little affection and a lot of understanding. She fit right in.

"I forgot to ask if you're vegetarian, so I made plenty of veggies in case," Cilla said, placing a giant dish of roasted potatoes, squash, turnips and onions in front of her.

"I'm not," Sara said, as Jake placed a carved pot roast on the table and she caught a whiff of delicious garlic and rosemary.

"Me either." Olly squirmed in his chair and rubbed his tummy. "That smells so good."

"It sure does." Sara accepted a healthy serving of meat and veg that Jake and Cilla dished out, and waited until everyone was served before starting.

"Aunt Cilla is the best cook," Olly said, despite his mouth being full.

"Thanks, Olly, but remember we don't talk when our mouth has food in it," Cilla admonished gently, her obvious fondness for the kid alleviating some of her earlier sadness.

Olly chewed fast, then responded. "But when food's this good, I can't wait to tell you."

Sara chuckled. "Smooth talker like his uncle, I see."

Jake's eyebrows rose. "You think I'm smooth?"

"You try." Sara found herself grinning at Jake across the table and for a moment, it was like no one else was in the room.

When Cilla passed the water jug, Sara blinked, filled her glass and passed it on.

"Be careful of young men who try to charm you," Cilla said, and Sara heard the wistful undertone, wondering if Cilla was warning her or herself.

"I think I can handle Jake." Sara eyeballed Jake with a boldness she didn't feel. "And if I can't, Olly will help me."

Olly glanced up from shoveling food into his mouth. "Help with what, Sara?"

"Never mind," Jake said, shooting Sara a loaded stare that implied he'd deal with her cheekiness later.

The banter continued as they ate, making Sara feel more at home than she had in ages. She liked the informality of eating in the kitchen, the warmth from the old Aga stove as comforting as the hearty food. Meals with Gran had been like this and she'd loved them. However, it had only served to reinforce how useless her mother had been when she'd been on the road with Vera. During those times, Sara had survived on TV dinners and tinned soups.

Annoyed that thoughts of her mother still had the power to sour her mood, she concentrated on her plate, realizing she'd cleared most of it when the others were still eating. A habit she hadn't been able to break, even fourteen months later—eating quickly to keep pace with her daughter so they could do fun stuff together after they finished.

"This is delicious," Sara said, forcing herself to slow down and push squash onto her fork at a snail's pace.

Mistaking her speed-eating for hunger, Cilla gestured at the serving dishes. "There's plenty to eat, so don't be shy in taking more."

"I'm fine, thanks," Sara said, blushing when she noticed her plate cleared quicker than Olly's. "I'm a fast eater."

Cilla locked eyes with her for a moment, her understanding obvious. She was a mother. She knew what it was like. But thankfully, the older woman didn't say anything and concentrated on her meal. Which she'd barely touched, now that Sara actually noticed.

Cilla cut small pieces of beef but pushed them around her plate. Same with the vegetables. Jake must've noticed too, because the second he finished he made a grand show of patting his belly and pushing back from the table.

"Sensational dinner. Thanks." He kissed Cilla on the cheek. "If you'll excuse Olly and me, we're going to check out some new shark app online."

Cilla frowned. "But we've got a guest."

"We'll only be gone a few minutes, won't we, Olly?" Jake said, at the same time Sara piped up with, "I'm fine."

Cilla's frown deepened. "Okay, but if you're not back in ten minutes, you don't get dessert."

Olly's bottom lip wobbled. "Uncle Jake, I know I bugged you earlier to look at that app before dinner, but maybe we can wait 'til much later."

Jake smiled and ruffled Olly's hair. "The girls won't eat our share of dessert."

Olly pinned Sara with a stare. "Promise?"

Sara held up her hand. "Promise."

"Yay." Olly pushed back from the table and ran from the kitchen. "Come on, Uncle Jake. I want to see this app real bad."

Jake sent Sara a pointed glare before following Olly at a more sedate pace.

When they'd left, Cilla gave up all pretense of eating and pushed her plate away, giving Sara the perfect in.

"Are you okay? You look tired." Sara chose her words carefully, not wanting to make Cilla feel worse than she already did, if her woebegone expression was any indication.

"Didn't sleep all night." Cilla squeezed the bridge of her nose, as if staving off tears. "There's no fool like an old fool."

Increasingly uncomfortable at having this conversation with a woman she didn't know well, Sara said, "You don't have to talk about it if you don't want, but it can help."

Cilla's shoulders stiffened for a moment, as if she was trying to steel her backbone, before she slumped. "That date last night?"

"Uh-huh."

"A disaster." Cilla scowled. "I never should've put myself in that situation in the first place, so it's my fault."

Wary, Sara hoped nothing too untoward had happened to this nice lady. "Situation?"

"Young men have needs." A blush stained Cilla's cheeks crimson. "My date is a young man. Forty-two, to be exact. Which makes me eighteen years his senior and supposedly wiser." She snorted. "So when a man asks me to his house, cooks me dinner, then expects more, I shouldn't freak out."

Oh dear. The conversation had moved from uncomfortable to downright terrifying. Sara didn't want to discuss Cilla's sex life, or lack thereof, now or ever.

"But I did. Totally freak out," Cilla continued, oblivious to Sara's awkward silence. "Told him to leave me alone."

From the audible devastation in Cilla's voice, Sara guessed this wasn't what she wanted.

"Do you like this guy?"

Cilla gnawed on her bottom lip and nodded. "He's sweet and gentle and utterly lovely."

"Which means he's perfect for you," Sara said, reaching out to squeeze Cilla's hand. "You're like that too."

Cilla blinked rapidly and Sara hoped she wouldn't have to deal with tears too. "Aren't you the slightest bit shocked by the age difference?"

Sara shrugged. "It's irrelevant if you both want the same things."

"I don't know what I want." Cilla deflated even more, if that was possible. "I'm so terrified of disappointing him that I don't want to take things beyond friendship."

Sara knew the feeling. After her marriage to Greg had imploded, she had no idea if she ever wanted to reconnect with a guy on that intimate level again. Jake made her feel things she hadn't felt for a long time, prompting her not to get too close. Being attracted to a guy was one thing, but following through and getting physical involved opening herself up on a deeper level, one she had no intention of exploring any time soon. Sara could empathize with Cilla. How much harder would it be for an older woman whose husband had died decades ago?

"Friendship is good—"

"But I want to be with a man again, too. It's been over twenty years."

Uh-oh. They were definitely entering icky territory and Sara needed a deflection.

"Chances are he's as bummed about all this as you are, so why don't you approach him as a friend and explain?"

Cilla shook her head. "I can't. Not after the way I ended things last night."

Sara wanted to trot out a few trite platitudes, like "Nothing is ever as bad as it seems" or "It'll all be better in the morning." But she knew that wasn't true. She knew firsthand, and had resented all those people who'd offered condolences when they didn't have a clue what it felt like to lose a child.

The best Sara could offer was honesty. "I can't profess to know what you're going through but if you ever need to talk, I'm always a short stroll away."

"Thanks, I appreciate it." Cilla reached over and hugged her, as Olly skidded into the kitchen with Jake on his heels.

"What's the surprise dessert, Aunt Cilla? Because I'm starving."

Cilla smiled fondly at Olly. "You only finished dinner five minutes ago. How can you be starving?"

"Boys are always hungry." Olly rolled his eyes. "Isn't that right, Uncle Jake?"

"You're absolutely right." However, the way Jake stared at her, Sara wondered if he meant for food.

"Then you'll love my lemon meringue pie," Cilla said, getting up to serve dessert while Sara helped Jake and Olly clear the table.

"Yum," Olly said, scraping scraps into the trash and handing the plates to Sara to rinse. "Not as good as Aunt Cilla's apple crumble, but still yummy all the same. Will you have one piece or two, Sara?"

"One, please," Sara said, and saw Jake eyeing her appreciatively, as if he didn't mind if she had seconds. "For starters."

As it turned out, Cilla's lemon meringue pie was so good they all had two pieces, but when it came time to clear the table again, Cilla shooed her away.

"Why don't you and Jake go for a stroll around the garden? Olly and I have this covered, don't we?"

Olly appeared torn, like he'd rather be walking outside than cleaning up, before reluctantly nodding. "Okay, I'll help clean up, because I'm family and Sara is a guest."

Cilla smiled, her first genuine smile of the evening, and Sara hoped their chat had helped. Even though Sara hadn't said much, she knew from experience that being allowed to offload to a good listener helped.

"You sure you don't need a hand?" Jake asked his aunt, who gave him a nudge in the direction of the door.

"Go," Cilla said. "It's a beautiful night out there."

Sara didn't mind walking off her dinner, but the moment the back door closed and that darkness she'd been looking forward to earlier enveloped them, she realized this stroll might not be such a good idea after all.

She didn't need the romantic ambience, not when she found Jake more appealing every time they met.

"How did your chat go?" Jake placed his hand in the small of her back to guide her onto the path and left it there, distracting Sara to the point she found it hard to put one foot in front of the other.

"You were right. Sounds like her date last night didn't go so well."

"If that guy hurt her, I'll kill him."

Jake sounded so earnest she smiled; his protectiveness was endearing. "I think it has more to do with her feeling out of her depth and not sure if she's ready for anything more than friendship."

"Oh."

Jake's one syllable sounded so uncomfortable Sara knew he'd understood more about what she hadn't said than what she had.

"I'm glad she had you to talk to," he said. "Thanks for that."

"Cilla's wonderful so it was no problem."

They strolled through Cilla's garden in companionable silence, the intoxicating fragrance of jasmine scenting the air, and when Jake slipped his hand into hers, Sara resisted her first instinct to pull away.

Walking hand in hand with a gorgeous guy through a darkened garden on a balmy evening felt decadent. Like a summer romance, fleeting and quixotic and too good to be true, but to be savored in the short term.

She'd confronted her fear of being around kids. Maybe she should allow herself to open up a little and just *feel* with a guy again too. Be in the moment without over-analyzing.

"Do you think she was trying to match-make by sending us out here together?" Jake stopped at the end of the garden, near a towering elm.

"Do you care?"

Because in that moment, with Jake staring at her lips like they were fruit ripe for the plucking, she sure didn't. Crazy, but it felt like the most natural thing in the world to be finally taking a chance on living again, despite her misgivings when they'd met.

"She initially warned me off you," he said, stepping closer, invading her personal space and setting her nerve endings alight. "Said you were too fragile and I wasn't around for long so I should stay away."

"And now?"

Sara held her breath as his fingertips skated across her jaw, his thumb gently raising her chin.

"Now, all I want to do is this."

He lowered his head and brushed his lips across hers, a kiss filled with hope and promises. A kiss as light as air. A kiss to reawaken dreams.

Dreams she shouldn't have because they couldn't go beyond this. Dreams that were foolish at best.

Yet when Jake's lips demanded more, Sara happily gave it, their tongues dueling with passion as he crushed her to him. Jolts of electricity sizzled through her body, sparking heat from her head to her toes and choice places in between, as, for the first time in forever, she experienced the kind of mind-blowing lust that eradicated common sense.

Sara had no idea how long they kissed, their soft moans the only sound in the still night. As their kisses deepened, Sara started to lose all sense of time and place. He devoured her and she matched him, a deep-seated desperation for pleasure rising from within.

Kissing Jake made Sara forget everything and for those interminable moments when their mouths fused, she allowed herself to just *feel*.

When they finally came up for air, they stared at each other in wonder, chests heaving, breathing raggedly in unison.

187

"That was . . ." Jake cursed softly under his breath and shook his head, lost for words.

"Wow," she helpfully supplied, and the bewilderment in his gaze gave way to wonder.

"*Wow* is an understatement." He ruffled the hair at the back of his head. "It's been a while for me."

"Bet it's been longer for me," she said, uncomfortable talking about this but figuring she owed him some kind of explanation for almost devouring him. "Greg, my ex, kept long hours at the office. I was too tired working full time and looking after Lucy after work to be interested in much else."

Jake nodded, like he understood. "Work was my life too. I dated occasionally but I haven't for a while."

"Let me guess: a while for you is like three months?"

He laughed at her teasing. "More like nine."

"Try eighteen," she said, with a grimace. "Even then, it was less than spectacular."

Jake's smile faded as he cupped her cheek. "We're not just talking about kissing here, right?"

"Right." She found herself leaning her cheek into his hand. "And please don't misconstrue what I said, and think because we shared a monumentally stupendous kiss that I'm going to sleep with you, but I feel like we should talk about this stuff, so there's no false expectations, you know?"

"Long speech." Jake caressed her cheek. "Just so you know, I don't have expectations."

"Good."

"But if that make-out session was any indication, we'd burn up the sheets."

She shoved him away playfully, laughing at his outrageousness. "Let's head back."

"Running scared?" he murmured, snagging her hand again as they turned for home.

"Maybe running toward those sheets?"

She snatched her hand out of his and sprinted away, feeling happier than she had in years.

If one all-consuming, all-powerful kiss could do this, she couldn't help but wonder what a roll in those sheets could do.

26.

Jake gave Sara a twenty-minute head start before returning to the house. Twenty minutes where he strolled the garden perimeter ten times, pulled a few weeds and sat on a bench, contemplating that kiss.

She'd cited an urgent bathroom visit as her excuse to head back and he'd let her go. He could imagine her sitting at the kitchen table with Cilla, having coffee and trying to pretend that they hadn't made out like a couple of randy teenagers.

Though calling what they'd done a make-out session was like saying Sara was pretty. Understatement of the year.

He could rationalize away his reaction to Sara as a case of neglected libido. But the way they'd gelled and melded and combusted? Like nothing he'd ever experienced before.

Dammit, he was hard again just thinking about it.

Sitting out here trying to get his head together wasn't helping. Nothing would help. He'd be awake all night regardless of whether he did another lap or ten around the garden, remembering the way she'd felt in his arms, the faintest floral fragrance of her skin, the softness of her lips, the tiny moans . . .

Muttering a curse under his breath, he stalked toward the back of the house. They hadn't had a chance to be uncomfortable with each other—she'd bolted that fast after the kiss—and the sooner they faced each other again the better. Maybe he could walk her home? Ask her out on a real date?

However, when he slipped through the back door, the house was silent and Cilla had left him a note on the table.

SARA HAD TO GO.
OLLY WAS TIRED SO I PUT HIM TO BED.
SEE YOU IN THE MORNING.

Well, guess that put paid to his grand plans to confront Sara and move past any potential awkwardness.

He paced the kitchen, as edgy as he'd been outside. It catapulted him back in time to the many floorboards he'd pounded in the kitchen back home, trying to work off tension caused by his father's verbal abuse.

Back then Rose would calm him down. She'd make fresh lemonade, PB&J sandwiches and talk to him about the most mundane things. Stuff like her favorite boy band at the time, the latest trash talk from school, her most hated teacher. He'd listen to her rambling, not particularly interested in the useless information she'd share but appreciating her soothing tone and the calming effect it had.

He glanced at the phone. Rose was allowed weekly calls and it had been six days since their last chat. Surely a day wouldn't make a difference?

Willing to risk the wrath of her supervisor, he dialed the number. Reception put him through to her supervisor, whose glowing endorsement of Rose's progress made some of his tension drain away before he'd even spoken to his sister. She put him through to Rose's room without a qualm.

As the phone rang, he almost hung up. What was he thinking, ringing his sister who was dealing with her own crap, in the hope she could talk him down off a ledge of his own imagining?

When she picked up, Jake vowed to make this a quick, stress-free call.

"Hey Sis, it's me."

"Jakey, so good to hear your voice. How's my darling Olly? And you?"

"Olly's fine. Missing you, but fine. And I'm great." His standard response for any period in his life, even if it was the pits. "You're sounding perky."

"I'm feeling good. Really good." Rose sighed. "Seriously, this is the best thing I could've done for Olly and me. I needed to get my shit together before I imploded."

"Know the feeling," he said, mentally cursing that he'd let slip so much without intending to.

"You're not so great after all, huh?"

That was his Rose, astute as ever. She wouldn't be satisfied with a brush-off, either. He'd tried that many times growing up and she'd never let him get away with anything.

"Being here in Redemption has helped. Caring for Olly, re-bonding with Cilla, hanging out with Sara—"

"Who's Sara?"

"Our neighbor. I mentioned her last week?"

"Yeah, but not in that tone." Rose snickered. "Your voice went all soft. Did something happen? Are you sweet on her?"

What could Jake say? That he wasn't just sweet on Sara, he was ga-ga for her in a way he hadn't been for any woman for as long as he could remember.

Sara challenged his previous status as Jilting Jake. Some of the ladies at work had dubbed him with the nickname after hearing some of his dating exploits on the airport grapevine, and it had stuck. Not that he'd cared. He'd never wanted a family, never wanted a long-term relationship or the risk that, when he came home from work at the end of the day, he might turn on the people he should love the most.

He'd tolerated enough of that from his dad growing up and he'd never wanted to risk finding out if he was like his old man. So he had dated frequently, never went beyond a few dates, and never grew emotionally attached.

What was it about Sara that challenged his preconceptions and carefully constructed plan?

"Your silence speaks volumes, Jakey. You not wanting to talk about her tells me more than if you were waxing lyrical."

There was no judgment in Rose's voice, only teasing, and he found himself relaxing.

"I like her, Rosey-Posey. She's amazing. And I think you'd like her too." Which brought him around to broaching the subject he'd tried to bring up last week. "Redemption has been good for me. And Olly. I really think you should consider staying here for a while once you get out of rehab."

"You can't be serious?" Rose snorted. "What about finding a job? I need a steady income to support Olly and make rent. You know that."

"The restaurant fired you without references. It'll be tough."

Jake heard Rose's muffled curse and felt like a bastard for bringing her down with a healthy dose of reality when she'd been so upbeat.

"It'll be easier to find another chef's job in New York City than that backwater place."

"There are a lot of restaurants here. And in the nearby towns. I reckon you could find a job here easily."

"A temporary one?" Her derision saddened him. "Olly's been uprooted enough. I don't want him to think we're moving to Redemption, only to find we're back in the city when it doesn't work out. I won't do that to him. I can't."

"Fair enough." He gave it one last shot. "But there's something about this place that has helped heal me. And I'm hoping it can bring you peace in the same way."

Very Dalai Lama of him, but it was true.

He'd been an emotional wreck when he arrived, operating like an automaton, getting through each day by sheer luck. Now, the nightmares had lessened and he didn't wear a permanent scowl as a badge of his guilt. Sure, Cilla probably had more to do with that than the town itself, but being in a new environment had certainly helped.

Then there was Sara . . . He knew she was more than a distraction, something to focus on other than the guilt. She was much more, but damned if he could figure out what to do about it.

"I'll think about it," Rose said. "But I'm not a country girl. Never have been."

"But maybe it's a good environment for Olly? He likes it out here. He's thriving."

He heard a sharp intake of breath and cursed himself for being so insensitive. He'd made it sound like Olly hadn't been doing so well before.

"We do okay, Jake. And I've pretty much been doing it on my own the last six months when you weren't around."

"Ouch." He deserved that. "You know I think you're an amazing mom, but Olly's life has been uprooted a fair bit lately. I just thought it'd be good for him to stay here for stability."

Rose blew out a long breath. "I said I'd think about it, okay? Don't push me."

"Would I do that?"

She chuckled, as he expected her to. "You've always been a bossy-boots."

"Just looking out for you, kid." And he always would. Their father had done a lousy job and Rose said Jake was the only guy she could count on in this world. He intended to keep it that way, until some intelligent guy figured out how great his sister was and captured her heart. Until that day, and an extensive vetting process, he was all she had.

"Thanks. Love you." She made a smoochy sound. "Tell my baby I'll call him tomorrow, okay?"

"Will do. Chat soon."

Jake hung up, feeling lighter. Rose had sounded like her old self and he was incredibly proud of how far she'd come in her rehab. Chatting with her had calmed him, had made him see things far more rationally.

Ironic, that in encouraging her to spend some time in Redemption recovering, he'd had a light-bulb moment.

What did he have waiting for him back in New York City?

An apartment he could easily sublet. That was it.

Redemption had been good for him temporarily. What if he made it more permanent? Hung around even when Olly reunited with his mom?

Not that he'd impose on Cilla any longer than he had to, but he could find his own place. Rent for the rest of the summer. Spend more time with Olly and Rose if she decided to move out here for a while.

The fact that it would give him more time to get to know Sara and see what could potentially develop between them . . . Well, that was an added bonus.

27.

Cilla had a killer headache that wouldn't quit.

She'd had it ever since she'd shrieked at Bryce like a banshee and run out on him.

He'd called her cell a few times and left messages. She'd deleted them without listening. What was the point, when nothing he could say would change facts?

She couldn't give him what he wanted and he deserved a woman who could.

"Were you playing matchmaker last night?" Jake strolled into the kitchen and grabbed an apple out of the fruit bowl.

"Good morning to you too," Cilla muttered, stirring the porridge with particular viciousness.

"Someone's in a bad mood." Jake took a bite out of the apple and leaned against the island bench, his intense scrutiny making her uncomfortable.

"Heard you on the phone last night. Were you talking to Rose?"

He bought her deflection or decided to let her off the hook. "Yeah, she's improving daily. Sounded really upbeat."

"When can Olly see her?"

It broke Cilla's heart, seeing the way that boy pined after his mother. Olly hid it well but she heard his tears some nights, saw the way he stared out of the window in the hope his mother would drive up to the house. Jake was doing the best he could, and their relationship had improved, but a caring uncle was no substitute for a mother.

"Not yet. But he can call her later."

"He'll like that." She took the porridge off the stove. "And to answer your original question, no, I'm not matchmaking. I just thought it was a nice night for a stroll."

Jake faked a sneeze that sounded surprisingly like "bullshit."

Cilla turned to face him. "Listen, want to know why I sent you two away? Because Olly dotes on Sara. I saw the way he hung on her every word, the way he lit up when she even glanced his way, and I don't want him getting too attached to her."

"What?" Jake's mouth hung open. "Olly's good for Sara and vice versa."

Cilla didn't condone naivety. Not when she'd had her own ripped away as a teen married to a monster. "I already warned you about this right at the start. Sure, Sara looks years younger compared to when she first came here, I'll grant you that. But what do you think will happen to her when Olly leaves and she feels like she's lost another child all over again?"

Jake frowned. "That's a bit dramatic, don't you think? You can't compare her grief at losing a child with missing Olly once he moves away."

"How do you know?" Cilla yelled, startled by her own vehemence. "I've never had a child die but I grieved every single day for years when Tam left. And even you . . ." She trailed off, horrified she'd given away so much. "When your father wouldn't let me see you and Rose anymore, I missed you so much it hurt. You kids had no idea how much you brightened my life when you stayed here. You helped me forget my own miserable life. You gave me purpose."

"I'm so sorry. I didn't know." Jake crossed the kitchen to hug her. "We missed you too."

Cilla allowed Jake to comfort her for a brief time before shrugging out of his embrace. The last thing she needed today was sympathy. She'd been treading a fine line since leaving Bryce, standing on an emotional precipice doing her best not to tumble off. If Jake was any nicer, she'd start blubbering and not stop for a week.

"I don't want to see Olly get hurt," she said, clearing her throat when her voice came out husky. "As far as he knows, his mom abandoned him, he's living with an old aunt he's never met, his uncle is his new guardian and the lady next door seems like an angel." She shook her head. "It's too much for a kid his age to handle."

"Olly's doing okay," Jake said, his expression closed off. "I have to head into town for half an hour and when I get back I'll take him fishing. Do you need anything?"

"No thanks."

Jake nodded and made for the back door, like he couldn't escape fast enough. What was it about men running at the slightest hint of anything to do with deeper emotional needs? Though considering she'd bailed on Bryce, she guessed the escape artist genes favored both sexes.

Shaking her head, she walked to the foot of the stairs, before calling out, "Olly, breakfast is ready."

Usually, he would scamper downstairs at breakneck speed, declaring how starving he was, and have a double helping of her porridge sprinkled with brown sugar and cinnamon.

Today, silence greeted her, so she called out again.

Nothing.

With an increasing sense of foreboding, Cilla climbed the stairs. Knocked on the door of Olly's room. And opened it when there was no response.

The bed had been slept in. But Olly's favorite ripped jeans, red T-shirt and holey sneakers were gone. Nothing unusual with that; he always came down to breakfast dressed. But the silence in the house made her edgy.

After a quick check of the upstairs bathroom and all the bedrooms, she padded downstairs.

"Olly, where are you?" she called out repeatedly, flinging doors open to check every room. He wasn't in the den, the living room or the downstairs bathroom, and in the kitchen, her porridge congealed on the sideboard with no little boy in sight.

Panic made her hands shake as she wrenched open the back door and scanned the garden. No flash of red. She ran outside and scoured her property, front and back. No Olly.

With her pulse pounding so loud in her ears she could hardly think straight, she ran inside and grabbed her keys. Maybe she could drive around, see if she spotted him walking in a nearby field.

Her first instinct, to call Jake, made her grab her cell. But she stopped, her thumb hovering over the call button. He'd freak out. He already carried around enough guilt over that plane crash and she saw it every day, no matter how much he tried to hide it from her. If he thought for one second Olly had run away . . . No, she was probably being overdramatic.

Perhaps Olly had gone for a morning walk without telling them. Or had popped over to Sara's house. However, a quick visit next door showed that Sara wasn't home and a scour of her garden proved Olly wasn't there either.

Fear tightened her chest as Cilla gripped the cell in her hand. There was one other person she could call other than Jake, the only other person in town she trusted aside from her nephew.

Bryce had a level head; he'd know what to do. He could help her search without making a fuss that could potentially scar Jake and Olly for life.

Without hesitation, she called him. He answered on the second ring, thank goodness.

"Cilla, thanks for calling me back—"

"I need your help."

"Anything," he said, without question, and if he were in front of her at that moment she would've kissed him in gratitude.

"I can't find Olly this morning. I've looked everywhere. Jake's in town and I don't want to worry him unnecessarily so I was wondering if you could help me search. It's probably nothing and he's just gone off for a stroll but I'm worried—"

"I'll be there in twenty minutes," he said, and hung up.

Cilla slipped the cell back into her pocket with a shaky hand. Bryce had come to her aid, no questions asked. A man of action. She should be grateful, but one thought pierced her worry.

Was I too hasty in giving him up?

While she waited for Bryce, Cilla retraced her steps, once again searching every inch of her house and its surroundings. She yelled out Olly's name until her throat ached. She checked every hiding place a boy would find tempting.

When Bryce arrived, he'd barely stepped from the car before she flung herself into his arms.

"I can't find him anywhere. Should I call the police?" She sniffled into his chest, finding the familiarity of his aftershave comforting, before she realized what she was doing and disengaged.

"Let's not jump to conclusions," he said, his expression grim despite his eyes seeming to eat her up and come back for seconds. "When did you last see him?"

"About half an hour ago. He was in bed so I popped my head in to say good morning before heading downstairs to make breakfast." She dragged in a deep breath to stop the quiver in her voice. "He seemed perfectly normal. Sleep-tousled but happy."

"So nothing happened? No argument?"

She shook her head. "I heard Jake say good morning to Olly a few minutes after I did and that was it."

"In that case, if you saw him thirty minutes ago, he couldn't have gone far." He glanced at her car. "I'd suggest we split up and drive a five-mile radius, but Olly doesn't know me and if I found him, he'd be more likely to bolt than come back with me."

"You really think he ran away?" Cilla's heart ached at the thought of that sweet little boy feeling so dejected that he had to abandon the only home he knew for now.

"No point speculating. Let's go find him." Bryce walked around his car and held open the passenger door, staring at her with a raised eyebrow when she hesitated.

But not for the reasons he thought. Being in the car alone with Bryce didn't terrify her as much as the thought of not finding Olly or, worse, discovering a tragedy had befallen him.

"I didn't call Jake because I didn't want to worry him unnecessarily. Do you think I should?"

Bryce's frown deepened. "Thirty minutes isn't long enough for little legs to get very far, so let's do a quick drive around and if we don't find him, we'll call Jake, okay?"

Cilla nodded, glad of Bryce's decisiveness. She'd done the right thing in calling him.

She slipped into the passenger side of his luxury vehicle, belted up and prayed. She prayed harder than she'd prayed for years, as they cruised the country lanes surrounding her house, working outward.

"Do you know what he's wearing?" Bryce glanced at her, taking his eyes off the road for a brief second, and the concern she glimpsed exacerbated her fear.

"Jeans and a red T, I think."

At that moment, Cilla spotted a flash of crimson in the vineyard on their left.

"There. I spotted something," she said, almost flinging the door open in her haste.

"Whoa. Hold on." Bryce pulled over and she was out of the car before it had come to a complete stop.

Bryce wasn't far behind. "Don't scare him," he said, laying a hand on her arm, the contact jolting her and making her panic in a different way: the way her body reacted when he touched her made her feel more alive than she had in years. Despite all her self-talk to ignore her attraction to this charming man, all he had to do was touch her and he bamboozled her all over again, her body humming to life in a way it never had before.

She could blame her body's reaction on her freak-out over Olly, on the fact that adrenalin was already flooding her system and maybe Bryce's touch had set it off, but she knew better, dammit.

"Come on, we're wasting time," she said, shrugging off his hand and running into the vineyard.

But she took Bryce's advice, not calling out to Olly. Instead, she pointed at the red flash weaving in and out of the vines. Bryce nodded and accelerated, his long strides meaning she had to jog to keep up with him.

When they got closer, Cilla's knees almost buckled in relief as she spotted a mop of dark curls above the red.

"That's Olly," she said, swallowing a sob that threatened to spill out.

"It'll be okay." Bryce snagged her hand and squeezed it before releasing, the brief contact less surprising this time and more welcome.

They picked up the pace and when they were close enough, Cilla held up her hand so Bryce would stop and she could move forward alone.

He nodded, his eyes filled with concern and understanding and compassion.

He really was a spectacular man.

But Cilla didn't have time to ponder her foolishness in letting him go. Not when she had a young boy who deserved her full attention.

She continued following Olly for a few paces, before her shadow fell across his and he spun around, letting rip a bloodcurdling scream.

"Olly, it's me," she said, crouching down to his level and holding his shoulders in case he decided to bolt. Her legs had turned to jelly in relief and she couldn't possibly have chased him at this point even if she tried. "Are you lost, sweetheart?"

Olly's lips compressed into a thin, mutinous line as he shook his head. Cilla's heart sank. Her earlier suspicions had been confirmed. Olly hadn't taken a morning stroll and lost his way.

He'd run away.

"Come home with me and we'll talk over a mug of hot chocolate." She squeezed his shoulders in reassurance. "With extra marshmallows, for energy." She glanced around. "You've walked a long way from home."

"Your house isn't my home," he blurted, tears filling his eyes. "I don't have a home. Mom doesn't want me anymore, Uncle Jake won't want me soon because I saw him kissing Sara and they'll get married and have their own kids, and you're sad all the time because I'm around."

He started sobbing and Cilla's heart fractured, and shattered into a million pieces.

This poor, poor child.

"None of that's true," she said, slipping her arms around him, relieved when he didn't pull away.

He sniffled into her shoulder. "It *is* true. I saw Uncle Jake and Sara kissing last night from my bedroom window."

For the first time this morning, Cilla felt like smiling.

"Sometimes grownups kiss because they like each other, not because they're going to get married."

He pulled away, indignation scrunching his cute face. "So they can't have kids if they're not married?"

That was a talk she'd save for another day, like in five years or so. For now, Cilla had to show Olly he was loved and that no one was going to abandon him again.

"How about we go get that hot chocolate and I'll answer all your questions, okay?"

Olly glared at her, his hands still clutching her top. "Okay. But Uncle Jake's going to be real mad I ran away."

"Why don't you let me handle Uncle Jake?"

Olly's frown cleared. "That sounds good."

"But Olly, you need to promise me something. You'll never run away again. And that if you're feeling sad or worried, you'll talk to me. Deal?" She eyeballed him, hoping he'd understand the gravity of the situation without being petrified.

After what seemed like an eternity, he nodded. "Deal. Can I get those extra marshmallows now? Because my legs are mighty sore from all the walking. And I'm feeling kinda sick in my tummy because I skipped breakfast."

"Let's go." Cilla took hold of Olly's hand and headed toward Bryce, his relieved expression making her want to tear up all over again. "Olly, this is my friend, Bryce."

"Hi." Olly raised his free hand. "I'm hungry."

"Me too, champ." Bryce fell into step beside them. "Can I join you for breakfast?"

Cilla's eyes narrowed. Sneaky.

When she glanced at Bryce, his guileless grin didn't fool her for a second.

"Sure," Olly said, oblivious to the sudden tension arcing over his head. "Aunt Cilla makes the best food. Totally yummy."

"I look forward to trying it," Bryce said, his deep voice yummier than anything she could concoct in the kitchen.

Ah hell.

"Wow, is that your car?" Olly tore his hand from Cilla's and ran toward it. "It's awesome."

"I like it too," Bryce said, and Cilla gladly tuned out as the two males made car talk all the way home.

Olly had ridden shotgun, giving her time to study Bryce's profile. Like that helped the turmoil churning her gut.

He was an amazing man. Beyond the kindness and the gorgeous exterior, his dependability drew her to him in a way she'd never thought it could.

After the way she'd treated him, he'd still come through for her in a crisis. No questions asked. No judgment.

As she stared at him, his straight nose, his strong jaw, the hint of a dimple as he chatted with Olly, she knew she'd never found him sexier than at that moment.

When they pulled up outside her house ten minutes later, Olly ran inside to wash up for breakfast. The poor kid really must be starving.

It gave her time to thank Bryce.

Before sending him on his way.

Her attraction to him hadn't dimmed one iota and she'd be damned if she turned into a masochist over this man.

Seeing him again, observing the kind of man he was firsthand, only served to make her want him more.

And that wasn't possible.

He opened the back door for her and she stepped out of the car, momentarily blinded by the sun.

"Thanks for helping me—"

Bryce's mouth locked onto hers, cutting off the rest of her sentence. Stealing her breath. Her sanity. For she kissed him back. Without hesitation. Without reservation.

Until she couldn't breathe and wrenched her mouth away, gasping for air.

They stared at each other in wide-eyed shock, their connection was that powerful.

But it couldn't be. Cilla had only let Bryce kiss her out of gratitude. Yeah, that had to be it. She couldn't contemplate any other explanation.

"You need to talk to Olly alone now. I get that," he said, cupping her cheek. "But I'll be at Don's Diner, waiting for that breakfast you're going to shout me."

"You'll be waiting a long time," Cilla said, her defiance tempered with a smile.

Even now, he was still thinking of her, knowing she wouldn't see him at his place, choosing a public place to put her at ease.

"Haven't I already told you? You're worth waiting for."

This time, his kiss was soft, gentle and all too brief.

She watched his car until she couldn't spot it any longer, her head a mess, her heart not far behind.

Bryce confounded her in a way she'd never expected. She'd spent the last twenty years as a happy widow enjoying her independence. She didn't need anyone for validation and she certainly didn't need some hot male barging into her life and turning it upside down.

But that's exactly what Bryce had done and, despite her shabby treatment, he'd been there in a heartbeat when she'd needed him most. That kind of dependability wasn't lost on her. She admired it. Respected it. So she'd shout him breakfast, be polite and end things between them on a more civilized note. It's the least she could do after the way she'd overreacted at his place.

Mind made up, Cilla trudged inside, steeling herself for the upcoming conversation with Olly. She'd been lousy with this stuff in the past. Tam had always clammed up when she'd tried to get her to talk and Cilla would be left floundering, trying to fill awkward gaps in conversation with meaningless trivia.

Their relationship now was testament to her failure as a mother, so if she'd made a mess of things with Tam, what could she do with a boy like Olly who had serious abandonment issues?

She had to talk to him before Jake did, though. Had to get more of an insight into Olly's thought processes before she told Jake everything. He was due back from town any second and she needed all the facts first.

Olly sat at the kitchen table, the picture of innocence. He held up his hands. "All washed and ready for breakfast. And that hot chocolate you promised."

"You can eat in a second," she said, sitting next to him. "But first we need to talk about why you ran away."

Olly sighed so loudly she had to stifle a smile. "I already told you. Nobody wants me."

"That's not true, sweetheart. We all love you and want you."

"Mom doesn't. I heard Uncle Jake talking to her last night. He said it'd be good for me to stay here, which means she doesn't want me anymore."

Oh boy.

"Olly, sometimes we only hear snippets of a conversation. Little bits that don't make much sense unless we hear everything. Maybe your uncle was suggesting your mom come here too when she's better, because you like it here so much?"

Olly's eyes widened. "I didn't think of that."

"As for listening in on other people's conversations, it's not very polite."

His face fell. "Yeah, I know. But I'd left Teddy downstairs and needed him to sleep."

"Fair enough."

So far so good. "As for me being sad, that has nothing to do with you being here. I love having you stay."

Olly brightened. "Yeah, that's right. You said I was family, not a guest."

Cilla nodded. "Exactly. Grownups can be sad for a variety of reasons but you could never make me sad. Unless you run away again," she threw in for good measure.

His solemnity made her heart swell. "Okay, I won't do it again. But do you think Uncle Jake and Sara like each other? Maybe they will get married and have kids and then they won't want to see me anymore—"

"Olly, your uncle loves you very much. And Sara adores you. Whether they have a relationship or not won't change that. Your uncle brought you here so you could have fun while your mom gets better. And even when you go home, he'll still be around. He'll always be around. As I will be."

Olly clapped his hands. "You mean it? You'll come to visit me when I'm back in the city?"

Cilla abhorred big cities and avoided New York City at all costs. The hustle and bustle scared her, one of the reasons she hadn't visited Tam. But Olly needed reassurance at a time like this, so she nodded.

"We'll always stay in touch." She leaned across to hug him. "We all love you, Olly. Don't ever forget that."

He hugged her back and as they eased apart, his stomach gave an almighty rumble.

Cilla laughed. "One hot chocolate and a bowl of porridge coming right up."

Jake entered the kitchen at that moment, arms laden with produce bags. "Thought I could teach Olly how to whip up a Mexican feast tonight."

Since they'd arrived, Olly had taken an interest in cooking. He was always hanging around the kitchen, measuring sugar or flour if she was baking, or wanting to stir the pot. The fact Jake wanted to do this with Olly was the best reassurance he could've given his nephew, even if he didn't know it yet.

"That would be awesome." Olly leapt from his chair and rushed over to help Jake unpack. "I'm so glad I didn't run away for long."

Jake stilled, his gaze flying to Cilla's. She gave a small shake of her head and thankfully, Jake didn't push. Instead, he worked alongside Olly, unpacking the groceries while she reheated the porridge, dished it up and made hot chocolate.

When Cilla glanced at her watch for the fifth time, Jake's eyebrow rose.

"Do you have somewhere to be?"

"I'm going out for breakfast," she said, glad that Olly was engrossed in eating and couldn't pipe up with his version of what he thought might be going on with her and Bryce.

"I'll walk you out then," Jake said, obviously keen to hear her version of Olly's running away caper.

Jake waited until they were outside at her car, sufficiently far from the house. "What the hell's going on? Olly ran away?"

Cilla nodded. "This morning. He didn't come down for breakfast and when I looked for him, he wasn't anywhere."

"Damn." Jake rubbed the back of his neck. "Why didn't you call me?"

"I didn't want you to worry 'til I figured out whether he'd gone for a walk and got lost, or had actually run away."

"What happened?"

"I called Bryce. He helped me look. It had only been thirty minutes since I'd seen Olly so we figured he hadn't gone far."

Jake slumped, a picture of dejection. "Do you know why he did it?"

"Because he thought no one wants him. Apparently he saw you and Sara kissing last night and thought you'd get married, have kids and wouldn't want him around."

Jake startled. "What?"

"In his mind, his mom's abandoned him. He's living with an old lady he didn't know before he got here." She patted his arm. "You're the only constant in his life since Rose went into rehab, so when he thought you were getting close to Sara and could potentially leave him too . . ." She shook her head. "He's a darling boy but kids tend to build elaborate scenarios in their heads that make them do crazy things."

"Should I talk to him about it?"

Cilla nodded. "Couldn't hurt. I reinforced how much we all love him and made him promise not to do it again."

"Thanks." Jake hugged her. "For everything. I couldn't have done any of this without you."

"You'd be surprised what we can do when we have to," she said. "I shouldn't be long. Having breakfast at the diner."

"Alone?" Jake smirked and damned if heat didn't flush her cheeks.

"None of your business," she said, giving him a shove in the direction of the house. "Go give that boy some TLC."

"While someone else gives you some, hopefully," Jake murmured, but loud enough she could hear.

Ignoring him, she got in the car and drove away.

She didn't need TLC. She needed a reality check. Or to give Bryce one, more like it.

She could do this. One quick breakfast and she was done.

Easy.

❦

Half an hour later, Cilla realized nothing about sitting across a table from Bryce was easy.

Despite the usual morning bustle at Don's Diner, they kept up a steady flow of conversation, only stopping to devour pancakes with maple syrup, bacon and eggs over easy.

Bryce pretended that her meltdown at his place hadn't happened and she was happy to play alongside him in Denial Land. It was a place she knew well. She'd lived there her entire marriage.

Bryce waited until a waitress had refilled his coffee cup before fixing her with a stare that smacked of interrogation. "Are we going to talk about what happened the other night?"

The eggs in Cilla's stomach curdled. So much for denial.

"Not much to say, really." She sipped at her water. It did little to ease the tightness in her throat.

"This thing between us isn't going to go away." He clasped his hands together and rested them on the table. "I won't give up on us no matter how hard you push me away."

Annoyed by the flicker of hope his sincerity sparked, she slammed the glass down harder than intended and water splashed everywhere. "This isn't the time or place to discuss it."

"Then name a time and place and I'll be there." He leaned forward. "We're adults. We need to deal with this."

"Don't patronize me," she said, wishing she'd never come. "I know we're adults. But what I meant was, there's no point discussing anything. You and me? Not going to happen."

To her surprise he stood, fished notes out of his wallet and flung them onto the table. "You've got avoidance honed to a fine art.

So when you're ready to face facts and not hide behind your past or whatever excuses you want to dredge up, you know where to find me."

"Nothing to face," she said to his retreating back, churlish and childish.

He ignored her and kept walking.

28.

ara hadn't been this jittery since Delivery Boy had asked her out on a date all those years ago.

She'd frittered the day away, alternating between cooking and cleaning the house, determinedly staying indoors to avoid any chance of a run-in with Jake.

Ridiculous, considering she wasn't a teen anymore and a kiss didn't mean anything beyond giving in to a spur-of-the-moment attraction. Because that's what they'd done. Given in to the temptation of a moonlit night, a balmy breeze and an extended dry spell. They'd both admitted as much.

It meant nothing. An impulse. A spur of the moment thing that shouldn't be given more than cursory attention. But all the dismissive rationalizing in the world couldn't detract from how amazing that kiss had been. In fact, *amazing* didn't come close. *Stupendous* didn't do it justice either.

"Damn it," she muttered, dousing the bath with bleach and scrubbing harder.

She didn't want to mull over how astounding that kiss had been. Waste of time, considering she didn't want to take it further. Because the more she replayed that kiss in her head, the harder it was to ignore how he'd made her feel for a brief moment: like she could envisage a future beyond guilt and sadness and retribution.

Scrubbing until her arms ached and the fumes made her head too fuzzy to think, she followed up her bathroom cleaning frenzy with a total kitchen cleanout. Mindless, repetitive, mundane activities designed to keep her busy and *not* thinking about that kiss.

By suppertime, she'd added watching reality TV and reading the same paragraph repeatedly to her distraction methods. When the phone rang, she'd dozed off, so it took her a few seconds to snatch it up and utter a breathless, "Hello?"

"Hey, it's me."

Damn. If she'd been awake and seen Jake's caller ID, she wouldn't have answered. So much for spending the day trying to forget that kiss. The moment he'd uttered those three words in his deep, rumbly voice, her body remembered every moment of his lips on hers, his hands all over her.

She managed a sedate, "Hey," which was better than hanging up, her first instinct.

"Sorry I didn't get around to seeing you today like I'd hoped."

"That's okay."

Better than okay. If his voice did these things to her insides, seeing him in person after that kiss would've sent her into meltdown.

When he didn't speak, she added, "Everything all right?"

"Not really." His heartfelt sigh echoed down the line and she found herself caring despite her self-talk to keep things platonic after last night.

"You sound overwhelmed."

"Olly ran away this morning."

"Oh my God. Is he okay?" Stupid question, because if he wasn't Jake wouldn't have waited until now to call her.

"Yeah, he was only gone for half an hour. Cilla realized and found him."

Sara had taken her eyes off Lucy for a few moments at a department store one time and she'd vanished. Those three minutes it had taken to find her at the nearby haberdashery counter had been the longest of her life. She knew the blind panic, the sick stomach, the icy numbness that invaded every cell.

"I'm sorry you had to go through that," she said.

"I had no idea 'til I got home. Cilla was a real trouper."

Jake sounded like he'd aged three decades and her heart went out to him.

"Olly seems really happy. Why did he do it?"

There was a long pause. "Apparently he saw us kissing last night, thought we'd get married, have our own kids, and not want him around anymore."

Stunned, Sara clutched the phone to her ear. "Hell."

Jake's dry chuckle held little amusement. "That was only part of it but basically Olly's got abandonment issues and we had to reassure him."

"Sure," she said, a familiar dread curdling her stomach. The dread of a parent worrying over a child. She'd done it with Lucy and had ultimately lost her.

No way could she start worrying about Olly. The fact that she was indicated she'd grown too attached already.

"I'm really glad he's okay. If there's anything I can do, let me know."

"Thanks. I was hoping we could go on a picnic tomorrow—"

"Sorry, I'm busy." It sounded harsh even to her ears so she softened her refusal with a legitimate excuse. "I'm under pressure prepping for the fair, so I'll be swamped for the next week or so."

"Okay." Jake sounded wounded and she gritted her teeth to stop from blurting how sorry she was for giving him the wrong idea with that kiss last night. "Talk to you soon."

"Yeah." Sara hung up and pressed her fingers to her eyes to stop the sting of tears.

This is what happened when she opened her heart again.

She'd been doing okay the last fifteen months. Coming to terms with her grief. Moving on.

Detachment was good. She'd made progress. But in letting Jake, Olly and Cilla into her life, she'd reopened old wounds.

Her actions had caused Olly to run away.

No way in hell would she be responsible for hurting another child again.

Ever.

With a heavy heart, Sara dragged herself upstairs to bed. Not that it would make much difference. She wouldn't be sleeping tonight.

29.

J ake gave Sara space for a few days.

He knew why she'd given him the brush-off.

Guilt.

The moment he'd told her the truth about why Olly had run away, he'd wished he'd lied. It had been a dumbass move. It wasn't until he'd hung up that he realized she'd probably blame herself for Olly seeing their kiss and running away. Hell, he'd done it himself.

But he'd been so morose all day, consumed by his own guilt, that he'd needed someone to talk to and she was the only woman he trusted next to Cilla. His aunt had returned from breakfast looking like thunder and he'd figured she'd done enough in finding Olly in the first place, so he hadn't wanted to burden her.

Rose hadn't been an option. She had enough going on without him adding his incompetence at caring for her son to the list. She would've freaked if she knew Olly had run away.

Sara had seemed like the perfect candidate to talk him down. Instead, he'd only served to bring her down too.

He'd wanted to see her the morning after their kiss. Had planned on taking Olly with him so it wouldn't be too awkward. But he'd arrived home to the news that Olly had run away and he'd spent the day showering attention on him to reassure him that his words weren't empty promises and that he would always be there for him.

Olly had seemed fine, with no lingering effects from his ordeal, and it wasn't until he'd tucked him into bed that Jake called Sara.

It had been four days now. Four days in which she'd probably been beating herself up. He'd respected her wishes in keeping his distance. But he missed her and wanted to know she was okay.

A phone call wouldn't cut it. She could give him the old heave-ho again too easily.

So he packed a container of leftover apple crumble from dinner, checked in on Olly to find him sound asleep, and told Cilla where he'd be.

She didn't say anything, but a quirk of her eyebrow spoke volumes. She hadn't mentioned the kiss but the fact he was heading over to Sara's at eight p.m. could be misconstrued.

"Won't be long," he said, feeling like a naughty schoolboy sneaking out to neck with his girlfriend.

"Okay." Cilla returned to her book, lips set in a grim line, like she wanted to say something but was trying hard not to.

He didn't stick around to hear what that was.

Walking to Sara's gave him time to mentally rehearse what he'd say. But all that went to crap when she opened the door. She wore cow-print pajama bottoms and a fitted black camisole, and had her hair in pigtails.

She was adorable.

But her frown didn't scream *welcome* so he turned on the charm.

"I brought you my world-famous apple crumble." He held out the container with a proud grin. "You haven't lived 'til you've tasted it."

"*You* made it?"

She made it sound like he had more chance of manning the next space shuttle than cooking an edible dessert.

"Of course. Would I claim I had if I didn't?"

The corners of her mouth twitched. An improvement on the disapproving frown. "Maybe not. Thanks for this. I'll have it later."

"Not so fast." He snatched the container out of her reach and held it aloft. "I haven't had my share yet and I've packed enough for two."

She gestured at her outfit. "I'm not exactly dressed for visitors."

"I'm a friend, not a visitor, and you could wear a hessian bag and still look gorgeous. So let's devour this delicious crumble and then you can kick me out." He semi-pushed his way in and with a resigned sigh she stepped aside.

"You're very pushy," she said, closing the door more loudly than necessary.

"So I've been told." He headed for the kitchen, pleased he'd got this far. Once she had a taste of his crumble, she'd be putty in his hands. He hoped.

"How's Olly?" she asked, setting out bowls and spoons on the table.

"Good. Our relationship has actually improved since his runaway stunt." He served the crumble into two bowls. "Made me realize exactly how vulnerable kids can be despite putting on a brave face."

"You know it was our fault," she said, sitting at the table and tucking one leg underneath her, looking like a forlorn waif.

"I thought that too, initially. Was beating myself up over it, before I had a chat to Olly and realized it was a whole bunch of stuff he's been bottling up. Mostly over missing his mom." He handed her a bowl and spoon. "So stop feeling guilty and pushing me away because of it."

"I'm not," she said, her gaze shifting away, her lie hollow.

"I'm not going to hurt you," he said, placing his hand over hers where it rested on the table. "You know that, right?"

"It's not you I'm afraid of." She snatched her hand out from under his and picked up a spoon. "I'm not good with getting too close to people these days."

"I think you've been doing just fine." He pointed at her bowl. "Now get some of that crumble into you and prepare to fall at my feet in gratitude."

"Better add monstrous ego to your dubious charms," she said, but at least he'd got a smile out of her.

"You mock, but wait 'til you taste it."

He watched her spoon a generous helping into her mouth, then wished he hadn't as her lips curved, reminding him of how soft they'd felt under his. Her rapturous expression wasn't helping either.

"Wow, you truly are a master," she said, mumbling between mouthfuls she couldn't shovel in fast enough. "This is divine."

"Told you so." He finished his serving quickly, not tasting much of it as he was fixated on Sara's mouth. "Seconds?"

She glanced at the empty container. "But there's nothing left."

"Who said I'm talking about crumble?"

She laughed and pointed at the door. "Get out."

"But you look so adorable in those cow PJs—"

"Out. Now." She playfully whacked him on the arm and he smiled, glad they were back on friendly footing.

"I've missed you, you know." He tried to reach for her but she slipped away, sliding her chair out of reach.

"I haven't missed you and I haven't lost sleep over it."

The faint dark circles under her eyes were testament to that lie.

"We should go out on a date."

"Maybe," she said, sounding less than enthused, her brows knitted in a frown. "Let me get this fair out of the way, then I'll think about it."

"My ego is smarting from that resounding endorsement." Meanwhile, silently, Jake pinned his hopes on the fact she hadn't refused outright.

Her tentative smile made something squirm in his chest. "Why don't you take your bruised ego home and let me do some more work before bed."

"Okay." When they stood, he swooped in for a kiss, catching her off guard.

He captured her mouth for a few delicious, illicit seconds before she pulled away.

"Go." She pointed at the door, her stare amused rather than disapproving.

"Yes, Ma'am." With a wink, he backed away, keeping his gaze locked on hers until he reached the door.

He had a date with Sara to look forward to after the fair.

Life was good.

30.

As Sara's final art class wound to a close and every child except Olly filed out, she came to a startling realization.

She was going to miss this.

Being watched by rapturous faces, being asked inane yet curious questions, being surrounded by youthful exuberance, had made her confront the darkness that had consumed her for far too long.

She'd never forget Lucy. She'd grieve for her darling little girl every day of her life. But the motley summer art class at Redemption Elementary had made her *feel* again and it wasn't as painful as she'd feared.

"Sara." Olly tugged at the hem of her smock. "You're the best teacher ever."

"Thanks, Olly." She tweaked the end of his nose. "And you're a talented artist."

"Really?" He fairly glowed with her praise as he cast a critical eye at the crayon sketch he'd completed. "But I just draw stuff. I don't burn wood like you do."

"There are many different types of art," she said, pointing to a stack of books on Andy Symes's desk. "Writers are artists. They paint pictures with words."

"I guess so." He looked skeptical. "Drawing stuff is more fun though."

"I think so too. Want to help me pack up?"

"Yeah, though doing art is more fun than packing up."

She laughed. "There's not much to do."

They worked alongside each other, putting away supplies and wiping down tables. Sara couldn't help but surreptitiously watch Olly, taking delight in his earnestness as he completed every task she set him.

He was one cute kid and she'd miss him when he left. Jake hadn't mentioned how Olly's mom was doing but she hoped for Olly's sake they'd be reunited soon. Children needed their moms.

"You're looking at me funny." Olly frowned. "Did I do something wrong?"

Busted.

Sara banished the image of Lucy that still popped into her head whenever she was around a sweet kid like Olly and forced a smile. "I'm looking at you funny because you've done an amazing job helping me clean up."

"Cool." He sat on the edge of a desk, legs swinging. "Are you coming to the fair with us?"

Sara had no intention of embarking on a family-like excursion with Jake and Olly, despite Jake's reassurances that Olly was okay after his runaway episode. She couldn't handle being responsible if Olly did something again because of her.

"I'll be at the fair, so I'll see you there."

Olly shrugged. "Okay. But if you don't come with us, Uncle Jake won't buy you popcorn and candy floss and corndogs like he promised me."

She smiled. "If I eat all that stuff, I might get a sore tummy."

His face crinkled in consternation. "I don't want to get a sore tummy."

"You'll be fine. Just don't eat too much." Wow, she was seriously out of practice at talking one-on-one with kids. She'd tried to lecture

Olly on the dangers of too much junk food rather than conveying a gentle warning. A real damper on his excitement.

"Don't eat too much what?" Jake sauntered into the class-room, immediately dwarfing it with his presence, and Sara couldn't help the way her heart fluttered when he looked at her with that irresistible mix of cheek and charm.

"Sara isn't coming with us to the fair, Uncle Jake, because she'll get a sore tummy if we give her too many treats." Olly rubbed his stomach. "But I'm fine so maybe I can eat her share?"

Jake laughed. "The secret to having a good day at the fair is to pace yourself, buddy. Not eating too much at once."

"I guess." Olly slid off the desk. "Is it okay if I go play with some of the other kids outside for a while?"

Jake hesitated and Sara knew why. After last week's stunt, he didn't want to let Olly out of his sight.

"I can see the kids in the playground from here," Sara said, pointing at the window and trying to allay Jake's concern about keeping an unobtrusive eye on him.

"Sure. Have fun," Jake said, shooting her a grateful glance.

Not until Olly had run out the door did Sara realize that maybe she shouldn't have been so quick to foster Olly's desire for play outside.

Because it left her alone with Jake inside.

"You've been avoiding me," he said, stalking toward her. Too big. Too gorgeous. Too everything.

"Told you I'd be busy with prepping for the fair." She took a step backward and her butt hit the edge of the desk.

With Jake invading her personal space, she had nowhere to go. Not a total downer, when she felt the heat radiating off him, when she inhaled his unique masculine scent.

"What's going to be your excuse when the fair's all done tomorrow?"

"I'll think of something," she said, unable to resist poking him in the chest when he mock staggered a little.

"You can't keep pushing me away forever." His smile faded as he snagged her hand. "I want to get to know you better."

"Why?" She wished her heart would stop pounding so darn loud so she could hear him better. Then again, did she really want to?

She didn't need Jake articulating reasons why they should go on a date. All the convincing arguments in the world wouldn't get her to change her mind. Getting attached to Jake—and Olly—could only end badly.

He stared at her for an eternity, his eyes trying to convey a message she had no hope of interpreting. He looked . . . haunted. A feeling she could empathize with.

"Because for the first time since the accident I feel like letting someone in," he blurted, before clamping his lips shut and taking a few steps back, his expression tortured.

"The accident?" Sara had to ask, despite his hunched shoulders and closed-off posture screaming that he'd said something he regretted.

A memory tugged at the edge of her consciousness. The day they'd been scouting fair locations, he'd looked sad and when she'd questioned him he'd joked about revealing their pasts one day over tequila.

Looked like she wasn't the only one whose past hid a wealth of pain.

"You don't have to talk about it if you don't want."

"I killed eighty-nine people," he said, his expression bleak. "I was an aircraft mechanic. Tired on the job one day. Had a gut feeling something wasn't right but ignored it. Went by the book as usual. Did routine final checks. Cleared a plane to fly. And it crashed."

His tone sounded so desolate, so bleak, she wanted to hug him. She remembered a commercial liner going down about eight months ago, but had switched off the news like she did most days. She had enough heartache in her life without adding to it.

"Aviation investigation cleared me but the guilt sits here," he thumped his chest, "and I live with it every frigging day."

Sara wanted to say "It's not your fault," wanted to take away his pain. But she'd never been one for trite platitudes, not after the many she'd endured following Lucy's death, so she settled for wrapping her arms around his waist and squeezing tight.

She'd done it instinctively, to comfort him, knowing all the hugs in the world wouldn't eradicate guilt but hoping it would help.

His arms came around her and they remained that way until Andy barged through the door and cleared his throat.

"Sorry to interrupt, folks, but most of the kids outside are being picked up by their parents and Olly's waiting."

Sara eased out of Jake's arms. "Thanks, Andy. We'll be there in a sec."

"Right." Andy fled, obviously aware of the tension in the room.

Sara touched Jake's cheek. "Thanks for opening up to me. We'll talk later?"

"Yeah." Jake scrubbed a hand over his face. "I promise not to be such a killjoy next time."

"Hey, don't do that." She took a deep breath, knowing she'd have to reveal a small hidden part of her to make him feel better. "I get it. I locked myself away physically and emotionally from everyone for over a year. Then I came here, and you and Olly and Cilla have given me hope." She blew out a breath. "Hope that I won't fall apart if I get close to anyone again and they walk away."

Understanding lit his eyes. "That's why you won't let me and Olly get too close, isn't it? Because we'll be leaving at some point?"

There was so much more to it, but for now, she nodded. "Self-preservation has been the only way I could handle the grief."

"I won't hurt you." He cupped her face, eyeballing her.

"Not intentionally, but I don't think I'm up for something fleeting." She eased out of his hands. "I'm not built that way."

He glanced out the window, a worry line bisecting his brows. "I've really got to go get Olly, so can I pop around tonight to carry on this discussion?"

Part of Sara wanted to hear what Jake had to say, wanted to see behind the tough-guy mask that hid inner depths she suspected lurked beneath the bravado. But that would contradict what she'd just said, and she had no intention of sending mixed messages to complicate an already fraught situation.

Her reluctance must've shown, because he rushed on.

"We can have a good friendship without the other stuff complicating it, if that's what you want," he said. "A friendship that can last beyond the time I'm in Redemption."

His sincerity settled it. Jake was right. She felt closer to him than any of the so-called friends she'd known for years, friends who rarely contacted her these days because they didn't know what to say or alternated between pussyfooting and false perkiness.

She could use a friend like him in her life.

"Okay. I'll see you tonight at my place."

"Great." He pecked her cheek and headed for the door, taking a tiny piece of her heart with him.

It had been tough keeping Jake at bay when he'd been a sweet charmer. Now that he had flaws and vulnerabilities and wasn't afraid to admit them?

It would be darn near impossible.

31.

Not cool, man, not cool." Jake glared at himself in the mirror, wishing he could erase today.

Starting in the morning, when he'd ventured near an airfield for the first time since the accident, and ending with blurting the truth to Sara at the school.

God, what a mess.

He'd never intended to tell her about the accident. He'd been dealing with it. Hell, ever since he'd arrived in Redemption he'd been too busy caring for Olly to obsess all day. It had only been at nights, when he lay in bed staring at the ceiling for hours, that he replayed the aftermath of the accident in his head.

Like a horror film stuck on repeat, he would see the smoke plume, the wreckage, the personal items strewn across the ground.

The toys had killed him the most. There'd been seven kids on board that flight. Seven kids who'd never get a chance to grow up because of him.

He turned away from the mirror in disgust. The only reason he'd told Sara the truth was because he'd wanted her to know he wasn't jerking her around. Wasn't some player who wanted to date her a few times with sex being the end game.

It wasn't like that with them. Hadn't been from the start, if he was completely honest. And while not being able to kiss her or touch her would frustrate the hell out of him, he'd meant what he'd said: if friendship was all that was on offer, he'd take it. He could do with a good friend.

He had drinking buddies back in the city. Guys he could call up to go to a ball game or hang out at a bar. But he'd been such a recluse since the accident that those guys had stopped calling about eight weeks into his funk.

He knew what drew him to Sara. On some innate level, he connected with her sadness. Because he felt it too. Every single frigging day.

That's why he'd visited the airstrip today. To confront his demons. To see if the nightmares would dim if he faced his fears head on. He'd heard in town that the couple who owned the local airfield were retiring, were selling up. It reminded him of his one-time dream, to own a hangar, servicing smaller planes and private jets rather than commercial liners.

Not that he wanted anything to do with planes anymore, but remembering his dream had driven him to check the airfield out. He'd wanted to prove to himself that he'd come a long way since he'd been in Redemption.

Sadly, he'd parked at the end of a runway on the outer perimeter of a fence, taken one whiff of diesel fumes, and dived back into his car.

Maybe he hadn't come as far as he'd thought.

Hopefully, tonight would help him forget his crappy day and solidify his relationship with Sara.

After saying goodnight to Olly and Cilla, he checked that he had everything packed in the trunk and headed over to Sara's. She thought they were staying in tonight. He had other ideas.

He knocked on her door, hoping he wasn't overstepping. What he had planned for tonight could be construed as a date. Which was what he wanted, to set Sara's reservations at ease, but she'd made it pretty clear she wasn't interested in short term. Maybe a moonlit picnic could be as simple as two friends eating supper?

Yeah, and maybe he'd be getting his pilot's license soon.

When she opened the door, Jake released the breath he hadn't been aware he'd been holding. She looked at him the same way despite knowing the truth about his demons, a beguiling mix of sincerity and sweetness, and it made him relax.

"Come on in," she said, holding the door open.

"Change of plans. We're going out."

She wrinkled her nose and glanced down at her sweatpants and hoodie. "But I'm not dressed for it."

"You're dressed fine for where we're headed." He held out his hand. "Ready to go?"

After the briefest hesitation, she snagged her keys off the hall table, took his hand and closed the door. "Should I be worried? You're not taking me night bungee jumping or anything ridiculous like that?"

Jake snapped his fingers. "Damn, you've gone and spoiled the surprise."

"Idiot." She laughed and bumped him with her hip. "Where are we going?"

"Not far." He opened the passenger door for her, wishing he didn't have to release her hand.

He liked the contact with her, no matter how brief. Friends held hands, right?

"Olly hasn't stopped raving about your art class all evening," he said, wanting to confront any potential awkwardness right off the bat. "You've inspired him."

"He's such a great kid."

He liked how her tone softened when she spoke of Olly.

"Best thing I ever did, bringing him here to Redemption while Rose recovers."

"You're a great uncle."

He shot her a sideways glance, found her staring at him with warmth and something more. Something he wanted to interpret as a deeper caring but didn't dare.

He returned his attention to the road and they made small talk, mostly about the fair. It only took five minutes to reach their destination, the oldest vineyard in the area, which had a picnic spot on the highest peak of the property. Locals in Redemption had used it for years and while it was technically private property, the Lanagans didn't mind people using it.

When he pulled the car over and switched off the engine, she said, "What is this place?"

"Lovers Lane," he deadpanned, laughing when she whacked his arm. "Come on, I've packed a picnic. Thought it'd be a nice place to relax."

She helped him lay the blanket on the ground and unpack the basket. He'd kept it simple: baguettes, cheese, strawberries, cider.

When they'd finished setting it out, she sat next to him, which he took as another good sign. At least she wasn't chastising him for picking the most romantic spot in Redemption. Not yet, anyway.

"This place is gorgeous," she said, tucking her knees up, hugging her legs and resting her chin on her knees. She looked pensive as she stared at the vines and he wished he could capture her whimsical expression in the moonlight forever.

"Haven't been here since I was a kid." He opened the cider and poured them each a glass.

"You started young, huh?"

He liked her teasing and he placed a hand over his heart. "I can solemnly swear that you're the first girl I've ever brought up here."

"Lucky me." Her eyes twinkled with amusement as he handed her a glass. "Though you know all this romance is wasted on a friend?"

"Is it?" He stared into her eyes, reading every shift in emotion: wariness, fear, excitement, hope. He could identify with all.

"Smooth talker." She clinked her glass to his and sipped at her cider, giving him the opportunity to broach the awkward topic of the day.

"You know what I told you earlier at school?"

Her hand stilled and she lowered the glass. "Yeah?"

"I just wanted to say you got me at a vulnerable moment so that's why I blabbed all that heavy stuff." He swirled the cider, staring into the amber depths. "I headed out to the airfield this morning. First time I've been near one since the accident."

Sympathy radiated off her. "That must've been tough."

"Tougher than I expected." He'd known facing his fear would be hard but he hadn't expected to feel so goddamn overwhelmed. He'd been filled with self-loathing, and had only averted being violently ill by driving away at high speed. Even now, twelve hours later, he couldn't shake the shame and the despair. "Couldn't even enter the place."

"Scars run deep." She placed a hand on his thigh, unaware that her simple stroking action, designed to comfort, was eliciting a reaction of a different kind. "Guess we've both learned that the hard way."

He tried to ignore the rhythmic stroking, not wanting to ruin the bonding moment. "That's another reason why I told you. Because I feel like we have a connection beyond the attraction stuff."

"You're attracted to me?" Her wry grin made him chuckle.

"Yeah. Go figure, huh?"

She patted his leg and removed her hand, making him wish he'd had the sense to anchor it there when he had the chance.

"Why did you do it? Go to the airfield?"

"To confront my demons." He screwed up his face. "And look how that turned out."

"It'll take time," she said, her voice soft and filled with under-standing. "A few months ago, I never could've envisaged myself in a classroom with kids."

"Has it helped?"

She nodded. "More than I could've imagined. Don't get me wrong, I still cry myself to sleep some nights, but it's getting easier to function most days rather than wallowing in self-blame."

Self-blame? Why would Sara blame herself for Lucy's death?

If Jake had any chance of getting closer to Sara, of getting her to trust him the way he trusted her, he had to know what had happened with her little girl. Had to know all of it.

"If you don't mind me asking, what happened with Lucy?"

Sara tipped the rest of her cider onto the ground, placed the glass back in the basket and took her time answering. He didn't push. She'd tell him if she wanted to.

"I loved my Lucy-Lou like nothing else. She was my world. I stayed in my marriage for her, long after I should have." She toyed with her hair, winding the ends around her fingertip. "But I loved my job too. Loved being a financial analyst. Found it challenging and rewarding. Worked hard to get promoted in the company."

Her finger twisted faster. "It was tough, working all day and looking after Lucy at night. And I often had to bring work home on the weekends, but I never let it interfere with our time together."

Her hand stilled, her eyes glazed in memories. "We did everything together. Walks in Central Park. Visits to bookshops. Play dates. I loved every second. But then I got a great opportunity, to present at a conference in Atlantic City."

Her voice hitched and he slid an arm around her shoulders in silent comfort. "Lucy had had a bad cold for over a week. She'd been to the doctor's, taken a course of antibiotics. Greg insisted she'd be fine, that he had it covered and if there was any change he'd call."

233

Her lips pursed like she'd sucked on a lemon. "I have to admit, the conference was amazing. Being surrounded by fellow analysts from all around the country, giving a kickass presentation, made me feel validated in a way motherhood couldn't."

She dragged in several breaths before continuing. "Final night of the conference, I was out partying so forgot to charge my cell. Was on my way back to New York City when the call came through that Lucy was in the hospital with breathing difficulties and a high fever. By the time I got home . . . A virulent strain of viral pneumonia, the docs said."

Silent tears trickled down her cheeks, making Jake's heart ache for her pain. "I didn't make it to the hospital in time. I didn't have a chance to comfort my baby or hold her or do something . . ."

Her audible anguish made him hold her tighter. "And I've blamed myself every single day since for not being there when Lucy needed me most. Maybe if I'd been there she wouldn't have—"

"Don't do that to yourself," he said, wishing he could do something, anything, to ease her pain. "There's nothing you could've done."

"Is that what you tell yourself every day to get over the accident?"

It was a low blow and he was sure she hadn't intended on it sounding so abrupt. But she had a point.

"Guilt eats away if you let it. Guess we both know that."

She nodded and rested her head on his shoulder. She fit perfectly into the crook of his arm and as they sat in silence, looking out over the moonlit vineyard, he wondered how on earth this felt so right when he'd only know this woman a short time.

"I've never told anyone all that," she said, so softly he barely heard.

"Ditto for me." He stroked her arm as she snuggled closer. "I think you're incredible, Sara, and I value the bond we share."

She looked up at him, her face inches away, her lips temptingly close.

234

"I feel the same way—"

He didn't let her finish, crushing his mouth to hers. She tasted sweet and tart, a tantalizing combination he couldn't get enough of as he devoured her.

She moaned as he eased her down on the blanket, the fervency of her kisses increasing as he smoothed her back, her hip, her ass.

Turned on to the point of pain, he rolled on top of her, savoring her gasp of awareness as he ground against her a little. When one of her legs wrapped around him, bringing her in tempting contact despite the clothing barriers, he had to remind himself where they were before he committed an indecent act in public.

Rolling back onto his side, he stopped kissing her with reluctance.

"Guess that answers the question of us being just friends," she said, running a fingertip down his cheek, lingering near his mouth, tracing his bottom lip, as he resisted the urge to suck it into his mouth.

"Guess so." He swooped in for another kiss, buoyed by her soft laughter as she gently shoved him away.

"But we take it slow, okay?" She eyeballed him and he glimpsed the remnants of fear.

"So that counts out a roll in the vineyard right now?"

Rather than push him away again, she fisted her hands in his T-shirt and shook him a little. "Don't tempt me."

"Tease," he said, kissing the corner of her mouth, wishing he could kiss her all over, all night.

In response, she jumped to her feet and dusted herself off. "Don't forget, it's been a long time for me."

"Me too." He kept a straight face with difficulty. "Does that mean if this ground is too hard, you'd be up for a little back seat action?"

"You're pushing your luck." Her laughter made his heart lighten. "Don't make me regret this."

He stood and snagged her hand. "I think we've both lived with regrets long enough."

If his sudden deviation into seriousness surprised her, she didn't show it.

"That's why I'm doing this. So I don't regret not taking a chance on us and having yet another thing to lament when you leave." She squeezed his hand. "I think it's worth the risk. *You're* worth the risk."

Crap, she had mammoth expectations of him. He hoped he'd never let her down.

"Right back at you," he said, defusing the tension with levity, but unable to shake the niggle of misgiving all the way home.

Was he in over his head with Sara?

32.

Sara was thankful the fair kept her busy the next morning. Four solid hours of manning the art stall, chatting with locals, accepting compliments from parents of her art students. And there were a lot of compliments, the kind that blew her away.

When she'd accepted Andy's offer to run a few classes, she'd never expected to enjoy them, let alone have the kids praise her so highly. Many of the parents asked if she'd considered running art classes out of school hours during the semester and she'd been flabbergasted.

She'd already decided to stay in Redemption permanently. The place was good for her soul. She had no idea if it was living in Gran's house surrounded by precious memories, or the laid-back atmosphere of the town, or the friendliness of the people in general, but Redemption had healed her in a way she'd hoped for but never counted on.

While she was financially secure for the moment, it would be nice to supplement her income and give something back to a community that had already given her so much.

She'd ask Andy Symes's advice later. Because the more she thought about it, the more excitement fizzed through her veins.

Teaching part-time pyrography classes would be great, a soothing balm for her soul and a way to foster children's love of art.

"Are all these pieces sold?" A familiar voice shook her out of her reverie. Jake leaned on the front of her stall, decidedly delicious in navy shorts, a pale blue polo and aviator sunglasses.

Her heart gave a massive *kathump* as she remembered last night and how much further it could've gone if they hadn't been lying in a vineyard under a moonlit sky.

"Only two left," she said, pointing to a matching pair of grape clusters hanging off a vine. "But I'm supposed to be saving those for Mrs. Minelli."

He leaned over and she inhaled, savoring the crispness of freshly showered male. "That old bat's purse strings are tied tight. She's probably promised half the stalls here she'd buy stuff."

"Be nice." Sara chuckled. "Though I think you're right. Her hands are empty."

"Cilla says she never donates to the hospital, whatever fundraising they do." He made a cross sign with his fingers. "Rumor has it she's blacklisted from the seniors' functions too because she's on the lookout for husband number three."

The thought of the wizened Italian lady who never wore anything other than black searching for a husband made Sara smile.

"Where's Olly?"

Jake jerked his thumb over his shoulder. "At the jumping castle with some of the kids he met at art class, under the supervision of Andy Symes."

"And Cilla? Haven't seen much of her today."

Jake grinned. "Think she's busy trying to avoid her boyfriend."

"Is he the dishy doctor who's been buzzing around between stalls, helping out wherever necessary?"

Jake frowned and mock pouted. "You think he's dishy?"

"Oh yeah." Sara loved teasing Jake, loved the banter they traded. She'd never had that with Greg, who'd been serious and driven since day one. "Makes me wish I had a cold so I could go see him."

"That's downright sick." Jake waggled his finger at her. "Cilla's got enough problems with the doc without you making a play for him." He slid his aviators down a little and stared at her over the top. "Not that you would, right?"

"Right," she said, laughing when he swiped his brow in relief. "But I find the whole grey hair thing on a young guy rather distinguished."

Jake snorted. "He's in his forties. He's not young."

Some of Sara's amusement faded as she glimpsed Cilla ducking behind the popcorn stand when she saw Bryce heading her way.

"Seriously, what's going on between them? Your aunt doesn't seem happy these days."

He grimaced. "Understatement of the year. She won't talk to me about it, which is probably a good thing. But I hate seeing her unhappy. She's had enough of that in her life before. She deserves better."

Sara had felt awkward enough talking to Cilla last time about her relationship and she really didn't want to do it again. But she knew what it was like not having anyone to talk to about the tough stuff. And Cilla would be her neighbor permanently.

"Do you want me to talk to her?"

Jake brightened. "Would you? I know I put you on the spot last time but she's not opening up to me and I'm worried."

"Ssh," Sara said. "She's headed this way."

Sara knew that if her expression mirrored Jake's, they looked like two naughty kids who'd been discovered with their hands in a cookie jar.

"Hey, Cilla, looks like the fair's a roaring success," Sara said. "Congratulations."

"Thanks to all of you." Cilla smiled but it did little to detract from the fatigue pinching her mouth and the dark circles under her eyes. Looked like she'd been losing sleep too. "Sergio's family are going to be thrilled."

"Glad to help." Sara gestured at her stall. "Only two pieces left to sell."

"I knew your wonderful work would sell out." Cilla glanced at her watch. "We're winding up in an hour so I'd better keep moving."

"Wait." Jake, who'd remained silent until now, bent down to kiss his aunt's cheek. "You've been amazing, organizing this entire event from start to finish. This town owes you big time."

To Sara's surprise, Cilla's eyes filled with tears.

"This town stood by me when I needed it most so it's the least I can do." Cilla blinked rapidly. "Helping out when I can is rewarding."

Considering how she'd felt after the art classes, Sara could empathize. Helping others was a great distraction. An alleviator of boredom. A way to focus on anything else but what niggled and annoyed a person until it was all they could think about.

"Looks like our new doc shares your sentiment," Jake said, and when Cilla stiffened and shot a quick glance over her shoulder, as if she expected Bryce to have materialized there, Sara knew Cilla needed to confront her demons or else it would eat her away.

"He's been helpful," Cilla said, her voice carefully controlled. "Everyone's pitched in."

"Are we all still meeting for a drink at the diner once the fair's closed?" Sara had planned on heading home, she was that tired, but it would give her a good opportunity to chat to Cilla in an informal setting. With a little luck, the good doctor would be around to further her cause.

"I'm beat." Cilla shook her head. "Thought I'd take Olly home and relax."

"Olly's looking forward to a burger at the diner," Jake said, then ducked down to murmur, "You can't keep hiding from the doc forever."

"Watch me," Cilla said, shooting Jake a scathing glare before hurrying off in the opposite direction to Bryce.

"That went well," Jake said, his tone dry.

"She's hurting," Sara said, her glance speculative as she saw a crestfallen Bryce watching Cilla's retreating back. "She's hiding it well behind a stoic mask but there's more going on than we know."

"It was the age difference initially," Jake said.

"There's more to it." Sara just knew it. A confident, independent woman like Cilla would be used to presenting a hardened front to the world. Judging from the snippets Jake had divulged, she'd been through the wringer in her marriage and the scandal that had followed her husband's suicide. She'd had many years to harden her hide, so the fact she was wearing her heart on her sleeve now because of Bryce meant Cilla was in deep.

"In that case, I should stay out of it." Jake held up his hands. "Secret women's business is complicated."

"I'll try to pop in this afternoon."

"And I'll make myself and Olly scarce." He crooked his finger at her. "Maybe later on, we can make ourselves scarce."

He wiggled his eyebrows suggestively and she laughed.

"We're taking it slow, remember?"

"Slow I can handle." His hand snaked out to capture hers, turn it palm up, then trace slow, concentric circles in the middle of it, making her squirm and setting long-neglected nerve endings alight. "But I'm not a snail."

When breathing grew difficult, she snatched her hand away. "Don't you believe the old fables about tortoises winning races?"

His lips eased into a wicked smile that made her pulse pound. "Let's get to the race first, then I'll show you how I use slow and steady to win the ultimate prize."

Sara swallowed as heat flooded her body. Jake was a master at flirting. Or maybe it had been too darn long since she'd had a guy pay her this much attention that he made her hot and bothered.

"Don't you have to man the soda fountain for a while?"

He grinned. "Nice deflection. I'll allow it for now." He captured a strand of her hair and tugged on it lightly, making her scalp tingle. "But later? It's time for the tortoise and the hare to . . . warm up."

Sara waited until Jake had left before fanning her flaming face. Looked like Cilla wasn't the only one who was in deep when it came to sexy guys.

33.

Cilla made her usual end-of-fundraiser speech to wind down the fair. She'd made enough of them to almost recite this one from heart. Which was lucky, considering she had a hard time stringing two words together with Bryce staring at her with obvious disapproval.

She'd dodged him all morning and if his glower was any indication, he'd noticed. But she had a feeling he'd corner her at the end of the fair.

So when her speech came to an end and he turned away and disappeared through the crowd, she couldn't have been more surprised.

He'd told her to face facts over breakfast at the diner, had said she could come find him when she did. Her initial ballsy response, not a chance, still stood firm. So why did sadness clog her throat as she watched him get into his car and drive away?

The only fact she had to face was the one that clearly stated they could never be anything beyond friends. And she'd been doing okay coming to terms with that. But every time she saw him, her heart gave an embarrassing flip-flop and her stomach joined the party.

Women her age didn't experience heart flutters or stomach rollovers. Or did they?

She'd shut herself off for twenty years. Longer, if she counted the deliberate detachment she'd fostered during intimate relations with Vernon. During his meaningless quick thrusts, she'd mentally list tomorrow's to-do list until he'd finished. She'd completed a lot of lists that way.

Now, whenever Bryce looked at her, it felt like her body sat up and howled. She tingled. All over.

Maybe it was time to go on a date with someone closer to her age? James Winsome had flirted with her over the last few years. A fifty-something widower who ran a successful winery in the region, he was known for two things: sublime chardonnay and exaggerated charm.

She'd always managed to deflect his attentions, fobbing him off with a joke or a laugh. Maybe it was time to see if her body could be assuaged with a man more her vintage?

As if she'd conjured him up, James appeared next to the stage and held out his hand to help her down.

"That was some speech, lovely lady."

Cilla would've usually ignored his hand. Today, she took it. "Thanks. And thanks for donating the wine. It sold like hotcakes."

"It's a good vintage." He winked. "Like me."

Cilla forced a chuckle. James still held her hand and . . . she felt nothing. No spark. No zing. No goddamn tingle.

"So when are you going to make an honest man out of me, and come out to the vineyard for some of my home cooking?" He squeezed her hand. "I'd love to show you around the place."

Probably starting with his bedroom.

Cilla should accept. She should put herself out there and start dating. Forget all about sexy young doctors who made her heart go pitter-patter.

But she'd been many things in her life and fickle wasn't one of them. She couldn't use James when his touch left her absolutely cold.

"Maybe I'll pop by one day if you're lucky," she said, tempering her refusal with a smile as she slid her hand out of his.

James made a mock gun with his thumb and forefinger, and cocked it. "I'll hold you to that."

Cilla wished he wouldn't but she returned his corny finger wave as he strolled away, looking every one of his fifty-odd years in brown corduroy pants, a checked shirt and a dusty cowboy hat.

"Damn you, Bryce Madden," she muttered under her breath. She knew she had to bring this situation between them to a head, but she had no idea how to go about it.

Time to do some serious thinking.

34.

After a long day at the fair, Jake was looking forward to spending some time with Sara. She'd agreed to come over for supper and Jake had been like an excited kid all day. So when his cell beeped with an incoming message, he hoped it would be her, saying she'd be over pronto.

He hadn't been able to forget their make-out session at the vineyard last night and judging by her upbeat mood at the fair today, she hadn't either. For the first time since they'd met, she'd appeared to enjoy his flirting, giving as good as she got.

However, when he glanced at the screen, the text was from Rose.

HEY BRO.
I'M READY 4 VISITORS.
WUD LUV 2 C OL ASAP!

Ignoring the wave of disappointment that washed over him, leaving him cold, he fired off a quick response. He should be thrilled that his sister had improved to the point of receiving visitors, not lamenting the fact he couldn't see Sara tonight. Rose's text meant she wouldn't be far off leaving rehab. Olly would be ecstatic.

"Is that Sara?" Cilla asked, bustling around the kitchen as usual, chopping and freezing herbs.

"No, Rose. She's up for visitors and wants to see Olly." Jake injected enthusiasm into his voice, hoping Cilla wouldn't pick up on his discontent. "I'll take him now."

After all Rose and Olly had been through, the least he could do was reunite the kid with his mom, even if it were only for a few hours.

"Isn't Sara coming over?" Cilla dried her hands, sat at the kitchen table, rubbed her foot and winced. "Though if her feet are half as sore as mine from manning a stall all morning, she's probably soaking in a bath."

"Yeah, but she'll understand."

While his nephew's happiness meant everything to him, he couldn't help but feel frustrated he wouldn't be seeing Sara tonight. He hadn't been this horny for a woman since his teen years and all he could think about was Sara, naked and warm and pliant in his arms.

She might've been coming over for supper but he'd planned on walking her home with the intent on getting some much-needed one-on-one time with her.

He hadn't planned on this setback and immediately felt guilty for seeing Rose's text as such. His sister had made amazing progress. He should be rejoicing, not trying to hide his disillusionment at not getting to spend time with his girlfriend.

"Why don't I take Olly to visit Rose?" Cilla stretched out her legs and wiggled her toes. "I'd love to reconnect with her. See if she wants to come stay when she gets out?"

Jake's heart leaped but he tried not to appear too eager. "You sure?"

It wouldn't be such a bad idea if Rose heard the invitation from Cilla. He'd already tried on the phone and she'd been less than enthused. Having it come from their aunt, who'd been nothing but welcoming since he'd arrived, might sway Rose in a way he couldn't.

It would also ensure his plans with Sara tonight didn't change. A purely selfish reaction to Cilla's offer but he'd be a fool not to contemplate it.

Cilla nodded. "Absolutely. I'd love to see her."

Jake wavered. As much as he wanted to see Sara, Olly was his responsibility. Rose was his sister. He should be the one to take Olly.

"You'd really be helping me out," Cilla said. "I'd like to get out of town for a night. Do some thinking. This would be a perfect opportunity."

When Cilla put it like that, how could Jake refuse? If Cilla needed thinking time to eradicate the sadness that hung over her like a pall, he'd facilitate it. And maybe get what he wanted in the process.

Did that make him heartless? He'd prefer to think of it as making it easier for everyone.

"Okay. A cleaner comes in once a week so my apartment should be spotless and if you can't find something, call me."

"We'll be fine," Cilla said, looking relieved he'd agreed. "Olly's a sweet child and I can't wait to see Rose again."

"Try to convince her to come stay, okay?"

"I'll do my best." Cilla glanced out the window, a faraway glint in her eyes. "This place is good for healing."

He couldn't agree more.

The next hour flew by in a blur of getting a very excited Olly ready to visit his mom, packing overnight cases and ensuring Cilla had directions from the recovery center to his apartment.

When Cilla and Olly left, Jake sank into the armchair in front of the fireplace and breathed a sigh of relief.

He loved Olly and adored his aunt but this would be the first night he'd have to himself since he'd arrived here.

While the prospect of yet another night alone would've made him maudlin back in New York City, he now cherished the silence that enveloped the house.

Though if he had any say in it, he wouldn't be alone tonight.

He should cook a meal, set the table, uncork some wine, put some music on. But all he could think about was having Sara all to himself and he didn't want to waste time doing any of that other stuff.

He texted her to come over and she responded almost immediately in the affirmative. Hopefully that was a sign she wanted this as much as he did.

As dusk descended, he strolled around the house, closing the curtains, switching on wall sconces and lamps, casting a cozy glow. Cilla had a lovely home, as warm and welcoming as she was, and he hoped it put Sara at ease.

He wasn't big on seduction. Had never had any use for setting moods or false promises. Not being emotionally invested in any of his previous lovers had served him well. But the way his heart bucked in his chest like a wild thing while he waited for Sara told him he was far more invested in her than was good for him.

A knock on the back door had him swiping sweaty palms down the sides of his shorts. Damn, he was nervous.

As was she, if her wide eyes and pale face were any indication when he let her in.

"Cilla's car's missing," she said, slipping past him before he could kiss her.

"She's taken Olly to visit Rose," he said, flicking the back lock and pulling down the blind. "Won't be back 'til morning."

Sara stilled, her gaze riveted to his. "So it's just us tonight?"

"Is that a problem?"

He sent a silent prayer heavenward that she wouldn't say yes.

It took her what seemed like an eternity to answer.

"Not at all." Her mouth curved into a coy smile that made him combust on the spot.

"I was hoping you'd say that." He advanced on her and she backed away, into the living room where a single lamp cast shadows. "Because I've been thinking about doing this all day."

Her back hit the mantel and she stopped. "Doing what? Chasing me around a room?"

"This," he said, vaulting the coffee table to land in front of her, grab hold of her, and haul her into his arms before crushing his mouth on hers.

There was nothing tender in the kiss and he couldn't help it. He wanted her too damn much. He should apologize, should take it slow, but Sara didn't give him the chance as she fisted her hands in his shirt and dragged him closer, plastering her body to his.

She matched him for frustration and passion, consuming him with hot, open-mouthed kisses that had them gasping for air.

He palmed her butt and she hooked a leg around him, bringing her heat in tantalizing contact. He groaned as she writhed against him, making soft, mewling noises that fired his libido into the stratosphere.

"You sure you want this?" he managed to say with his last ounce of chivalry when she trailed kisses along his jaw, down his throat.

"Absolutely." She eased back to look him in the eye. "I want you."

"Feeling's entirely mutual, sweetheart." Not breaking eye contact, he hoisted her into his arms and took the stairs at a reckless speed.

Her wild peal of laughter made him nuzzle her neck, tickling her with his stubble until she was breathless from laughing.

Her laughter died when he laid her on the bed and towered over her, reaching for the first button on his shirt.

"I promised you real slow, remember?" He slipped the button through the loop. "So first I'm going to strip and then I get to watch you do the same."

The tip of her tongue darted out to moisten her bottom lip. "You know the wait's killing me, right?"

"It'll be worth it."

∾

Sara couldn't breathe as she watched Jake slip his shirt off his shoulders. He was magnificent. Broad chest. Strong pecs. Smattering of hair. Tanned.

She wanted to run her hands over every inch of him.

The moment "inch" popped into her head her gaze automatically dipped to the bulge in his shorts.

"Do you want to see all of me?" His fingers snagged the zipper and her mouth went dry.

She nodded, gnawing on her bottom lip as he slid the zipper down, grating metal the only sound in the room apart from her ragged breathing.

When the shorts fell to the floor, air whooshed out of her lungs.

When the boxers followed, her jaw dropped.

Now she could understand why Jake was so confident.

"Your turn," he said, holding his hands out.

She took them, allowed him to pull her to her feet.

"I want to touch you," she said, not waiting for permission as her palms skated across his chest, his abs, his hips.

She heard his sharp intake of breath as her hand slid lower, heard his muttered curse as she wrapped her hand around him and stroked.

He stilled her hand. "You know how I wanted to take this slow? You keep that up and you'll be disappointed."

Batting her eyes in faux innocence, she said, "Trust me, nothing about you is disappointing."

His rueful grin tinged with pride made her laugh and she released him.

"One of us is way overdressed," he said, reaching for the zipper on the back of her sundress. "And if you won't strip for me, looks like I'll have to do the honors."

"Be my guest."

He eased the zipper down as far as it could go, then pushed the straps off her shoulders. She shivered as the cotton slid down her body and pooled at her feet, leaving her breasts bared.

"Holy hell." He stared at her like she was the most beautiful thing he'd ever seen and it empowered her to hook her thumbs into the elastic of her white cotton panties and slowly push them to the floor.

As Jake's hungry gaze slid over her body, Sara had never felt so exposed. Yet strangely, she didn't feel vulnerable.

This was Jake.

The man who'd helped her confront her demons. Who'd been gentle and supportive. Who hadn't pushed or judged, but had been there for her while she healed in this town.

This was *Jake*.

The man she wanted more than she'd wanted anything in a long time.

When he took her into his arms, she came alive, as if waking from a long slumber. Every touch, every caress set her alight, making her crave release with every heartbeat.

He loved her with his tongue and his mouth and his hands, until she shattered into a million floaty pieces.

Still wanting more.

Wanting it all.

He gave it to her. This wonderful man thrust into her, filling her, completing her, making love to her until she was mindless and boneless and shameless.

Sara didn't care.

For the first time in a long time, she felt alive.

35.

Jake woke to the first slivers of a cool dawn peeking through the blinds and an armful of hot woman snuggled into his chest.

Disoriented, he blinked several times and glanced at the woman.

It all came flooding back.

Sara.

Over him. Under him. Satisfying him in a way he'd never thought possible.

They'd had an incredible night. How many times had they done it? Four? Five? It didn't matter. What mattered was the fact she was here, right by his side and he liked it. A lot.

For the first morning in nine months, a smile crept across his face. At last, he had something to smile about.

He had no idea how they'd make this work. He hadn't planned on staying in town beyond Rose's rehab stint. Hell, he couldn't even enter the local airfield without freaking out. Then there was his apartment back in New York City. And a host of contacts he'd built up over the years in the industry, should he ever need a change of direction in his career.

If there ever was a time he needed a change, that time was now.

But then there was Sara. Sweet, sassy, seductive Sara.

He couldn't see her leaving Redemption. Not after she'd left her pain behind and seemed comfortable in the house she'd inherited. But it was more than that.

This town had saved her.

He'd watched her at the fair, had seen her deep in conversation with many of the locals, the joy on her face when she sold her pieces. She'd even appeared comfortable around the kids from her art class who'd stopped by her stall, a far cry from the woman who'd bawled when she'd first laid eyes on Olly.

No, he couldn't see her heading back to the city. Which meant he had some serious thinking to do.

He hadn't needed the phenomenal sex last night to cement what he already knew.

He'd fallen for Sara.

And he wanted to explore what that meant for the both of them.

She wriggled a little and sighed, her eyelids fluttering. The corners of her mouth curved a little and he hoped she was dreaming of him.

His cell buzzed on the drawers next to the bed and he froze. Dawn phone calls couldn't be good and his fears immediately focused on Olly or Cilla or Rose. He prayed to God they were safe as he carefully slid his arm out from under Sara, who appeared to sleep in a catatonic state and couldn't be roused despite him shifting to reach for his phone.

He grabbed the cell, padded into the bathroom, slid the door shut and allowed himself a deep breath before glancing at the screen.

Rose.

Trying to stay cool, he hit the answer button. "Hey Rosey-Posey, everything okay?"

"No." Her voice was barely above a whisper and his heart sank.

"What's wrong?"

"I need to see you, Jake. Now."

Hell. "I can be there in an hour if I leave now."

Jake wanted to ask a million questions but she sounded so lost, so forlorn, that he didn't want to be responsible for tipping the balance. So he focused on the one topic guaranteed to put a smile on her face.

"Olly must've loved seeing you yesterday."

"That's what I want to talk to you about," she said, her tone bordering on shrill. "Get here as fast as you can."

She'd hung up by the time he'd said, "Okay." Not good. He hadn't heard her sound so desperate since the night she'd called him, hysterical, to say that Olly's father had been found dead of a drug overdose.

He got dressed at record speed and tiptoed back into the bedroom to scrawl a quick note for Sara. She hadn't stirred and he allowed himself the luxury of watching her sleep peacefully for a few seconds before writing a brief explanation, then slipping out the door.

He tried to focus on their night together on the drive to the rehab facility but instead, a variety of scenarios, all of them bad, kept flashing across his mind.

Had Rose had a relapse? Had she checked herself out then realized her mistake? Had Cilla said something to put her in a funk? What would happen to Olly if Rose couldn't get her act together?

The sixty-minute drive took him forty-five at this early hour and he found himself holding his breath as he waited to be admitted to Rose's ward.

The night nurse on duty, about to clock off, shot him a compassionate glance that did little to settle his nerves. What the hell was he walking into?

Thankfully, Rose appeared alert and calm as she sat by the window in her room, dressed in yoga pants and a hoodie. With her hair in a ponytail, she looked like a teenage waif.

She turned as he entered the room and leapt to her feet. "Thanks for coming so quickly."

He crossed the small room and hugged her, wishing he could infuse her with some of his strength. For that's how he felt these days, like Redemption had made him stronger. He wasn't the same guy who'd left New York a few months ago in search of help for his nephew and had ended up helping himself in the process.

"You've got me worried, Sis. What's up?" He perched on the side of her bed, hoping that whatever had upset her he could fix it.

"I need to get this all out in one go without you interrupting, okay?"

"Okay." Foreboding strummed his spine. This sounded bad.

"I'm a lousy mom and seeing Olly with Aunt Cilla yesterday reinforced it. He's like a different kid. He looks healthy and happy in a way he never did with me."

She started pacing, taking three steps and turning back, and when he opened his mouth to respond she held up her hand. "Let me finish. I know you want me to recuperate in Redemption when I get out of here, and Cilla put forward a strong case too. So I'm considering it. But Olly's better off with you for a while. I'm not strong enough to leave here yet and . . . honestly? I won't be for a while."

"How long?"

She hesitated, as her shoulders sagged. "I don't know."

This was worse than he expected. Olly was Rose's life and if she didn't want to get out of here ASAP to be with him, she must be in a bad way.

"Did you relapse?"

She snorted. "How? You think they have a mini-bar stocked full of vodka in these rooms?"

He bit back the logical response: If she was allowed visitors now, any one of her friends could've snuck alcohol in.

"Olly adores you, Rose. You're all he talks about—"

"That's not true. He kept mentioning Sara, like she hung the moon and stars." She resumed pacing. "Aunt Cilla said she's great."

And she's my new girlfriend, Jake wanted to say. But now wasn't the time and place to get into the logistics of his love life. He needed to find out what was bugging Rose.

"Yeah, Olly took a few art classes with her."

She nodded. "He told me. He also said she's your girlfriend and he saw you kissing."

Rose's smirk reminded him of the way she used to tease him when they were kids. He liked it.

"Kids are blunt," he said, smiling. "Sara and I are . . . involved."

Could he sound any more pompous?

Predictably, Rose screwed up her nose. "Involved? That's a new one."

"I really like her. She's incredible."

Now he sounded like a sap. But he didn't care. Like Redemption, Sara had helped him come alive again. Not that he felt only gratitude for her. Oh no. He felt far, far more.

"It's the first time I've ever seen you like this." She shook her head, but not before he'd glimpsed the sheen of tears. "I'm happy for you. You deserve it."

"We both do," he said, and to his horror, she burst into tears.

Not just tears. Sobs. Gut-wrenching sobs that made him want to slay whatever demons haunted her. For now, all he could do was hold her and comfort her and wait until she was ready to talk.

When the sobs petered out to sniffles, they eased apart and sat on the bed.

"You've been through some tough stuff and you've always come out on top, Rosey. You've got a stronger backbone than me. So why are you talking crazy, saying Olly's better off without you?"

"Because I'm not blind. I can see how well he's doing." She looked away, swiped a hand under her nose. "I want you to have custody of him—"

"What the—"

"He's better off with you." She raised her tear-stained face to eyeball him. "He's a different kid now, Jakey, and that's because of you. *You* did that. You're more capable than me. You can handle the hard knocks when I can't. Plus, you can give him everything, and Olly deserves the best in life—"

"Stop talking shit." Jake leapt to his feet and started pacing, stunned she'd suggest such a thing when she loved her son more than anything. "Olly is your *life*. You adore that kid. You've slaved for years to provide him with everything."

Shocked his sister would even consider giving him custody of her precious son, he stopped in front of her and glowered. "So what the hell is really going on?"

She took her time answering, knuckling the tears from her eyes. "I'm scared. Freaking terrified." She hiccupped and raised bloodshot eyes to his. "What if I end up like him?"

Jake didn't have to ask who the "him" was. Their father. The bastard. Ruining lives even from beyond the grave.

"With the alcohol, you mean?"

Rose shook her head. "I only drink to forget. I can control it if I want to."

"Then why don't you?"

"Because I have to forget . . . I *need* to forget." She grimaced, her hand shaky as she tucked a strand of hair behind her ear. "It still makes me mad. Every time I think of what he put me through, the fury sweeps over me and the only way to calm it is by drinking."

"There are other ways—"

"Don't lecture me, Jake. Not now." She plucked at the edge of the bedspread. "When I get that angry, that's the worst time of all, because I'm terrified I'll lash out at Olly . . . like he did with us."

"Hell, Rose, don't give him so much power. We both did enough of that already when the old bastard was alive."

His gut roiled at the memory of what they'd endured as kids. "You and I are nothing like him. *Nothing*. You love Olly. You'd do anything for him, including holing away here to get yourself together. The old man never loved us. Never treated us as anything other than nuisances to be tolerated or abused. And we put up with it because we had to. But not anymore."

He took hold of her hands. "It took me years to get over our childhood. I still get the occasional nightmare. But I made a choice a while back, not to waste any more time lamenting what happened back then. That bastard took enough of my life. I won't give him the satisfaction of stealing any more."

Rose stared at him, wide-eyed and wary. "Do you ever wish we'd done things differently? Maybe run away or fought back?"

"We were kids. We did the best we could."

A lone tear trickled down her cheek. "I never thanked you for protecting me. Because I know you did. You took the brunt of his brutality—"

"Stop. You don't need to thank me. I did what I had to do, just like you do with Olly." He squeezed her hands. "Seriously, Sis, you're a great mom. You should be proud of that amazing kid you've raised all on your own." He eyeballed her. "You. Are. Nothing. Like. Him. Always remember that."

After what seemed like an eternity, Rose nodded. "Thanks. I've never told anyone else all that stuff, about me being terrified of ending up like Dad. Only you could truly understand and you haven't judged me. You've made me see things in a different way."

"I'm always here for you, Rosey-Posey, always. And I don't ever want to hear you talk crazy about giving up custody of Olly to me, got it?" He hugged her tight, blinking to dispel the moisture stinging his eyes. "You're never alone."

"Aunt Cilla said that too." She pulled back. "I really want to concentrate on the therapy side of things here for a while, get my head straight, then I think I will come to Redemption."

"That's great. In that case, I'd better stick around town a while longer."

Her tremulous smile lightened his heart. "Like you need an excuse. Sounds like you've got your hands full with this wonder woman Sara."

"I can't wait for you to meet her."

Rose had met the occasional casual girlfriend he'd taken to functions, but no one who'd meant as much to him as Sara.

"Take care of Olly for me, okay?"

"Always."

This time, their hug was more affectionate than desperate.

"Call me if you need me," he said, pausing at the door. "Any time. Day or night. I'll be here."

She blew him a kiss. "Love you, Jakey. You're the best."

"I know." He grinned, relieved when she grinned back. "Talk to you soon."

His grin faded as the door closed behind him. He'd kept his fury in check in front of Rose, but the residual anger against his father and the long-reaching consequences of his cruelty made him want to thump something.

But he'd be a hypocrite if he didn't practice what he preached, and on the drive back to Redemption, he let the anger go and focused on something more positive.

Getting back to Sara.

36.

A week after the fair, Cilla was no closer to peace.

She still felt edgy and annoyed and off-kilter.

She knew why, too. Bryce was ignoring her, just like he'd said, leaving the ball in her proverbial court. But her vow of "He'd be waiting a long time" for her to contact him was wearing thin.

She'd seen him several times at the hospital, when she'd popped in to see Sergio and finalize the funds raised with his parents. She'd seen him grabbing a coffee at the diner. She'd even seen him jogging late at night when she'd been doing volunteer dinners for the seniors' center.

Each and every time, she'd become breathless and wished a pox on him. But he looked better than ever and wouldn't do much beyond a brief nod to acknowledge her existence.

The man could out-stubborn a goat. Then again, what had she expected? For him to continually chase her only to be rebuffed? She'd got exactly what she'd wanted: for him to keep his distance. She should be ecstatic. But the last seven days had been tough, seeing Jake and Sara so happy. She was thrilled for them, but when was the last time she'd been really, truly happy?

Probably when she'd given birth to Tam, which was . . . what? Forty-two years ago? Damn, she was a sad case. Maybe she should go out with James after all? The mere thought made her shudder and she picked up the pace, needing to get home and start dinner. Dinner for one, considering Jake and Olly were eating at Sara's tonight. She'd begged off their invitation, citing fatigue after a long day at the hospital and a little much needed "me time," when the truth was she couldn't face another dinner feeling like a third wheel. At least, not at the moment.

If she could hold out until Bryce left, she'd be okay. Back to her staid life, just the way she liked it. So why did the thought leave her cold?

As she exited the back door of the hospital and headed for the car park, she spied a lone figure in the grotto, a small circular space surrounded by hedges with a park bench in the middle. It had been built originally as a peaceful place for people to wait while their family or friends had surgery, but it had become redundant over the years after the new cafeteria had been built.

As she neared, she saw Bryce sitting on the bench, his elbows resting on his knees, shoulders slumped, like he was bearing an invisible weight.

She stopped, startled by her first instinct—to go to him and hold him. To comfort him. To ease whatever burden made him look so vulnerable.

Before she could second-guess her decision, she entered the grotto. He didn't look up until she sat next to him, his surprise quickly masked by a carefully neutral expression.

When he didn't speak, she said, "Are you okay?"

"Fine." His short, clipped, monosyllabic response indicated he was far from it.

"Usual post-rounds tiredness?"

He straightened and shrugged. "Something like that."

An awkward silence stretched between them and Cilla wished she'd never approached him. Small talk had never been her forte.

And she couldn't broach any subject remotely connected to the two of them.

Eventually, he half-turned to face her. "What are you doing here when you're usually doing your best to avoid me?"

She settled for honesty. "You looked like you could use a friend."

"Is that what we are now? *Friends?*" He made it sound like they were sworn enemies. "Because I sure as hell don't treat my friends the way you've treated me."

To her mortification, tears stung her eyes. "It's complicated. You know that."

"Doesn't have to be."

Thankfully, he turned away to continue staring at the jasmine bush, giving her time to compose herself. Time she needed as she dashed her hand across her eyes.

"I know why you're pushing me away," he said, continuing his intense study of the bush. "You're wracked by guilt."

"You don't know the first thing about me." A sliver of anger pierced her sadness. "And you never will."

"I called Tamsin."

She jumped. "What?"

"You heard me." He stood and she leapt to her feet so he wouldn't tower over her. "I was sick of all the BS and I wanted to get an insight into the woman I care about, so I tracked her down and called her."

"How dare you?" Cilla puffed up in outrage, wanting to slug something, preferably him. "Who the hell do you think you are?"

"I'm the man who's been in love with you for twenty-five god-damn years!" he roared, his gaze tortured as he stepped away. "Don't you get it, Cilla? I'm not bullshitting. I'm not an abusive prick. I'm not Vernon!"

Stunned by his outburst, she glared at him. "You don't know the first thing about Vernon—"

"Actually, I do. Tamsin told me. All of it. And I'd hazard a guess that when she went away to college, things only got worse." He ran a hand over his face. It did little to erase the devastation twisting his features, and he hadn't even lived through it. "Not all men are like that bastard. And feeling guilty because you stuck out the marriage for Tamsin's sake yet she left anyway isn't helping. Tamsin loves you but every time she's around you she feels the weight of the past stifling her and you look so sad and remind her of everything that went wrong back then—"

"Shut up." She jabbed him hard in the chest. "Just shut the hell up!"

Bryce bloody Madden was presuming to tell her about her daughter? Worse, why the hell had Tam told him all that crap?

Cilla shook with rage as Bryce stared at her with pity.

That was the final straw.

"We're going to have this out, once and for all." She grabbed his shirtsleeve and all but dragged him out of the grotto. "We'll talk at your place."

Bryce shrugged off her grip but he followed her along the path bordering the back of the hospital that led toward his house. They didn't speak, which was good, because Cilla couldn't have forced a single word past the lump of anger lodged in her throat.

He'd called Tam for insight into her life. What gave him the right? As for Tam, Cilla had never felt so betrayed. Tam had never said any of that stuff to her. Her own mother!

When they reached Bryce's cottage, he opened the door and she pushed past him, stomping into the darkened living room. She'd been so gung-ho to give him a piece of her mind in private that she hadn't realized the effect being back here would have.

The last time she'd been here, he'd cooked her dinner, plied her with charm and banter, and then made her body sing with a mere kiss. The memory made her hands shake and she planted them on her hips, ready to blast him.

But when he switched on the lone lamp in the room, some of Cilla's fury fizzled. He looked like she'd kicked him where it hurt the most.

"You want to tell me I'm an asshole for delving into your private life? Go ahead. You want to berate me for caring? Have at it." He held his hands out to her, like he had nothing to hide up his sleeves. "But know this, Cilla. I'm one of the good guys. I'm not spinning you a line. Or jerking you around. Or playing some lame game while I'm in town. I'm so damn mad at you for doubting me and for pushing me away when I've wanted you since I was seventeen years old and that hasn't waned—"

Cilla lost her mind and kissed him. Initially to shut him up. But as his arms slid around her waist and hauled her close, she kissed him for another reason entirely.

Because he made her feel good. He made her feel alive. He made her forget.

And that's what Cilla wanted to do tonight. Forget.

Forget every rational reason why she shouldn't do this.

Forget her fears and self-esteem issues.

Forget her past.

And just live.

She didn't allow herself to doubt as Bryce undid her skirt, ripped off her panties and buried his tongue in her.

She didn't stop him from pleasuring her until she was gasping for air and her knees had buckled.

She didn't analyze or rationalize when he hoisted her up against the wall, buried himself deep and thrust repeatedly until he yelled her name and she came apart.

She didn't do any of those things because from the first moment Bryce had touched her, it felt right. And what they'd just shared had been magnificent. Desperate and wanton and passionate. The way two people who cared about each other should be.

"You okay?" His gentle kiss brushed her lips. "I didn't mean it to be like that . . . I mean, I'd dreamed about it but not like that and—"

"You talk too much."

She kissed him to shut him up again.

Her excuse and she was sticking to it.

37.

Sara had spent the last week existing in some weird dreamlike state, the same odd floaty feeling she'd had when Delivery Boy had asked her out all those years ago.

She had the same tummy tumbles and heart pitter-patters, the same goofy grins and vivid daydreams.

But this time, the object of her fantasies liked her back and it was a heady feeling.

Jake was incredible. Attentive and caring, sweet and funny. And the kind of unselfish lover who made her feel like a goddess.

They'd spent a lot of time together, doing fun stuff with Olly during the days, then naughty stuff beneath the covers at night. It had been an amazing week, culminating in dinner at her place tonight where Olly had helped her cook fajitas and they'd eaten cross-legged on her living room floor.

But something was making her uneasy and she couldn't figure out what it was. She'd initially attributed it to being happy for the first time since Lucy's death, so maybe the niggly feeling was guilt. She'd pondered it at length, had analyzed it from every angle, but what she had with Jake was too good to make her feel guilty.

Her musings had taken a different route then, and she'd wondered if spending so much time with Olly was making her uneasy. But she'd dismissed that as nonsense because she'd got past her funk where kids were concerned.

So what the heck was making her this edgy?

Olly ran into the room and skidded to a stop in front of her. "Uncle Jake has gone home for a minute to get my flavored milk. He'll be back soon."

"In that case, why don't you sit here and we'll chat." She patted the floor next to her. "Or maybe we can tell stories."

"Cool." Olly flopped onto the floor and rested his back against the sofa. "My mom tells good stories but she's still in that hospital place getting better."

Sara had no idea how much Olly knew about Rose. Jake had told her plenty but she didn't want to make the mistake of divulging too much, so she gave a noncommittal murmur.

"I really like hanging out with you and Uncle Jake." Olly glanced up at her, his expression serious. "If my mom doesn't come home, can I live with you and Uncle Jake and you be my mom?"

Sara froze. Not that Olly's scenario would ever come to fruition, but the moment his question had penetrated her loved-up fog, she knew what had been nagging at the edge of her consciousness.

In getting too close to Jake, she'd opened herself up to the possibility of commitment. And commitment ultimately led to complications she couldn't contemplate, like living together and children.

When she didn't answer, Olly looked crestfallen. "It's okay if you don't want to—"

"Sweetie, anyone would love to have you live with them but your mom will be home before you know it."

A spark of hope lit his eyes. "You think?"

"I know." She slid an arm around his shoulders and hugged him tight. "She loves you very much and I bet she's counting down the days 'til you're with her again."

"I miss her a lot." He leaned into her, in that snuggly way that only kids could do.

It broke her heart that she'd never have the chance to do this with Lucy again, but for now, she relished the feel of a warm little body tucked into hers.

"Will you and Uncle Jake have kids? Because I'd sure like someone to play with."

An image of a tousled haired, blue-eyed boy sprang to mind, a boy the carbon copy of his father, and it steadied her resolve like nothing else.

She couldn't have Jake's or any other man's baby.

"You've got plenty of friends in town," she said, deflecting his initial question and wishing Jake would hurry up. "Shall we get the ice cream ready while we're waiting for your uncle?"

"Yeah." Olly leapt to his feet. "Can I have chocolate sprinkles on mine?"

"Absolutely."

Rattled by Olly's innocent questions and the deep-seated yearning he'd stirred up with his cuddle, Sara needed some time to compose herself. "Would you like to watch cartoons while I get the ice cream ready?"

"Yeah, that'd be cool." Olly sat cross-legged on the floor and waited for her to turn on the TV.

With his elbows propped on his knees, chin resting in his hands, he looked adorable and she wanted to scoop him up and snuggle him tight.

Sadness clogged her throat and she swallowed before turning her back on him and marching into the kitchen.

This is what came of opening herself up to the possibility of attachment. If a simple embrace brought on tears and this much emotion, she was already way too attached to Olly. To his uncle, too, but she wouldn't think about that now. Blubbering over the ice cream would be uncool.

Uneasy, she busied herself getting out the bowls and spoons, trying not to remember how she used to do the same for Lucy and how much her little girl had adored anything strawberry flavored.

She was sure Olly had said he wanted chocolate sprinkles on his ice cream, but she wondered if he'd want that if he knew all she had in the freezer was strawberry.

"Olly, do you still want chocolate sprinkles on strawberry ice cream or do you prefer it plain?"

Olly didn't answer and she shook her head. What was it with kids and TV? Or any electronic device, for that matter, that sapped their focus.

"Olly? Did you hear me?" She yelled louder this time but silence greeted her.

Ignoring a twinge of apprehension, she huffed out an exasperated breath and marched back to the living room.

To find Olly gone.

"Olly?" Trying to keep her tone steady, she glanced around the room, like he'd miraculously appear.

Mentally chastising herself for being foolish, she walked down the hallway toward the bathroom. "You in there, Olly?"

The lights were off.

Hell.

"Olly, where are you?" She ran from room to room, her panic rising as she searched to no avail.

By the time she'd scoured the whole house, her heart was pounding so loudly she could hardly hear herself think.

Then she spied the front door. It was closed but unlocked, and she froze, a thousand horrific scenarios flashing through her head.

No one locked their doors in Redemption. But she hadn't been able to break the habit since arriving here. Which meant either she'd forgotten to lock the door after Jake and Olly had arrived . . .

Or Olly had unlocked it and snuck out.

Chills racked her body and she started to shake. Logically, she would've heard him unlock the door, open it and close it behind him. But all logic had fled and she was now in full-blown panic mode.

Dragging in deep breaths, she gave it one last shot.

"Olly, if you're here, you need to come out now!" She bellowed. "Otherwise you'll be banned from TV and treats for a month."

An empty threat she wouldn't have any control over, but sometimes kids reacted to threats when they wouldn't listen to reason. Not the best parenting, but when desperate, moms used what they could.

She heard a scuffling sound behind her and spun around, sagging against the wall in relief when she spied Olly crawling out from a wicker basket that Gran used to store wool in.

"I don't want to be banned," he said, managing to look fearful and contrite at the same time. "I used to play that hiding game with Mom and she'd pretend she couldn't find me and I'd be really quiet like a mouse, then I'd leap out and surprise her." Olly wrinkled his nose. "Only it didn't sound like you wanted to be surprised."

Tears burned Sara's eyes but she willed them away. Crying in front of Olly would only scare him and she didn't want to taint a game he obviously liked playing with Rose.

But he'd taken ten years off her life and she had to say something.

"I didn't know you were playing a game, Olly, so you scared me."

"Sorry, Sara." Downcast, he stared at his feet, biting his bottom lip.

"It's okay," she said. Her legs finally felt strong enough to move, and she crossed the room to squat in front of him. "Maybe you save that game to play with your mom, okay?"

He nodded and raised his head. "Can I still have ice cream?"

"You bet." She ruffled his hair and he bolted toward the kitchen, the incident forgotten.

If only it were that easy for her.

As Sara switched off the TV and followed at a more sedate pace, she knew she'd received the wakeup call she needed.

She couldn't do this anymore.

Couldn't pretend like she was okay entering into a potential relationship with a man, no matter how incredible he was.

Because those few moments when she couldn't find Olly had reinforced why she could never have kids again.

She couldn't go through that kind of panic, that mind-altering dread when something happened to a child under her care.

She couldn't be a mother, ever again. She couldn't risk losing another child.

It had almost killed her when Lucy died; she could never go through it again.

And that meant ending things with Jake now, before they got in any deeper.

Jake found them a few minutes later, adding sugary toppings to strawberry ice cream, but Sara could barely look at him as he came through the door.

Intuitive as ever, Jake put the milk into the fridge and came to stand close, his hand resting in the small of her back. "Everything okay?"

"Yeah." She brandished the toppings in her hands. "Sprinkles or chocolate?"

He ducked to whisper in her ear. "You're sweeter than any of that stuff so can I have you?"

She forced a laugh and squirmed away. "There are children present."

"When there's ice cream in front of Olly, he wouldn't hear an explosion." Jake paused then and scrutinized her closely. "You sure everything's okay? Did something happen when I was next door?"

"Everything's fine."

But it wasn't, and Sara counted down the next thirty minutes until they finished dessert and Jake had to take Olly home. Cilla had texted him and said she wouldn't be home tonight, for which Sara was doubly thankful. It meant Jake couldn't come back over to her place and that, hopefully, Cilla and Bryce had resolved their differences.

Thanks to Olly's presence as they said goodbye, Jake couldn't interrogate her either.

It was for the best. She needed some time to think. Time to devise a way to extricate herself from this relationship before she got in too deep.

As she trudged upstairs to draw a bath, she ignored her voice of reason, which insisted it was way too late. She wasn't just in too deep with Jake; she was in so deep she was drowning.

38.

Jake was nursing his second coffee the next morning when Cilla breezed through the back door, wearing yesterday's clothes and a grin that took ten years off.

"About time you did the walk of shame," he said, raising his coffee mug in a toast.

"Hush now," she said, her laugh soft and melodic. "I'll have none of your smart comebacks, you hear?"

He chuckled and pushed out the chair opposite with his foot. "Sit. I'll get you a coffee."

"I've already eaten," she said, and blushed. "Bryce made me breakfast."

"So you and the doc are back on speaking terms?" he dead-panned, well aware the glow his aunt sported attested to more than a late night chat with the doc. "Good for you."

"Bryce is a good man," she said, her blush intensifying. "I may have misjudged him."

"It's good to see you so happy," he said, meaning it. If anyone deserved happiness, his aunt did. "But please let me know if you're planning any shenanigans around here so Olly and I can make ourselves scarce."

"Don't be ridiculous." Her glower hardly packed a punch when it was accompanied by a satisfied smirk. "How was dinner at Sara's last night?"

"Good." At least, it had been until he'd popped back here to grab Olly's favorite strawberry milk.

When he'd got back to Sara's, she had been tense and jumpy, at complete odds with the woman he'd spent the last week with. He'd tried to pry the information out of Olly when they'd got home, but in typical distracted six-year-old fashion, Olly had been more intent on getting his bedtime story read than discussing what he'd talked about with Sara.

He'd wanted to call her but he knew she could fob him off too easily over the phone, so he'd bided his time until now.

"Your dour expression says otherwise." Cilla sat opposite him. "Did something happen?"

"Not that I know of, but toward the end of the evening she became fidgety and edgy, like something was wrong."

Cilla hesitated. "You don't think you've been spending too much time together?"

He shook his head. "She's been happy the last week. We both have. I left her alone with Olly for a few minutes and when I came back she was different."

Cilla frowned. "She's been at ease with Olly for ages now, so it's not that."

"I know, but it must be something."

Damned if he knew what it was, despite mulling all night.

"Why don't you ask her?" Concern clouded Cilla's eyes. "I'm not sure if this is relevant, but I saw her packing her car with what looked like an overnight case as I was driving up."

"Crap." Jake stood and headed for the door. "Can you watch Olly for a few minutes?"

She nodded. "Take your time."

Apparently Jake didn't have much time, though: as he sprinted along Cilla's driveway, he saw Sara locking up. He vaulted the hedge between their driveways and jogged toward her, belatedly realizing he looked like a desperate lunatic when she stared at him in surprise.

"You're leaving?" Not his best opening. Her lips compressed into a thin, unimpressed line.

"Heading back to the city for a few days," she said, annoyingly unflappable as she opened the driver's door and leaned down to fling her handbag inside. "Scouting a few galleries that are interested in showing my pyrography pieces. I emailed them pictures a while back."

"You never mentioned it," he said, icy dread making him numb. They'd talked a lot over the last week and not once had she mentioned the possibility of her work taking her back to New York City.

He felt like a chump, when all he'd been thinking about was ways he could viably stay in Redemption and make their relationship work.

"It's something I've been toying with." She shrugged. "Worth testing the waters to see how I go."

"Yeah," he said, because what else could he say without sounding churlish? "Hope it goes well."

"Thanks." She made a grand show of looking at her watch. "I'm running late, so I'd better go."

"Just like that," he said, unable to keep the rancor from his tone.

She flinched a little, which he took as a good sign. Meant she wasn't totally indifferent to what they had, no matter how much she was trying to prove otherwise.

"Listen, Jake, this isn't the time or place to have this conversation, but I can't do this."

His blood chilled. "Do what?"

"Have a full-blown relationship. The kind of relationship that ends in commitment and kids and the works." She tapped her chest.

"I'm not cut out for that anymore. I can't do it. And it's not fair on you for me to pretend otherwise."

"Whoa." He held up his hands. "You're jumping way ahead. Why can't we just have fun for a while?"

Her mouth drooped. "Because we both know we're beyond fun already."

He had no comeback for that because dammit, she was right. What they had far surpassed what he'd had with any other woman and he didn't want to give it up.

"I don't want to hurt you, Jake, and I'm scared that's what will ultimately happen if we keep dating." She took a deep breath and blew it out again before continuing. "Let's cool it for a while and stay friends, okay?"

It wasn't okay, not by a long shot. But he couldn't think of one damn thing to say to change her mind.

So he stood there like a dummy and watched the woman he loved drive away.

39.

Sara spent the next ten days in New York City, visiting galleries and talking up her work. A few showed interest; most dismissed her as a kooky artist who burned wood for a living.

She didn't care. She already had her heart set on running art classes in Redemption and the knock-backs didn't sting as much as she'd expected. What did sting were Jake's emails and texts and phone messages.

She screened all her calls. Listened to the messages he left with a heavy heart. But his emails got to her the most. Brief yet chatty, they painted a picture of life in Redemption that she knew intimately and missed. Dish of the day at the diner. Funny anecdotes about Olly. Updates about Cilla and Bryce's burgeoning romance.

It made her ache with longing. It also made her wonder if she'd had anything with Jake beyond the illusion of happy families.

Because that's what they'd done for that amazing week together—play happy families. They'd spent seven perfect days that encapsulated a summer vacation: swimming at the town pool, afternoons in the park, bike riding, roller-skating, picnics and lying on a blanket reading in the backyard.

It had been idyllic and special and too good to be true. As she knew all too well, when everything seemed perfect, it was an illusion and inevitably ended.

Sadly, another side effect of breaking up with Jake seemed to be a return to insomnia. Though this time around, she didn't cry herself to sleep from missing her child; she tossed and turned, missing the warmth of Jake's big, strong body wrapped around hers.

The boutique hotel apartment had lost its appeal too. She missed Gran's house. Missed the large kitchen and comfy bed and sprawling backyard. She missed her pyrography tools most of all.

She had to go back. Just one more day . . .

Cilla had told her tomorrow would be the day Rose came out of rehab and Jake would take Olly back to her.

That meant Jake would leave Redemption for good.

And she could start the arduous task of forgetting him and Olly and how they'd helped bring her back to life.

On a deeper level that she'd never acknowledge, she'd miss them the most. She'd grown used to hearing Olly's belly laughs, his amusingly blunt comments, his infectious giggles. She'd enjoyed Jake's company; the way his eyes crinkled when he smiled, the special way he had of staring at her, his deliberate flirtation.

Jake had awakened her body in ways she'd never imagined and Olly had made her secretly yearn for a child's innocence again.

Once they left, she needed to put both behind her.

Jake would soon give up pestering her when she maintained her silence, and would move on. Hopefully, she wouldn't have to see him again. Much easier to remain distant when she didn't have a sexy guy trying to persuade her in person.

Yes, tomorrow would be the day. Jake would be out of her life and she'd return to Redemption.

In the meantime, another twenty-four hours stretched before her in which she'd battle to forget the man who'd stolen her heart without trying.

40.

Jake had been a madman the last ten days. Grouchy. Irrational. Touchy. Until Cilla had sat him down and made him see sense.

He'd ranted against Sara when she hadn't returned his emails or texts or calls. Had said maybe Olly had been the real attraction between them; that he'd been an adjunct to her desperate need to make up for her lost child. He hadn't told her about Rose possibly coming to live in Redemption, so as far as Sara knew Olly's departure was imminent, and her fleeing to New York City proved that theory.

Cilla had called him a few choice names for his outlandish speculation and told him to wake up to the truth.

Sara had lost everything. Her child. Her husband. Her home. Her job. Her previous life.

She'd found acceptance and permanency in Redemption.

But when Olly left, Jake probably wouldn't be part of that permanence. Sara would assume he'd leave. And that could be why she was ending it before it had begun.

When Cilla laid it out like that, it all seemed so simple.

So Jake set about proving to Sara that he was in this for the long haul. Which was why he'd hightailed it to New York City and now waited at her front door, rocking on the balls of his feet, resisting the urge to constantly check the documents in his jacket pocket.

She'd already buzzed him into the apartment building so he hadn't wasted his time in turning up.

Now he needed to convince her that the place they both belonged, together, was Redemption.

She took her time answering the door and when it opened, he struggled not to bundle her into his arms.

"What are you doing here?" No greeting and she hung on the door, keeping it half closed. Not so glad to see him obviously. Hopefully, he could change that.

"We need to talk." And he wouldn't stop until he'd convinced her they belonged together. "Can I come in?"

She hesitated, and for the first time since he'd arrived, his confidence plummeted. The conversation they had to have wouldn't pack the same punch while he was standing on a doorstep.

"I'm heading out soon, so you haven't got long." She opened the door wider and stepped aside.

"It won't take long."

He entered the small studio apartment and had a flashback to the first time he'd entered his. He'd loved living in New York City, loved the buzz and the vibe. It had been a far cry from his upbringing in that pokey house with Rose and his father. He'd reveled in the freedom.

But after the accident, his apartment had become a prison. Dreary. Confining. Depressing. It hadn't been until the last few months in Redemption that he'd realized how much he'd needed to escape. Now, with what he'd done to prove his commitment to Sara, he hoped he'd be sticking around Redemption for a long time.

"Do you want something to drink? A soda?" She perched on the back of a small sofa, looking like she'd rather be anywhere other than here.

"You don't need to play hostess for me," he said, stopping two feet in front of her. "I just want to talk."

If his proximity bothered her she didn't show it, apart from a telltale sharp intake of breath that she released slowly.

"I thought we'd already said everything that needed to be said." She eyeballed him, daring him to disagree.

"Actually, you spoke, I listened last time. Didn't mean I agreed with any of it." He reached into his pocket and pulled out the documents. "I get it. You were running scared. You think a relationship will lead to marriage and kids and that terrifies you because of what you went through with Lucy."

She scowled. "You can never 'get it' because you have no freaking idea how painful it is to lose a child and I hope to God you never will."

He faltered. Maybe their relationship *had* been about Olly all along.

"Tell me this. Were you only interested in me because you were using Olly as some kind of surrogate kid and I was just part of the package?"

Her mouth dropped open a little before her eyes narrowed and she shot him a venomous glare that should've scorched him on the spot. "You really think I'm capable of doing something like that?"

"No, but you haven't answered my question."

"You're an idiot," she said, shoving him away and moving to the other side of the sofa. "What you and I had was nothing to do with Olly. No child could ever be a substitute for Lucy and I'd never use anyone the way you just suggested." Her chest heaved with indignation. "I can't believe you think I'd use *you* like that, not after what we shared."

Hope flickered to life. "So it was real? You and me? All of it?"

After several long, tension-fraught moments, she nodded. "Of course."

"Then did you run because you think I'll run too, once Olly's back with Rose?" He glanced down at the paper in his hand, surprised to see he'd clutched it so tight it had wrinkled. "Because I won't. I'm staying. In Redemption."

Her eyes widened in surprise. "Why?"

Jake inhaled a deep breath. Here went nothing.

"Because I'm in love with you and I want to have a real relationship for the first time in my life." He thrust the document at her. "And I'm hoping you'll see how serious I am once you take a look at that."

Sara appeared shell-shocked as she took the papers and unfolded them.

He waited, his fingers curling into fists. He shook them out, willing the nervous tingling away. If this failed, he had no idea what he'd do. He'd be stuck in a town with the woman he loved, who didn't want anything to do with him.

Sure, he'd be near Rose and Olly and Cilla for a while, but being so close to Sara and not being able to have her—it would drive him insane.

Her gaze flew across the document and when she finally looked up, he let out his breath.

There were tears in her eyes. Whether of joy or sadness, he had no idea.

"You bought the Redemption airfield?" She glanced at the papers again and shook her head. "Why? When you couldn't even go near the place last time?"

"To prove I'm in this for the long haul." He thrust his hands in his pockets to stop from reaching for her. "I faced my fear for you, Sara. I'm going to open up a charter school. Have a small fleet of planes. Hire instructors. Get back in the game. Because I want to stay in Redemption and make a life with you."

"You did this for *me*?"

To his horror, she burst into tears. The documents slipped from her fingers and fluttered to the floor.

"There's not much I wouldn't do for you," he said, finally allowing himself the luxury of hauling her into his arms.

It reminded him of the first day they'd met, when she'd cried unashamedly. Now, like then, he wanted to hold this woman forever.

When her crying stopped, he eased back and captured her face with his hands. "So what do you think? Can we make a go of this?"

Her tear-stained face looked so forlorn he wanted to hug her again. "You're right, I'm petrified of us getting in too deep because you'd end up wanting kids and I'm not sure if I can go through that again."

"How about we take it one day at a time? Save the kids until we see if we can survive living together?"

Her eyebrows rose. "You want to move in?"

"If you'll have me." He mock frowned. "Otherwise, with Rose and Olly at Cilla's, I'll be bunking down in the hut at the end of the runway."

Her tremulous smile had him wanting to punch the air in victory.

"Okay, you can move in, on one condition."

He grinned. "Anything."

"That you let me love you back." Her arms snaked around his neck. "You're the best man I've ever known, Jake. And if I have to face my fears, I'm glad it's with you by my side."

Jake didn't cry but at that moment he came pretty damn close.

"Deal," he said, a second before their lips met in a fusion of understanding and hope and love.

Best deal of his life.

41.

ould this get any better?" Bryce lay sprawled on his side in the long grass, propped on his elbow, as he watched Cilla gather herbs. He looked like a model, lying there shirtless, his chest dappled with sunlight.

A chest she'd explored in intimate detail, with her tongue and her lips and her hands. Heat scorched her cheeks at the memories they'd created over the last three weeks. Memories she could hardly believe were real, they were that spectacular. Memories to base a future on, which is what they were fast moving toward.

"It could get better," she deadpanned. "If you were naked."

His slow, sexy grin made her heart pound. "I love the sex maniac you've become."

"Your fault," she said. "Never knew I had it in me."

"Oh, you've got it, sweetheart, and then some." He sat up and patted the spot on the blanket next to him. "Why don't you come sit and I'll prove it to you?"

"Rose and Olly will be back from Sara's any minute," she said, but sat next to him anyway. "And Jake's due back from the airfield to pack the last of his stuff."

"Damn. I'll have to wait." He nuzzled her neck. "Not too long, I hope."

"You're insatiable." She bumped him away playfully, loving the way her body reacted to him now she'd let go all her reservations.

"Only for you." He kissed her lips, slow and lingering. "I've waited too long so I'm making up for lost time."

"Actually, that's what I wanted to talk to you about."

Cilla knew she was crazy for even contemplating what she was about to ask him.

But circumstances had changed.

She'd changed.

And this marvelous man was such a huge part of that she couldn't let him go.

"You know how you keep bugging me to spend more time together?" Heck, was she really about to say this?

His face lit up. "You're moving in with me? Fantastic, because we can—"

"Actually, I was thinking perhaps you could move in here? I know Rose and Olly will be around, and that may cramp our style a bit, but my place is big enough for all of us and—"

"Yes. Hell yes." He cupped her face and kissed her until she saw stars. "You have no idea what this means."

Actually, she did. Because she'd come to learn over the last few weeks that Bryce was as much of a loner as she was. He hadn't been in a serious relationship and he'd never lived with anyone. So wanting to live together was akin to making a full-blown declaration of their insanity in falling for each other, despite the age difference.

When he finally let her come up for air, she added. "I know you said you don't want children. But having Olly around for a while will give you an idea of whether you do. Then maybe we can foster, make a real difference in some poor kid's life, if that's what you want to do?"

He stared at her, his ebony eyes wide with shock. "You'd do that for me?"

She nodded. "If that's what you wanted."

She mentally searched for the right words to tell him how much he meant to her, then settled for the truth. "Bryce, I had no idea I could be this happy. No clue that being in a relationship with a man could be filled with joy and laughter, not pain and devastation. You've opened my eyes in a way I'd never thought possible and I'd like to thank you for that."

He blinked rapidly but she saw the sheen of tears. "You don't have to thank me. I'll be here for you. Always."

That surprised her. His locum stint would be ending shortly, hence her magnanimous invitation for him to move in. She knew it would only be short term, and she wanted to spend as much time with him as possible.

"You don't have to make any promises you can't keep—"

"Ssh . . ." He placed a finger against her lips. "I've applied for a permanent residency at the hospital. No idea if I'll get it, but the fact they've liked having me around the last few months should hold me in good stead."

Incredulous, she opened her mouth, closed it again, before finally getting her brain and mouth to work in sync. "You're staying?"

He smiled. "Already regretting that offer for me to move in?"

Bryce. Living with her. Permanently.

It should scare the bejeesus out of her, but it didn't.

Since she'd opened her heart to him, she knew he was exactly where she wanted him to be: by her side.

"Not at all, roomie."

"So that's how you see me, huh?" He eased her down onto the blanket and rolled his strong body on top of hers. "As a roommate?"

"A roommate with benefits," Cilla said, a second before his lips covered hers, silencing her fears and doubts, and giving her hope for an amazing future.

EPILOGUE

Sara had been back in Redemption a month when the bomb detonated.

Not an actual bomb, but one that would have far-reaching consequences and the potential to cause emotional devastation and fallout.

Just when everything had been going so well.

Jake's sister Rose had moved into Cilla's place next door and Jake had stuck around for a while, just to make sure she was doing okay. But because he spent most of his time at Sara's place, especially the nights, she'd taken the colossal step of asking him to move in with her.

Living with a man again was huge for her. Monumental. Then again, as she stared at the plastic stick with the blue cross on it for the hundredth time, nothing could be as monumental as this.

Pregnant.

The worst scenario she'd contemplated as a result of her relationship with Jake. It had freaked her out enough to think about it possibly happening sometime in the future. But now?

A baby.

She turned the stick around again and again. It didn't change the result.

Positive.

She was going to have a baby.

She waited for the panic to set in. For her chest to tighten and restrict her breathing. For her hands to shake. For a cold sweat to break out over her body.

It didn't come.

The longer she stared at the stick, the calmer she felt.

Gran had always said things happened for a reason. Sara had never believed it. She didn't believe in fate. But this town had healed her. Healed her enough to take a chance on an amazing man like Jake.

Maybe she'd been meant to have this baby?

It wasn't like they'd been trying. She'd been absolutely sure about not trying, ever. But latex wasn't foolproof and it looked like what had once been her biggest nightmare could prove to be a godsend.

"Hey, you done in the bathroom yet?" Jake stuck his head around the door. "We have to go or we'll be late and you know how Bryce frets over his barbecues . . ." His gaze landed on the plastic stick as she tried to hide it behind her back. "What's that?"

"Uh . . . well . . ." She couldn't think of one rational thing to say so she settled for waving it at him. "We're going to have a baby. Surprise!"

Jake's jaw dropped and he flung open the door and barged into the bathroom. "What?"

"I'm pregnant, and before you ask how, condoms aren't one hundred percent effective," she said, almost defiantly, as if this was somehow his fault. Which was totally untrue, but now that Jake knew the truth, she was suddenly nervous.

"What the . . ." he shook his head as his lips eased into a grin. "We're having a *baby*?"

"Uh-huh."

His grin faded as his concerned gaze flew to hers. "How do you feel about it? Are you okay?"

"Never been better." She took hold of his hand and placed it on her flat stomach. "This special child is going to have two parents who love and adore it as much as they do each other."

Jake's doting gaze radiated delight and she choked up. "I love you."

"Right back at you." Tears of joy trickled down her cheeks and he pulled her close, enveloping her in his strong arms.

He didn't say anything as she blubbered against his shirt. He didn't have to. She had never felt so cherished, so protected, as she did in his arms.

When she stopped sniffling, he eased away and stared down at her, the sheen in his beautiful blue eyes alerting her to the fact she wasn't the only one overwhelmed by elation.

"I never thought I could be this happy," he said, brushing her lips in a feather-light kiss. "Never thought I was worthy, 'til I met you."

"Stop." She pressed her lips to his. "You'll start me blubbering again."

He traced a tear track with a fingertip. "And I'll kiss them away."

She smiled. "Olly's going to have a cousin. Hopefully that means Rose will stick around for a while."

Jake's glance turned sly. "I know another way to make her stick around."

"How?"

"A wedding." Jake picked her up, spun her around, before coming to a stop so she could slowly slide down his body. "Gorgeous Sara, will you marry me?"

Her heart expanded with love for this incredible man but she shook her hand. "I don't need a wedding ring to have a baby. We can live together, see how it works out—"

"The ring isn't for the baby. It's for me," he said, so solemn her breath caught. "I love you, Sara. I'll never stop loving you and I want us to be a family. So what do you say?"

There was only one thing Sara could say.

"Yes," she said, and he let out a whoop of delight. "I love you and I'd love to be your wife."

"I'm sure glad I came to Redemption." Jake kissed her. "Best move I ever made."

Sara felt the same way.

In this town she'd found healing and compassion and love. So much love.

A new start.

A new beginning.

A new life.

She couldn't wait to live it.

ACKNOWLEDGMENTS

After being published for eleven years, I still pinch myself that my job involves taking a smidgeon of an idea from my subconscious, brainstorming it and getting the words down on paper to form a complete story. It's exciting when my characters come to life on the page and that was especially true for this story, which I couldn't write fast enough.

But writing is a solitary occupation and once the story magic leaves my fingertips, other people become involved to make the publishing dream a reality.

So my heartfelt gratitude to the following people for making this particular dream come true:

Sammia Hamer, editor extraordinaire, I'm so thrilled you love this story as much as I do. It has been a fast, exciting ride from receiving "The Call" from you to publication, and I look forward to a bright future with the fantastic team at Amazon Publishing.

Katie Green, fab editor, whose insights during the revision process really made this shine.

Jennifer McIntyre, for her tight copy edits and for making me giggle in parts.

Soraya Lane, who made this all happen after reading the first three chapters and outline of this story. You're a star, Soraya. Your generosity and kindness mean so much to me. I can't thank you enough. And I value our daily chats so much, even when kids demand most of our time!

Natalie Anderson, you're a great motivator and your pep talk when you were last in Melbourne really kicked me into gear. Writing this story in six weeks was the result. Thank you!

My street team, Nic's Super Novas, for always being there to brainstorm a title or character name or give encouragement.

My amazing boys, you are the loves of my life. Every single book I write is for you (even if you can't read them yet!). You make every single day brighter with your smiles and hugs. Love you, infinity.

My hubby, for being my number one cheerleader.

My parents, for their unswerving support.

And last but not least, my readers. Thanks for your loyalty, your fan mail and for buying my books. I hope you have as much fun reading my first women's fiction novel as I did writing it.

ABOUT THE AUTHOR

 Nicola Marsh is a bestselling, multiaward-winning author, who has sold more than six million copies worldwide. Her first mainstream romance, *Busted in Bollywood*, was nominated for Romantic Book of the Year 2012. Her first indie romance, *Crazy Love*, was a 2012 ARRA finalist. Her debut young adult novel, the supernatural thriller *Banish*, was released in 2013, and her YA urban fantasy *Scion of the Sun* won the 2014 National Readers' Choice Award for Best Young Adult Novel. Marsh is a *USA Today*, Bookscan, and Barnes & Noble bestseller, and a 2013 RBY (Romantic Book of the Year) and National Readers' Choice Award winner. She has also won several CataRomance Reviewers' Choice Awards, and been a finalist for a number of awards, including the Romantic Times Reviewers' Choice Award. A former physiotherapist, she now writes full-time. Her other loves are raising her two little heroes, sharing fine food with family and friends, and her favorite: curling up with a good book!